JAMIE SHARPE & THE PIRATES OF BARBARY

Praise for *Jamie Sharpe & the Pirates of Barbary*

Bush's latest, *Jamie Sharpe and the Pirates of Barbary*, is his greatest. Surprising, full of danger and intrigue, it grabs you and won't let go.

Reed Farrel Coleman, *New York Times* bestselling author of *Sleepless City*

Gary R. Bush's latest novel, *Jamie Sharpe and the Pirates of Barbary*, continues the adventures of the intrepid young hero as he battles both new and old foes in this rip-roaring adventure story which finds him taken captive and then left to fend for himself in a foreign and hostile place. Bush writes in an entertaining fashion, combining a compelling storyline with a historical insight that will keep you turning the pages. If Robert Louis Stevenson were to be reincarnated in the Twenty-First Century, he would be Gary R. Bush.

Michael A. Black, author of the Trackdown series, including *Devil's Vendetta*, *Devil's Breed*, and *Devil's Reckoning*

Jamie and his crew are classic heroes, surviving war and empire as they fight for love and freedom in the great Age of Sail. Each adventure makes turning the pages like eating popcorn at the movies. This is a can't-miss series for all lovers of stories grand and glorious — *Pirates of Barbary* will keep you gripping your seat as Jamie overcomes pirates, sultans, and treachery to make his escape from a tragedy straight out of a Greek myth. Make a place on your shelf next to Forester, Bush's Jamie Sharpe has earned his place alongside the venerable Horatio Hornblower.

Rick Ollerman, author of *Mad Dog Barked*

This is the stuff from which dreams are made: heroes and rogues and swashbuckling derring-do that brings to mind the verve and excitement of those long-ago but never forgotten Saturday morning serials. Bravo to Gary R. Bush for his engaging storytelling. I await Mr. Sharpe's next outing.

Gary Phillips, author of *One-Shot Harry*

Young adults and adult readers who look for high adventure and an 1800s setting involving pirates will find *Jamie Sharpe & the Pirates of Barbary* a captivating story that tells of former shipmates taken captive by brutal pirates.

Readers of the prior Jamie Sharpe story, *Seas of Treachery*, will find that old enemies emerge to challenge the friends, albeit with new strengths and weaknesses: "Jamie walked off. Horace seems to have grown a bit, he mused. Geoff is still the same small tyrant he's always been."

From kidnappings and slavery to the politics of a world affected by seafarers, pirates, and struggles for wealth and control, Gary R. Bush brings to life the 1800s, in which sailors in the Mediterranean and around the world struggled with pirates that harbored their own nefarious agendas.

From daily life on the high seas to Jamie's increasing realization that he needs to do something drastic to influence the American Navy's projected attack on Tripoli, history comes to life in a series of adventures and encounters that pit Jamie against forces beyond his control.

As he evolves a relationship with Claire that involves redemption and money, he also cultivates a changing sense of the world and his place in it.

Libraries and readers looking for historical fiction infused with pirate action and political and social insights will find *Jamie Sharpe & the Pirates of Barbary* replete with a fast pace and satisfying action that does not require prior familiarity with either the prior book or the times.

Jamie's search for a way out of the dilemmas that ensnare him in issues of slavery, freedom, and financial struggles makes for an involving, action-packed adventure that educates readers almost subliminally.

Jamie Sharpe & the Pirates of Barbary is a vivid story that will resonate with the clash of swords and ideas, ideally sparking lively discussion and debate in historical fiction book club circles, as well as young adult readers.

D. Donovan, Senior Reviewer,
Midwest Book Review (June 2023)

JAMIE SHARPE & THE PIRATES OF BARBARY

Gary R. Bush

THREE OCEAN PRESS

Library and Archives Canada Cataloguing in Publication

Title: Jamie Sharpe & the pirates of Barbary / Gary R. Bush.
Other titles: Sail into treachery | Jamie Sharpe and the pirates of Barbary
Names: Bush, Gary R., 1942- author.
Identifiers: Canadiana 20230455603 | ISBN 9781988915463 (softcover)
Subjects: LCGFT: Novels.
Classification: LCC PS3602.U895 J35 2023 | DDC 813/.6—dc23

Editor: Kyle Hawke
Cover and Book Designers: PJ Perdue and Kyle Hawke
Cover Image: Rebecca Treadway
Author photo: James R. Boylan

Three Ocean Press
Vancouver, BC
778.321.0636
info@threeoceanpress.com
www.threeoceanpress.com

First publication, June 2023

To my late parents,
Arthur and Ida Bush,
who were always there for me,
through good times and bad.

And finally, to Stacey
for her support and
for always being there.

Acknowledgements

To my writers' group, Heidi Skarie, Barbara Deese, and Stan Trollip, whose advice and constructive criticism made me a better writer.

To my editor, Kyle Hawke, who pushed me to do better and found the errors I never saw. To Rebecca Treadway, the cover artist, who brought the characters to life. And to PJ Perdue, whose design skills brought all the elements together.

A Note on Translations

The translations of various languages are included for the benefit of readers, but no knowledge of any language but English should be necessary to read this book. The specific choices for translation are a convenience, more modern than would be the versions spoken at the time of these events. Some of them may be in dispute. Any errors are mine.

Prologue

Aboard the USS *Constitution*, September 10, 1803

"WE'RE QUITE NEAR the Straits of Gibraltar," Midshipman Bradford Welles said, turning to his companion. "Are you anxious to go to war, Charles?"

"Well, it might be a change," Midshipman Morris answered. "Commodore Preble has kept us busy. All those standing orders. What was the last count, one hundred and six?"

Brad chuckled. "One hundred and seven actually. The latest: officers must set an example of probity and good manners. 'Blasphemy, profanity, and all species of obscenity or immorality are peremptorily forbidden' and we officers are not to tolerate 'such disorderly and despicable practices amongst the men.' It's not that I mind those orders, but it's the tirades and sarcastic jibes he hurdles at us. I don't know what to make of him."

At nineteen, Charles Morris was a wise and experienced midshipman who had already seen action in the Quasi-War with France.

Morris put his hand on the younger man's shoulder.

"I joined the navy as an acting midshipman in '99, when I was fifteen. I received my warrant a year later. In that time, I've seen enough bad officers to know a good one when I see one. Commodore Preble is a very good officer. Trust me, Brad, you'll be glad you sail under him. You'll learn much from him and he's already noticed your proficiency at navigation. I wish I had your schooling. When I entered the service, hardly any officer owned a sextant or much less knew how to use one. I myself have been grateful for your instructions. Mind what you learn from the good officers, and even some of the men, and you will go far."

"I shall heed your advice," Brad said, fingering the locket around his neck.

Morris smiled. "You're going to break the chain on that locket the way you've been toying with it."

Brad blushed. "I suppose. You know it holds the picture of someone quite dear to me."

"Indeed. I saw the girl come aboard before we sailed. If you don't mind me saying so, she is quite a beauty."

"Maisie Sharpe, the most beautiful girl in all of New England."

Morris nodded. "Is she not the sister of your friend who disappeared? Accused, he was, of running off with the family fortune."

"A damn lie!"

"What's the real story?" Morris cocked his head.

"I believe Jamie was the victim of foul play perpetrated by the Cutts family. I too might have been one of their victims had I not stayed aboard ship that night. I only pray that he lives." Brad gripped the hilt of sword. "In fact, I intend to have a duel with one of Simon Cutts' cronies, a Midshipman Horne, aboard the *Philadelphia*. Once we rendezvous with the rest of the squadron, I intend to call him out. My friend George Walling, who was supposed to be aboard this very ship, was to act as my second. But, as you know, he too disappeared, just before we sailed. He was, I'll wager, a victim of foul play. I know George well — he wouldn't have given up the opportunity to sail for anything." Brad shook his head in sorrow. Regaining his composure, he added, "I would be honored if you would act in his stead."

"Aye, I will. Despite the fact that the commodore doesn't approve of dueling."

"I know, but Horne has insulted me and, if I'm to retain my honor, I must challenge him."

As dark descended, both men were standing watch when they saw a strange vessel, large enough to be a ship of war, come within close range. The commodore was alerted and came on deck. He ordered the crew to come to quarters as silently as possible.

"What ship is that?" Commodore Preble called through his speaking trumpet.

"What ship is that?" came the reply.

Again, the commodore hailed and again came the same reply. Brad, standing next to Preble, noticed his patience had come to an end.

The commodore raised his speaking trumpet and said, "I am now going to hail you for the last time. If a proper answer is not returned, we will fire a shot into you."

From the strange ship came a quick reply. "If you fire a shot, we will return a broadside."

"Damn," Preble muttered under his breath, a curse that made Brad smile. "What ship is that?" he called one last time.

"This is His Britannic Majesty's ship *Donegal*, eighty-four guns, Sir Richard Strahan, an English commodore. Send your boat on board."

Preble leaped to the rolled hammocks arranged on the rail as a protection against gunfire and grabbed the mizzen shroud. "This is the United States ship *Constitution*, forty-four guns, Edward Preble, an American commodore, who will be damned before he sends his boat on board any vessel." He called loudly to his crew. "Blow your matches, boys."

Brad was in charge of the swivel guns on the quarterdeck. He ordered his gunners to get their fuses glowing by blowing on their lit ends. Excitement coursed through him, ready to follow the commodore's orders.

But there would be no action this night. Soon, a boat arrived with a lieutenant from the other ship. It turned out it was not the *Donegal*, but the frigate *Maidstone*, thirty-two guns.

"I'm sorry, Commodore, for our rudeness. We didn't see your ship until we were hailed. We needed time to order men to quarters. We didn't expect an American warship to be here."

"Your explanation is satisfactory," Preble said. "Apology accepted."

☸ ☸ ☸

"Well," Morris asked Brad later. "What do you think of our commodore now?"

"A brave man. He nearly fired on a British vessel, assuming it was a ship of the line and not a frigate. Even more, we are near their strong base at Gibraltar."

"Yes, a leader with enough fortitude to challenge the greatest navy in the world will have no fear of a petty tyrant like the Bashaw of Tripoli."

Chapter 1

The Mediterranean Sea, Southwest of Malta
September 1803

"I DON'T LIKE this weather," Captain Maxfield Collins said to his first mate, who had just come on deck and taken the wheel. Collins clamped down hard on his clay pipe, snapping the stem. He cursed and threw the pipe over the lee rail.

"Aye, sir," his first mate replied as he fought the helm of the schooner *Barbara Allan*. "I'm afraid we're being driven closer to North Africa. The wind is blowing us toward the lee shore. It looks like we're in for a squall. He pointed with his chin toward the towering clouds just aft."

Jamie Sharpe was young for a first mate, only sixteen, but already an experienced sailor and no longer a boy.

"If the British hadn't pressed most of my crew at Malta, I would have sailed two weeks ago and avoided this foul wind," Captain Collins said. Then he looked over at Jamie. "But had I sailed earlier, I wouldn't have met up with you and George Walling. You'd be stranded in Malta, or worse, being held for trial."

"I'm grateful, Captain," Jamie said, holding the wheel steady, straining with hard muscles. He scanned the sails and asked, "Sir, may I suggest we take in the topsails?"

Collins nodded. He called out, "Haul in the upper and lower topsails."

Men scrambled up the rigging of the foremast, stepped out on the yards, and hauled in the topsails. Jamie eased off the helm and began a tack to the northwest.

"That's better," Collins said. "I'm going below. The deck is yours, Mr. Sharpe."

Several minutes later, George Walling emerged from the cabin, followed by Mateus Balduino, a Portuguese sailor. Both were dressed in foul weather gear. George carried a tarred jacket and wool cap. He handed them to Jamie.

"Best put these on," George said, "the glass is falling. Captain sent me to help batten down the hatches."

Jamie nodded. He turned the wheel over to Mateus, who was familiar with the Mediterranean and its weather.

"Keep this heading, North Northwest," Jamie said, putting on his rain gear.

"*Sim*, North Northwest," Mateus repeated, gripping the wheel.

George called all hands. They jumped to secure the hatches, stretching canvas over them and tying down the heavy fabric with rope.

The wind picked up and snapped the canvas free of the forward hatch before it could be battened down, knocking two sailors off their feet.

George ran forward and grabbed the flapping cloth. While George was a few inches shorter than Jamie's six feet, he was much broader across the torso. Born with a strong body and with years of working as an apprentice to his blacksmith father, he was physically powerful. He soon had the hatch tied down.

George returned to the quarterdeck just as the skies opened up, drenching the schooner with heavy rain. Mateus had trouble holding his heading, so George added his muscles to the wheel.

"Do you have any idea where we are?" George shouted to Jamie over the roaring storm.

"I took a reading at noon yesterday, the last time we saw the sun," Jamie yelled back. "At that time, we were 34 degrees, 55 minutes, 80 seconds North by 12 degrees, 56 minutes, four seconds East. About thirty-seven nautical miles southeast of the isle of Lampedusa. God knows how far south we've sailed since then. I'll help Mateus with the wheel. You had better get some sleep before your watch. If things get bad, I'll send for you."

George threw Jamie a casual salute and went below.

Jamie and Mateus brought the schooner about, tacking northwest.

❁ ❁ ❁

At end of watch, Captain Collins relieved Jamie of the deck.

"I've asked Mr. Walling to check the cargo. He'll relieve me when he's through." He gripped the rail and looked aloft. "When the weather clears, I want lookouts in the rigging. We're in Barbary waters now. With Tripoli at war with the United States, I take no chances. Also, I want cannon practice as soon as possible."

"I'll see to it, sir," Jamie said. "I'll take a turn around the deck before I go below."

"Do that. Then get some hot food. That Portagee you brought with you, Dimas Mendes, is a fine cook. I'm going to ask him to ship with me on my next voyage."

Jamie smiled. Dimas and Mateus weren't the only survivors from the slave ship *Beneficence* he and George had brought with them. There were eight sailors, although two were recovering from injuries. Then there were the others chained below — five evil men who Jamie had the misfortune to know.

Jamie entered the small galley where Dimas, the cook, was stirring a large pot of bacalhau, a Portuguese dish of salted cod, potatoes, and onions, topped with eggs. Although the food was foreign to Jamie's New England palate, it was delicious and a far cry from the usual ship's fare of salt pork and ship's biscuits. Captain Collins had the foresight to bring hens aboard, so the men would have fresh eggs.

After eating, Jamie retired to the small cabin he shared with George. Jamie kicked off his shoes, hung up his hat and jacket, and swung into his hammock.

His life had taken a strange turn since graduating from Captain Bullard's School of Instruction in Navigation, Mathematics, Seamanship, and Artes Liberales in June, three short months ago. How cocky he'd been back then. So sure of himself, a bit of a braggart and swashbuckler. But the next terrible months had changed him. Money entrusted to him was stolen. He and George had been kidnapped and taken aboard the slave ship *Beneficence*, meant to be marooned on the coast of West Africa. However, fate had intervened and the ship was wrecked in the Mediterranean. What was left of the crew of that ill-fated ship had been saved by a Maltese ship and delivered to Malta where Captain Collins had offered passage home.

Jamie pulled up his blanket and immediately fell asleep.

Suddenly, he was awakened by screams coming from the hold, followed by shouting and violent curses. He swore silently, jumped from his hammock, checked his pair of steel Highland pistols, stepped into his shoes, and went below.

By the light of lantern hanging from the overhead, he surveyed the five men manacled to the bulkheads, but he was drawn to the one screaming and rolling about the deck. The others were shouting at the man to shut up.

"I'll break your damn head if you don't stop that caterwauling," the largest of the prisoners bellowed, straining at his chains.

"Belay that, Billy Scars," Jamie commanded.

The big man scowled, but sat down.

George joined Jamie in the hold, carrying a small cask of rum. "Doctor Harris could wake the dead with his screams."

"If only he could. How many poor devils did he kill with his surgery?" Jamie asked. He handed his pistols to George and took the cask. "Watch the rest of them. I'll tend to Harris."

Harris screamed louder. "I need rum, I need drink. For God's sake, I'm dying."

Jamie poured a dram into a tin cup and pressed it to the doctor's lips. Harris, wild-eyed and shaking, gulped the liquor down as if it were water.

"God bless you, sir," he managed to croak. "More, I need more."

Jamie poured another small amount down the doctor's gullet. "That's enough for now. Get some sleep."

Harris collapsed against the bulkhead.

"Why don't you sew him up in a hammock and toss his worthless carcass over the side?" Billy Scars laughed.

Harris sobbed and fell into a restless sleep.

Jamie looked over at the prisoners. The most dangerous, Billy Scars, a giant of a man, was feared throughout the seafaring world.

His face scared and pockmarked, hence his sobriquet. His real name was William Mars.

Next was Bruiser McPhee, ex-pugilist from the London prize ring, his pushed-in nose red as Malmsey wine. Then there was Hector Woolly, another hard man. He and McPhee were hired on the *Beneficence* as guards to keep the slaves in line. Neither were real sailors.

Finally, there was Simon Cutts. Eighteen, tall, muscular, blond, handsome enough to charm the ladies of Boston, but all of it a façade. For underneath his fine features and behind his cold blue eyes, was the heart of a treacherous coward and an arrogant bully. He glared at Jamie, but chained as he was, could do nothing but plot revenge.

"How long," he asked, "are we to be kept below, manacled like—?"

"Like slaves?" Jamie finished for him, unable to hide his disgust. "You're situated better than any slave would be in one of your vessels, squeezed so tight they couldn't turn over. You get the same food as the crew, you are brought up on deck twice a day for air and exercise. So shut your mouth. I'm tired of your whining."

Jamie and George left the captives.

"There are days," George said, "when I'd push the lot of them overboard."

"I as well, but we aren't savages like they are."

"Keep your mouth shut the next time Sharpe comes down here," Billy Scars admonished Simon Cutts.

"What?" Simon looked stunned. He was not used to underlings addressing him in that manner.

"Keep your mouth shut and bide your time. Sharpe's a fair man and that makes him weak. He'll drop his guard and, when he does, we'll take the ship. Most of the crew is our old shipmates. We can put the fear o' God into them. They'll follow our orders 'cause they be afraid of us. Fear's a great persuader. We'll get our chance. Now I'm for sleep."

With that, Billy Scars rolled over on his side and shut his eyes.

Chapter 2

THE NEXT MORNING broke clear and sunny. The wind was still blowing hard from the north. The captain ordered men aloft while Jamie and George took charge of cannon practice. They had taken instruction when they attended Captain Bullard's school and, as a lad of ten, Jamie had been in action against French privateers in the United States' Quasi-War with France.

The *Barbara Allan* carried four six-pounders, two to a side, along with six swivel guns mounted along the rails. The swivels had a three-inch bore and were loaded with grapeshot. None of the crew was trained cannoneers, although two of Jamie's friends, Fenton Webb and Mateus, had some experience. They were put in charge of the swivel guns.

Practice consisted of loading the cannons and aiming them. After two hours, Jamie felt the gun crews were ready to fire a few shots. Several wooden barrels were set adrift and used as targets. Two shots out of six hit their marks.

"It's the best we can do," Jamie said to George. "Should we run into trouble, it will be up to you and me to aim these things."

George shrugged. "Hopefully, we won't run into trouble and we'll get out of enemy waters soon."

At noon, the three officers took readings of the schooner's position. After consulting charts, the consensus was they were about 115 nautical miles from the city of Tripoli.

"This does not bode well," Captain Collins said. "We must make haste and leave these foul waters."

The topsails were set and the schooner ran a new tack, but beating against a strong wind made for slow going.

At two o'clock by the ship's clock, a lookout called, "Sail ho!"

"Where away?" Captain Collins asked, reaching for his telescope.

"Off the larboard bow, about five miles."

Collins focused his glass in that direction. "I see her, but can't make her out. Mr. Sharpe, I need your young eyes. Climb the mainmast and see if you can identify her."

He handed Jamie his telescope. Jamie hung the scope over his shoulder, jumped to the rigging, and scrambled to the top. He put the glass to his eye and watched the vessel closing rapidly from the northeast.

"It's a xebec," he yelled down. "Three lateen sails, running on a beam reach. She's flying the flag of the Kingdom of Naples." Jamie focused the telescope. "She's carrying cannon — at least fourteen, six- or eight-pounders by the look of them. Swivels too. She soon will be in hailing distance. I estimate she's making fourteen to sixteen knots."

"Come down," Captain Collins ordered. "I want you on the larboard guns. Mr. Walling on starboard. She may be friendly, but the Barbary pirates have been known to fly false colors. I will take no chances. Pass out muskets, cutlasses, boarding pikes, and hatchets."

Mikkel Holgerson was the ship's bosun. Along with Einar Gunnarson, they were the two Swedish members of Captain Collins' crew not pressed into service by the Royal Navy. Collins had them command the men with hand weapons.

Orders were carried out swiftly as the two vessels closed.

A hail in English was called from the xebec. "Aboard the schooner there, heave to and identify yourself."

Captain Collins picked up his speaking trumpet. "What ship is that?"

"We are His Majesty Ferdinand the Fourth, King of Naples' ship *Lupo*. Now, heave to and identify yourself or we shall open fire."

"He speaks perfect English," Jamie said, "albeit with an Irish accent."

"Aye," Collins replied. "Sir John Acton, an Englishman and a Catholic, is prime minister of Naples. It wouldn't surprise me that he has an Irish Catholic in service."

"Now, I want you to move those larboard cannon to starboard. The xebec is closing on that side."

Jamie gave the order and gun crews obeyed.

Collins shouted back, "This is the schooner *Barbara Allan.*"

"Of what nationality?" The English speaker on the *Lupo* called.

"American."

"Heave to and prepare to be boarded."

"The hell you say," Collins called back. "You have no right to stop my schooner, let alone board her."

His defiance was answered by a cannonball crashing into the mainmast, bringing it down, and crushing Einar Gunnarson.

Not waiting for an order, Jamie fired his own cannon and the ball struck the deck of the xebec. George opened fire as well and his shot took out the mizzenmast of the *Lupo*. The two remaining cannon also opened fire but both shots sailed over the xebec. As the gun crews reloaded, the *Lupo* closed with the *Barbara Allan* and dropped her mainsail boom across the schooner's deck, holding her in place.

Suddenly, men dressed in loose-fitting garments with turbans upon their heads, some waving swords and pistols, sprung from where they were hiding beneath the rail and grappled the boat with hooks.

"Corsairs!" Jamie yelled. "To arms!"

He fired his pistols into two of the pirates as they swarmed over the deck, drew his sword, and cut down a third man. Some of the pirates held scimitars clenched in their teeth and had their pistols jammed in their belts. Others screamed "*Kalb masihiun qadhir!*"

The crew of the *Barbara Allan* didn't understand the Arabic curses, but it mattered little at that point. They fought back with fists, pikes, cutlasses, hatchets, and muskets. George used his musket as a club and brought down several pirates.

Fending off a corsair with his cutlass, Captain Collins yelled to Bosun Holgerson, "Get below! Free and arm the prisoners."

The Swede obeyed and ran below. A few minutes later, Billy Scars, followed by McPhee and Woolly emerged on deck and entered the fray. The three large men laid into the pirates, swinging cutlasses.

Simon hesitated at the hatch until he was attacked by a pirate and struggled in desperation with the man. He brought his cutlass down on the pirate's head. His will to live overcame his innate cowardice.

Doctor Harris was nowhere to be seen.

Jamie wrestled a large corsair who had a death grip on his throat. He struggled to break free. He locked his hands together, brought them up fast, and broke the pirate's hold. Then, Jamie punched him hard in the larynx and tossed him into the sea.

Holzman, a German sailor from the *Barbara Allan*'s original crew, was felled by a scimitar blow across his neck. Maarten De Klerk, one of Jamie's men, died from a pike thrust through his body. Holgerson was wounded but continued to fight. Despite a broken hand, John Green, a Wampanoag Indian in Captain Collins' crew, impaled a huge corsair using a boarding pike as a spear.

Captain Collins' normally ruddy complexion turned gray. "Jamie, lad, they'll not take the *Barbara Allan.* Get you below and open the seacocks."

Jamie grabbed an ax and ran below. He found Doctor Harris tapping a rum cask.

"I've no time for your worthless hide now. But if I were you, I'd get on deck before the boat sinks."

Jamie reached the hold and, using the ax, he broke the seacocks and the water began to rush in.

He returned to the deck, where the struggle was still going on, but it was obvious the pirates were winning. Jamie rushed to Captain Collins, who was pinned to the deck by two of the corsairs. One of them thrust a scimitar into Collins' left side. Enraged, Jamie cut both corsairs down with his ax.

"Captain, is it bad?"

"The worst, Jamie. It's a mortal wound. Did you open the seacocks?"

"Aye, sir," Jamie said, holding back tears. "I smashed them, so they can't be replaced."

"Good lad. Survive, Jamie. You've a good head on your shoulders. Don't let the pirates kill you. Surrender. Our navy will win in the end and you and the men will be rescued. Survive." His voice failed there and Jamie heard the Captain's last breath as Collins eyes glaze over and Jamie gently shut them.

Jamie gave a cry of grief and turned to see more pirates enter the fray. He dropped his ax and sword.

"Surrender!" he shouted.

The crew saw the futility of fighting on and dropped their weapons. The pirates overwhelmed and dragged the defeated men aboard the xebec.

The remaining crew of the *Barbara Allan* was herded into the waist of the xebec as Arab sailors menaced them with sword and pistol.

A man of average height, broad across the chest and shoulders, his wide face covered with a curly brown beard, stood on the quarterdeck. He had a stub of a nose and his cheeks were crossed with broken blood vessels. He was dressed in splendid clothes and a red-and-gold turban was wrapped around his head. He stroked his beard and addressed the prisoners in a rough voice.

"Well now, sure'n if it ain't but a small prize of infidels I be taking. Hardly worth the effort, but still ye may bring some profit. At least a few of you look sturdy enough. You are now property of his highness, Yusuf Karamanli, the Bashaw of Tripoli. I am Kemal Rais, Captain Kemal to you. This is my ship, *Aldhib*, 'Wolf.' And I've captured a fine schooner that will bring a good price, along with its cargo."

"But you're English," Simon Cutts cried, horrified.

"Never that!" He slammed his fist on the rail. "Born Padraic Curran in County Wicklow, Ireland, I was. Saw me brothers killed in '98 at the Massacre of Dunlavin Green. It was enough for me. Catholic or Protestant, a plague on both of them, the *kalb masihiun*, Christian dogs. Now I'm a member of the true faith, Allah be praised."

A renegade, Jamie thought. Not the first European to abandon their heritage and join the Barbary pirates.

One of the pirate crew said something to Kemal and pointed to the sinking *Barbara Allan.*

"What the hell!" Kemal screamed. Then he yelled in a mix of Arabic and English, waving his arms in direction of the sinking schooner.

Some of the pirates jumped back to the schooner and began to unload as much cargo as they could. One of them dragged up Doctor Harris, who was still clutching the rum cask. Harris was flung in with the rest of the captives, the cask left rolling on the deck.

Cargo was tossed from ship to ship, but finally Kemal Rais gave the order. The grapples were loosened and the pirate ship moved off.

Jamie watched in sadness as the schooner *Barbara Allan* slipped beneath the waves. His gloom was interrupted by Kemal.

"Now, identify yerselves."

Cutts pushed forward. "I'm Simon Cutts, rightful captain of the brig *Beneficence*. My father is Nehemiah Cutts of Boston, Massachusetts and Charleston, South Carolina. Some of these men led by that one there," he pointed to Jamie, "mutinied and took my ship. I demand you arrest them. My father will pay you a great sum of money."

Kemal stepped down from his perch on the quarterdeck, looked Cutts up and down and then struck him in the face.

"Do I give a tinker's damn who your father is? Never demand anything from me, *kafir*. That's *infidel* to you. I should cut off your head, but you're worth more to me alive, now that I know you have a rich father." He turned to one of his crew. "Throw him with the others."

Cutts was tossed to the deck, where he lay sniveling.

Kemal motioned for Jamie to come forward. "So you took the ship from him, did ye now?" He pointed to the spot where the *Barbara Allan* went down. "I done the same, took the ship from me own captain, and offered me services to the bashaw."

"Not the schooner, Captain," Jamie replied. "It was a brig I took from him."

Kemal stepped closer to Jamie. "You have courage. I see that in your eyes and I saw you fight. Join the true faith and you can be part of me crew. For sure'n, I could use a fightin' man with guts like yours."

Jamie thought carefully before he answered. It wouldn't be prudent to anger the man that held his life in his hands.

"I must decline, sir. I have a duty to return to my home and avenge my family and my honor from Cutts and his father."

"Your name."

"James Montgomery Sharpe, sir. First mate of the schooner *Barbara Allan*."

"Montgomery, eh? Irish branch?"

"My grandfather is Scots, sir, but I'm an American."

"Well, that is your misfortune," Kemal said, tugging at his beard. "Our countries are at war and you won't be returnin' home soon. And maybe never."

And so it went with each member of the crew. George was as careful as Jamie in his answers. The English captives claimed that Great Britain was at peace with Tripoli and they should be freed when the xebec reached port.

"I hate the English," Kemal said with fire. "As far as I'm concerned, all of you are Americans, for you sail on an American ship. You are the property of his highness, Yusuf Karamanli."

When it was Billy Scars' turn, Kemal looked him over and grinned. "Now here's a specimen of a man! You should bring a good price. Unless, of course, ye take the true faith."

Billy Scars looked the corsair captain in the eye. In his rough rumble, he asked, "What do I got to do, sir?"

Kemal smiled. "Surrender to Islam, take instructions from an imam — a holy man — and a wee bit of surgery. The latter might hurt, but I had it done. What say you?"

Without hesitation, Billy Scars said, "I'll do it. Captain."

"Well, ye answered quickly enough, but until we reach port, you are a prisoner. I'll allow you some freedom. Betray the trust and I will disembowel you."

Kemal Rais gave an order in Arabic and the men of the *Barbara Allan* were forced to strip naked. Those who resisted were beaten and had their clothes ripped from their bodies. Each was handed a single dirty shirt and a pair of pantaloons.

What possession and weapons they had were piled on deck, where the Arab crew fought over them. One Arab cut the throat of another as they fought over Simon Cutts' officer's coat, which he had retained since the sinking of the *Beneficence*.

A gunshot and a shout of "*Tawqf!*" broke the mêlée.

Kemal Rais stood on his quarterdeck, a smoking pistol in his hand. He pointed a swivel gun at his own crew. "*Waqf 'aw 'ana sawf tabadul li'iitlaq alnnar*," he said in a cold hard voice. It didn't take a translator to understand he meant to shoot his own men if they didn't stop.

The men grumbled but went back to combing through the things in a more orderly fashion. Kemal himself picked up Jamie's sword and pistols along with his chronometer, sexton, and copy of Bowditch's *American Practical Navigator.*

"Now, these I can use. A timepiece like this will serve me well. And this sword, a Ferrara blade if I'm not mistaken, and two steel pistols. The book might be of some interest."

He tested the flexibility of the blade and marveled at it.

Jamie felt miserable and angry that his treasured possessions were taken from him. The sword and pistols had been given to him by one grandfather, the chronometer by the other. Yet he'd be damned if he'd let these pirates know. He continued to show a brave face.

"Won't Murad Rais be jealous that I have Scottish weapons superior to his?" Kamal crowed.

The name Murad Rais was not unknown to Jamie and George.

"The Scotsman Peter Lyle," Jamie whispered. "He turned Turk and became known as Murat Rais after he was captured in the brig *Betsy* out of Boston in '96. So there are least two renegades in the Tripoli navy."

Suddenly one of the Arabs cried out, "*Dhahab!*" He waved a money belt.

Jamie recognized it as his own. He had relieved it from Simon, who had taken it from him when he was kidnapped. Now the pirates had it. He clenched his fists but could do nothing.

"Gold!" Kemal Rais said, jerking the money belt from his crewman's hand. "It will make up for the loss of the schooner. Me master will be pleased."

The xebec changed course and retrieved any flotsam from the schooner that might prove useful. A few spars were brought aboard. The pirates had managed to get several chests of silk, a number of wine barrels, casks of rum, and boxes of opiates off the *Barbara Allan* before she sunk, but not the sulfur Captain Collins had purchased in Sicily. Jamie was glad of that, for sulfur was used in making gunpowder.

Kemal looked over the loot. Pointing to the wine and rum, he said, “These I can sell to the Jew and Christian merchants. It is forbidden for those of the true faith to partake of spirits.”

However, Jamie noticed Kemal ordered barrels of wine and the rum casks set aside with his personal loot.

Doctor Harris lay on the deck, among the sick and injured. “Could I have a bit to drink, Captain?” he begged.

“Drink, is it?” Kemal asked. “I’ll give you all you want.”

He turned to two of his crew and said something in Arabic. They picked up the doctor and tossed him overboard.

“Drink all ye want,” Kemal yelled, laughing in morbid delight. “The sea will see ye get yer fill.”

Jamie and George watched stunned as Harris floundered, screamed, and sunk beneath the waves. Then Kamal shouted another order and the sick and injured followed Harris over the side. Mikkel Holgerson was first to go under, followed by Walker, the topmen injured in the fight. Then the last three sick or injured were consigned to the depths. John Green fought off two of the pirates before Kemal shot him and had his body tossed overboard with the others.

Screams of “Help!” faded fast as the rest of the wretches were swept away. Jamie and the *Barbara Allan*’s crew watched in horror. Some began to shout, but being under the gun, they could do nothing.

Jamie turned to George and said, “Remember what Yoro, the Old African, told us? Slavers threw the sick and injured overboard. Some of those men were slavers, but I can’t help but have some pity for them. Walker wasn’t a bad fellow. My grandfather once said, ‘War is vile and no side is pure at heart.’ I believe that could apply to Walker.”

George nodded, his face doing nothing to hide his disgust at what he’d just witnessed.

Kemal Rais bellowed above the din of the noise on deck. “You infidel dogs, get below! We sail for Tripoli. We should have no trouble a’tall, as your navy is no longer blockading the harbor.”

The crew was shoved and kicked into the hold. The hatch cover cast the space into darkness.

Jamie crawled about until he found George.

"Not the first time we found ourselves in the dark." George gave a mordant laugh, remembering the time they spent in the hold of the *Beneficence*.

"It seems every time we jump out of the frying pan, we land in the fire." Jamie slapped the hull in anger. The savage feeling he had for Cutts returned and now he added Kemal to his books – and Commodore Morris, for all the good it would do.

"Mr. Eaton told me Commodore Morris had no stomach for war, but to give up the blockade is criminal."

George laid a calming hand on Jamie's shoulder. "Commodore Preble's on the way, with our friend Brad aboard. Preble'll show these villains a thing or two," George said. "It may be too late for us. I've read what they do to slaves in Barbary."

"It is never too late, my friend," Jamie said, regaining some of his composure. "We still live and, as long as we do, we have a chance. We shall never give up."

Chapter 3

Tripoli, North Africa

THE DAY WAS WARM, the sun brilliant, the water an azure blue. A beautiful day.

Dressed in his finest clothes, Kemal Rais stood on the quarterdeck of his xebec and watched as his men dropped anchor in Tripoli harbor. Without seeming to notice, he was humming an old Irish tune, "Galway City."

"I'm a happy man," he said aloud, although none of his crew understood his English. "Gold and rum, only poteen and gold would be better."

Breaking out of his introspection with a sigh, Kemal turned to matters at hand.

"Prisoners bring!" he commanded in his broken Arabic.

Kemal was certain it was not a beautiful day for the twelve forlorn men prodded out of the hold. They, plus one, were all that were left of the crew of the brig *Barbara Allan.* Each man was dressed in rags and chained hand and foot.

The thirteenth, a giant of a man, exited last, unchained. A wicked smile crossed his scarred, pockmarked face. The notorious William Mars, better known as Billy Scars, seemed to take great pleasure in seeing his former shipmates in such straits. One of the most feared men sailing the ocean had in the parlance of the time *turned Turk.*

Kemal pointed across the harbor to Tripoli. "You *kalb masihiun,* Christian dogs, this is your new home."

The xebec's crew lowered the longboat and dropped a ladder over the starboard rail.

The chains were struck from the prisoners and they were ordered into the boat to take position at the oars. Two heavily armed Arabs took seats in the bow. The big man was directed to the tiller. Finally, Kemal took his place in the stern sheets.

"Row, you useless lubbers," Billy Scars ordered.

The prisoners had no choice other than to pick up the oars and start rowing.

"Steer for the castle," Kemal said, pointing to the northeast.

Among the prisoners sat three young men tied together by fate.

Simon Cutts, eighteen, his once-cruel blue eyes now full of fear, shook as he pulled at his oar. How did he, master of the *Beneficence*, heir to the Cutts' fortune, an honest slaver, come to this? His thoughts turned to pleading. *God, why are you punishing me? Please save me. I've done nothing to deserve this. It was the fault of Jamie Sharpe. He took my ship and let the barbarians capture us.*

George Walling, the blacksmith's son, sat on the bench behind Cutts. He should have been a midshipman in the United States Navy. Thanks to Cutts, he was now a slave of the Bashaw of Tripoli. He was frightened as well, but was determined not to show it. *There is always hope. Others have been captured and been redeemed.*

Jamie Sharpe, the third member of the trio, was chained behind George. Fire was still in his heart. Despite his circumstances and the fear he also felt, the irony that Simon, the former slaver, was also a slave made him smile.

As the longboat came about, Jamie took in his surroundings. A tall wall surrounded the town of Tripoli. Several forts with heavy artillery sat at strategic points.

The castle itself was a huge dark pile of red stone, with walls he estimated to be nearly one hundred feet in height. It scared him to think he would be a prisoner in such a formidable place, but he planned to learn its weaknesses.

When the boat neared the beach, the bedraggled crew was commanded to jump into the surf and drag the vessel ashore.

Wet, tired, and hungry, they dropped to the beach, where they were greeted by rows of janissaries, the elite Turkish soldiers, armed to the teeth with swords, pistols, knives, and muskets.

A few kicks and spittle issued by the janissaries brought the captives to their feet. Shoved and hit with flats of swords or musket butts, they were forced into the castle. They were marched through corridors and up and down stairwells until they were thoroughly confused. Finally, they found themselves in a great room with a marbled floor and porcelain and enameled walls — the throne room of Yusuf ibn Ali Karamanli, the Bashaw of Tripoli.

Chapter 4

JAMIE GAZED AT the bashaw, who sat on a silken gold-colored cushion that rested on an inlaid mosaic throne. At 37, Yusuf ibn Ali Karamanli was a man in his prime. Tall, though slightly overweight, he presented a virile figure. He was richly dressed in a robe of ruby-red silk, embroidered with gold and silver threads. His diamond-encrusted belt held two gold-mounted pistols and a saber with a golden hilt in a beautiful scabbard. He wore a large white turban set with jewels. A long black beard brushed his chest.

His muddy brown eyes looked over the captives. When they met Jamie's, he frowned for a moment, then whispered something to a blond-bearded man standing next to him. This man, too, was elegantly dressed: a blue silk shirt, a short vest filigreed with silver threads and billowing pantaloons. A tall white turban adorned with ribbons did nothing to hide his slight stature. A sneer crossed a rather dissipated face and he uttered a short, barking laugh. Kemal crossed his arms and returned the sneer to the blond-bearded man. The bashaw beckoned Kemal to him and, in French, commanded him to speak.

Fluent in the language, Jamie listened intently.

Kemal made a low bow and said with a heavy accent, "*Seigneur, j'offre des cadeaux.*"

"Show me the gifts," the bashaw answered in better French.

Kemal handed over a money belt he had taken from Simon Cutts. "*D'or.*" In his poor French, Kemal continued, "Coins, a lot is of English gold Paper money is also. Six thousand pounds is total."

"How much did you take for your ain self?" the man with the blond beard asked in Scottish-accented English. It occurred to Jamie that the blond man must be Peter Lyle, the renegade Scot now known as Murad Rais.

Kemal turned red and reached for one of the Highland pistols he had taken from Jamie.

The renegade Scot drew his own weapon.

The bashaw jumped to his feet and rattled off something in Arabic. The men put away their weapons, looking at each other with poisoned eyes.

Kemal, still red with anger, spoke to the bashaw in bad French once more which came out to Jamie's ear as "Highness, how many insults I receive from this scoundrel?" He pointed at his accuser. "Me, not Grand Admiral, captured Americans." Kemal stuck out his chin. "I got gold and wine, silks, opiates, and strong captives and one rich. He sneaked out of Gibraltar when Americans blockaded it, even abandoned his ship, *Meshuda*."

"Ai! Enough." Yusuf jumped to his feet. "Two of my best captains fight like dogs over scraps." He turned to Murad. "You, my beloved son-in-law, must not denigrate Kemal Rais. He has brought us treasure. And you, Kemal Rais, while we honor you with praise, never draw weapons in our presence, unless it is for our protection."

"*Oui, Majesté.*" Kemal bowed his head.

"Now tell me of the prisoners."

Kemal smiled and pointed to Billy Scars. In his twisted French, he said, "Have seen you ever one like this? A fighter, ox strength, and the true faith to become. The others, all strong men also." He pointed to George. "And this one..." He singled out Simon. "This one, his rich father will pay pretty, will ransom his son. He is strong also and serve to you until redeemed."

Jamie hid a smile as he listened to Kemal's tortured French syntax.

Simon spoke up in French, his voice shaky. "My father is very rich. He will pay the ransom."

"We shall see," Yusuf replied. "Until then, you are my slave. Now, step back."

A man, toothless, wrinkled, and bent with age, leaning heavily on a staff, came forward and looked the captives over. He let out a shrill cry and stamped his staff upon the floor, then pointed to Dimas, cackled, and limped away.

Dimas shook with fear. The other prisoners were stunned, but before anyone could say anything, all of them were marched out of the throne room except for Billy Scars.

Down they went, deeper in the great hulk of the castle. Jamie tried to memorize the various twists and turns as well the many flights of stairs, but the maze was too much for him.

Eventually, they were led to a small courtyard surrounded by high walls. Once in, the guards slammed a gate behind them, locking it.

"'Ey," McPhee said. "'Ow about some vittles? We ain't et for nearly two days."

Several others took up the cry, but to no avail. They were locked up without food, still wet from the surf, and exposed to the open sky. Some sat down on the cold stone floor, wondering about their fate. Poor Dimas could not stop shaking. Others stayed away from him as he prayed aloud.

Fenton Webb joined Jamie and George where they sat in a corner. Jamie related what he heard in French to Fenton. "No love lost between the renegade captains."

"Perhaps we can use that," George said.

"If you're planning an escape, count me in," Fenton said. "But I don't know how we'll ever break loose. This whole city is a fortress. Hell, them walls would be near impossible to climb and I'm a right monkey at climbing. We ain't going to be redeemed like Cutts."

"Cutts isn't leaving any time soon. By the time his letter reaches his father and the ransom is arranged, it will be months." Jamie noted. "I will try to get a message to my family as well. Until we know what they're going to do to us, we can do nothing but wait."

They waited with hunger eating at their bellies. As darkness fell, the cold winds and fog off the Mediterranean chilled them to the bone until their bodies began to shake and their teeth to chatter. They tried to get some sleep with neither warm clothes nor even a sailcloth to cover the cold stone floor. They clung to each other for warmth but suffered just the same. Despair permeated the air as each man pondered his fate.

Chapter 5

THE NEXT MORNING, they were roused by the guards and counted, then coarse black bread with the chaff still in it was issued to each man. They were herded through the labyrinth of the castle to a courtyard below the bashaw's balcony.

The bashaw made an appearance, accompanied by Murad and Kemal. Yusuf said something to Murad, who translated to the men below.

"You are slaves. Obey all orders. You!" He pointed to Dimas. "You will work as a cook in the castle kitchen. The marabout, the old holy mystic, so decided."

Dimas let out a huge sigh and muttered, "*Mãe de Deus.*"

"If there be any among you who are mechanics, carpenters, coopers, smiths, or have other skills, who are willing to work at their trade, they shall be paid. If not, you will be compelled to do other work."

"George," Jamie whispered. "Tell them you're a smith."

"Why should I work for them?"

"Because you'll earn money and may learn things. Money will buy us things that might help in our escape. Take the job."

George shrugged and stepped forward.

"I'm a blacksmith," he declared.

An Englishman named Byrd raised his hand. "I was a sailmaker's apprentice."

"Any others with skills?" Murad asked.

"I'm a sailor, a subject of His Britannic Majesty," Upton, a man from Canada, shouted. "Give me a ship and I'll sail out of this hellhole."

Murad exchanged words with the bashaw, who spoke to the guards in Arabic.

"This will be a lesson to you all," Murad said.

The guards seized Upton and threw him to the ground. Two men picked up a long wooden board that had a rope passing through two holes near the center, forming a loop. The loop was placed over Upton's ankles. The guards twisted the loop tight around them and raised the soles of his feet. One guard sat on his back. Two other guards each picked up heavy date palm branches and, with all their might, began beating on Upton's bare feet.

"Damn you to Hell," Upton cursed. But soon his curses turned to cries of anguish. After a hundred blows were struck, the poor man was untied and lay on the ground, whimpering in aguish.

"The bastinado, I read of it," George whispered to Fenton Webb. "A terrible punishment."

"Aye. I heard of it from another sailor, first time I seen it. Sickening," Fenton muttered, turning away. "I guess sea captains ain't the only cruel ones," he added, his sarcasm hardly masked.

"Be careful not to incite the guards," Jamie warned. "We must stay fit as possible."

"That is all," Murad said. "You will now work."

Orders were issued in Arabic. George and Byrd were separated from the others and led back into the castle. The remaining men, including poor Upton supported by two others, were marched out of the castle and to a quarry to break rock.

☸ ☸ ☸

The sun beat down on the men and the guards struck them with staves if they slacked off. No leniency was shown. Finally, after hours in the merciless sun, the guards picked out Jamie and Simon Cutts. They handed each of them two leather buckets and gestured for them to follow. They walked nearly a mile to a well.

"This is your fault, Sharpe," Cutts said. "You took my ship and let us be captured. When my father redeems me, I'll see you are hanged for mutiny."

"Mutiny? How about you being hanged for piracy? You stole my sloop, you stole my gold, and you kidnapped me. Simon, you're the one that got us in this mess. You put the British sailors over the side. Do you think the Royal Navy will forget that?"

Cutts burst into tears.

"Simon, that won't help. Be a man. If they see weakness, they'll make your life even more miserable."

The guard, as if he understood, hit Cutts across the shoulder with his stave. "*Eajal!*"

Cutts howled and dropped his buckets.

The guard struck him again. This time, he bit his lip and picked up his buckets.

They reached the well and the guard prodded Cutts to lower the bucket. "*Ma'*," he said.

"*Ma'?* Water?" Jamie asked.

"Wa-ter," the guard answered. "*Ma'*."

"*Eajal?*" Jamie asked.

The guard made a fast motion with his hand.

"*Eajal.* Hurry?" Jamie made the same motion as the guard.

The guard nodded.

"What the hell are you doing, Sharpe?" Cutts demanded as he drew the bucket from the well and filled another one.

"Learning the language. It will come in handy."

"Thinking of turning Turk, are you?" Simon sneered.

The guard prodded Cutts again.

Jamie pointed to the bucket and made the motion for drink.

"*Ma'?*" The guard made the same motion. "*Yashrab.*"

"*Ma'?* Yes? *Yashrab*, drink." Jamie cupped his hands and drank.

The guard did the same and prodded Simon to drink. Simon grimaced at the taste of the brackish water.

After filling the buckets, the guard quickly motioned with his head to pick them up. "*Eajal.*"

Jamie nodded. "*Eajal*, hurry."

The guard smiled, showing gleaming white teeth. "Hur-ee."

They picked up the buckets and started back to the quarry. The guard began to point to objects, like rocks and trees and sky. He would say them in Arabic and Jamie would repeat them.

"Ain't you the good little pupil?" Cutts muttered.

Jamie ignored him. By the time they got back to the quarry, he had memorized twelve new Arabic words, those for bucket, quarry, sea, and house among them.

He pointed to himself. "Jamie Sharpe." He then pointed to the guard.

The man nodded, pointed at his own chest, and said, "Zafir."

Jamie repeated the name and smiled. He may not have made a friend, but he found a teacher, a man willing to show an infidel the true way.

The slaves found shade and were grateful for the water even if it was acrid. Some better-dressed slaves came to the quarry carrying loaves of black bread and tureens of olive oil.

"This is your food," one of them said in English with a strong Italian accent. He was a short wiry man about forty, his dark hair going grey. "Eat. You will see no more today. But if you have money, I can get you some more. Or if you prefer something stronger, I can get you palm whisky."

"We have no money, you damn rascal," Fenton Webb said. "The Turks took what we had."

"They are not all Turks," he replied in a know-it-all manner. "Some are Arabs, other Berbers, often called Moors. And still others from south of the Sahara are Black people."

"I noticed," Jamie said, "a gang of Blacks and whites working together on the other side of the quarry. Are they all slaves?"

"Some, not all." The man smiled. "This is not like Europe or America, where only Black people are enslaved. If one is not Muslim — white or Black — and if sold or captured, they are slaves. There are Black people who are not slaves. The bashaw's favorite wife is Black and she is a Muslim, so not a slave." He pointed to himself. "I was captured as I said by the corsairs, but many of the Black people were captured by other tribes or the Blue Men and brought along the caravan routes to North Africa."

"Blue Men?" Fenton asked.

He shrugged. "I've only heard they were blue and had no faces."

"Never heard of men with no faces," Fenton said. "Though a sailor once told me he saw a dragon off the Gulf of Guinea."

"What's your name?" Jamie asked pleasantly. He was determined to learn as much as he could from whomever.

"Marco Cardullo. I'm from Messina, Sicilia. I've been a slave for fourteen years. I was taken from my ship. I was the mate."

"Fourteen years?" Fenton whistled in awe.

"*Si.* While my *capitano* was redeemed, I and the rest of the crew remained slaves. The *capitano*'s family had money. Alas, mine had none. So you see, I'm here." He shrugged. "When you call me a damn rascal for asking for money, I sell what I can to redeem myself. It is common for captives to make money. Our masters don't care. In the end, it will come to them."

"Take no offense, Marco." Fenton said, offering his hand. "We are in the same fix."

"*Si.*" Marco took Fenton's hand and Jamie's as well. "But I warn you, there are others of my countrymen, as well as Maltese and those from Napoli, who would cheat you and rob you. Be on your guard."

"Thank you," Jamie said. "We will."

A wail was heard from the town. The overseers went to the buckets, washed, laid out rugs, and prostrated themselves on the ground.

"What are they doing?" Fenton asked. "And what was that howl we heard?"

"The *howl*," Marco answered, "is the *muezzin*, a sexton, calling the faithful to adhān, prayer. A good Muslim must pray five times a day. It is so written in their holy book, the Qur'an. It is one of the five pillars of their faith."

"What are the other pillars?" Jamie asked. "An old African in America told me of one. Something about Allah and his prophet."

"*Si.* That one is Shahada. It says there is only one God and that is Allah and Muhammad is his prophet. This is the first pillar of Islam.

"What are the others?"

Marco scratched his head. "Salat is the five daily prayers. Zakat is charity. Sawm is fasting during the month of Ramadan. And finally, the Hajj, a pilgrimage to the holy city of Mecca, in Arabia, during the twelfth month of the lunar year."

"Now I must go back, before the guards beat me. *Arrivederci.*"

"Thank you, Marco," Jamie said, as the Sicilian left.

"What good's that information?" Fenton ran his hand through the stubble on his head.

"Knowledge is power, according to Sir Francis Bacon. We need to know as much as we can about our captors."

"I ain't educated like you. The only bacon I know comes from pigs, which are mighty scarce around here, so I'll take any bacon I can get. But that Sir Francis must have been one smart man." Fenton laughed aloud for the first time in days.

"One of the great philosophers," Jamie commented. "I read some of his works when at sea with my father. I didn't understand it all then, but when we get free, I shall read him again. Now, while the guards are at prayer, let's see what we can do for poor Upton."

Upton lay on his side. Despite his injuries, he had been forced to break rock. Large pieces were brought to him and, with a small hammer, he broke them into smaller bits. He moaned as Jamie and Fenton approached.

Jamie looked at the soles of the sailor's feet. They were swollen, crossed with cuts, and black and blue. Jamie took his ration of water and washed Upton's feet and applied the olive oil he'd been issued.

"Mr. Sharpe," Upton said. "I thank thee. I did not stand by you on the *Beneficence* and for that, I'm sorry. Now you've given me your water and oil."

"What went on aboard ship is over. We are in this together. I had a drink at the well and what is a gill of oil but five small ounces? Now, eat the bread and oil, for they will force us back to work soon enough."

Chapter 6

NEAR SUNDOWN, the weary prisoners were marched back to the castle, urged on by the overseers with strikes from their staves and sharp barks of "*Eajal!*"

Instead of the open courtyard where they had spent the previous night, the men were herded into a small storeroom where there was not enough space for all of them to lie down.

Jamie and Fenton stood over Upton, who they made sure was given room to lie down. It became even more crowded when George, Dimas, and Byrd were pushed in a few minutes later.

George shoved his way through to Jamie and Fenton. George was dirty, covered in soot, and smelled of a wood fire.

"I was lucky to get my hands washed before they booted me in here," he said, wiping his face with the back of his arm.

"What are they having you do?" Jamie asked.

"Assisting a gunsmith to repair muskets."

"To kill or capture more Americans." Fenton did nothing to hide his disgust. "I'd spit if my mouth weren't so dry."

"Aye," George whispered, holding out a little cloth bundle. "But I've stolen a bit of black powder. I'll try and get more. Perhaps we can make a grenade. I wish I could have done a bit of sabotage on the muskets, but the old Turk gunsmith was too savvy." He shook his head.

"Don't do anything that might get you in trouble. Be a model prisoner." Jamie then gestured toward Upton. "Mustn't let that happen again."

"I have some money. I was actually paid." George reached into the waistband of his pants and pulled out two coppers. "I think they're called bohunseen. The old Turk spoke a little French. He said they're worth about six centimes apiece."

"A near-fortune," Jamie said. "I met a Sicilian today who said he could get us food for a price. The two loaves of the awful black bread and less than a gill of oil won't sustain us long."

"Here." George handed the coins to Jamie. "Buy what you can. The old man said he'd pay me this much every day. I'll bring more tomorrow."

"We'll spend half and save half. Money speaks many languages."

❁ ❁ ❁

The next day, it was back to the quarry and work in the unforgiving sun. When Marco showed up, Jamie called him over and presented him with one of the copper coins.

"What can you get us with this?"

"Vegetables. Carrots, scallions, greens, turnips. I can get you a pot to make soup in. But it will take more than a few coppers. I can get you meat, but again it is not without cost."

"If you trust me, I'll get you some money in a few days. We'll pay for the pot and more vegetables."

"How can I trust you? Where would you get the money?"

"Our friend is a blacksmith and the Turkish gunsmith he's working for pays him every day, two of these coppers. I'll try and find a way to make money as well."

"Can you write?"

"English, French, Latin, and a little Greek."

"Perhaps Kemal Rais could use you as a scribe. He speaks very bad French. He can neither read nor write it. I can contact him. If he will take you on, I will advance you the money, for interest of fifteen percent."

"Ain't that a bit high?" Fenton Webb interjected.

"Cheaper than anyone else."

"I'll pay it." Jamie figured a man who has survived fourteen years in captivity would do anything for money and fifteen percent, though high, would be worth it to get food for himself and his comrades.

The next day, Jamie gave Marco another copper and the Sicilian promised he would deliver the pot and the vegetables that evening.

"I have not made contact with Kemal yet, but I will try tomorrow. My cousin Tomaso is Kemal's majordomo. He will approach his master."

"Tell him to say this: my father is an important sea captain and owner of ships and a counting house. Sharpe and Company is known in Europe and America."

"Your family has money?" Marco cocked his head.

"We did until that one" — he pointed to Simon Cutts — "stole it. But my father has ventured to China to regain our fortune. He's back in America now." Jamie had Captain Collins word on that.

"If you can convince Kemal Rais your family has money, it might make it easier for you," Marco said with a smile. He wasn't sure Jamie was telling the truth, but he would be paid either way.

"You have a great deal of freedom for a slave, Marco," Fenton said. "How is that possible?"

"I've earned the trust of my masters over the years."

"Have you ever thought of escape?" Fenton asked.

"Thought of it? Yes. But where would I go? That way" — Marco pointed west — "would be to Algeria or Tunis. There, I would be another slave and worse off than I am now. South is the desert. If I didn't die of thirst, the Bedouins would take me, perhaps kill me. The same is true to the east — nothing but desert and wilderness between here and Egypt. Finally, if I were to steal a boat, I would never get out of the harbor. It is full of shoals and rocks. And there are forts with guns everywhere. No, my friend, escape is not possible. Please don't think of trying it."

Fenton nodded, his shoulders slumped in despair.

That evening, the cooking pot was delivered as promised, along with some vegetables and a few scraps of wood for a fire. George used flint and steel and got the fire going.

"Gather 'round," Jamie called to his cellmates. "I've bought this pot and these vegetables from one of the Sicilian slaves. The money came from George Walling. We will share, but only if you add some of your rations to the pot. After today, we must provide our own fuel. Pick up what scraps you can find. Anything that will burn, including animal dung. Now, who is with us?"

Most of the men agreed, but Simon Cutts asked, "Why should we share our meager rations with you?"

"Aye," Bruiser McPhee agreed. "Why should we?"

"You ain't too smart, McPhee," Fenton Webb said. "The soup will be more nourishing than just the bread and oil."

Even Hector Woolly, McPhee's friend, nodded his head. "It makes sense, Bruiser."

He threw his bread and oil into the pot. The other prisoners followed suit. Simon stood by as they did, but finally tossed his rations into the pot.

The vegetables gave the soup some added flavor. Byrd, the sailmaker, approached Jamie.

"Here's another copper. Use it to buy what you can. I'll give more when I'm able."

Dimas said he would try and get salt from the castle kitchen, for the soup lacked that needed ingredient.

The next day, Jamie and the men returned to the quarry and were told to load a cart with the rocks. Once loaded, the overseers made the men haul the heavy vehicle to the harbor and start rebuilding the walls.

"They've donkeys, camels, and horses," Fenton complained, "but they make us their beasts of burden."

"Animals are too precious," Jamie said, straining as he pulled. "They can always get more slaves."

They reached the city walls and were herded toward a large breach that faced the harbor. There, slaves were constantly stirring cement before it could cure. Jamie and the others were told to apply the caustic material to the wall to hold the rocks in place. Their hands burned and eyes teared from the alkalis in the mixture.

Jamie and the other seamen, whose hands had been toughened by hard work and salt spray, suffered the least. Still, they were cut and bleeding. Jamie noticed Simon Cutts' hands were bleeding more than the others. They never had toughened up on the voyage.

During Muslim prayer, Jamie led the crew to the beach and they washed their hands in the water, scraping off the dried cement. Simon cried out as the saltwater stung his bleeding hands. Jamie could *almost* pity him.

That evening as they trudged back to their prison, the men picked up scraps of wood and any other combustibles they could find for the cooking fire.

Marco delivered vegetables and a piece of goat hindquarter.

"I bought this from a Jewish butcher. The Jews don't eat that part of the animal."

"Have you contacted Kemal Rais about me being his scribe?"

"He is at sea. You'll have to be patient."

Several weeks went by as Jamie and the men worked either in the quarry or on the walls. Marco provided food as long as he was paid.

Simon became more and more morose, but his hands were toughening up, even if he wasn't.

Finally, after three weeks of hard labor, Marco came to Jamie.

"You will start working for Kemal Rais tomorrow. So will one called Simon Cutts."

Simon! Jamie thought. *Can I never be rid of him?*

Chapter 7

THE NEXT MORNING, instead of being sent to work, the men of the *Beneficence* were brought to a small courtyard where Murad and Kemal were talking to two men in European dress. Jamie noticed the angry look on Kemal's face, while Murad's was contented.

Murad walked forward and addressed the men. "Those of you who are Dutch, step forward."

Two men moved to the front, their faces flushed with fear.

One of the Europeans joined Murad. "I am Antoine Zuchet, consul in Tripoli for Bataafse Republiek. If you are men of Holland, I've come to redeem you, for we have a treaty with His Majesty Yusuf ibn Ali Karamanli, Bashaw of Tripoli. I have two names, Elmo Van Dreesen and Broos Roijakker. Come with me — you are free men."

The men whooped for joy and ran to Mr. Zuchet. Van Dreesen grabbed the consul's hand and kissed it.

The other European announced in a haughty manner, "I am Mr. Langford, consul to Tripoli for His Britannic Majesty George III. If there be any of his majesty's subjects among you, step forward."

Immediately, Upton limped up. "I'm Gerald Upton of Halifax, Nova Scotia."

Hector Woolly started to move, but his friend McPhee grabbed him.

"Don't. If you go with him, the Royal Navy will hang you for sure."

"I'll take me chances. I'd rather be hung by an Englishman than be a slave to these Turks."

"Yeah, well," McPhee said, "I'll turn Turk just like Billy Scars before I'll be hung."

Byrd handed Jamie a few copper coins.

"Use it for food," he whispered.

He then raised his hand and stepped forward.

"Is that all?" Langford asked.

No one else stepped up. Out of the original fourteen survivors of the *Beneficence*, all that was left were Jamie, George, Simon Cutts, Fenton Webb, Bruiser McPhee, Dimas Mendes, Mateus Balduino, and of course, Billy Scars.

Jamie and Simon were held back while the others were marched off to work. Jamie noticed Simon smiling.

"Why are you so happy?" Jamie asked.

"I'm too precious to work at hard labor. My father will redeem me. I'm sure I will be treated well. You, on the other hand, are probably destined for some menial work."

This time, Jamie smiled. He knew he was to clerk for Kemal Rais, which probably wouldn't involve lifting more than a pen.

Kemal snapped his fingers and told the young men to follow him. They walked out the castle gate and into the town. Two heavily armed guards led the way.

It was still the cool of the morning as the guards elbowed and shouldered a path through the crowded, dusty, dirty, and narrow streets of Tripoli.

Here and there, date palms grew wherever they could take root. The buildings were low, no more than two stories high, made of stone, and washed white with lime.

Jamie took note of the occasional paving stone, which looked to be of Roman origin. As they turned a corner, they came to a large marble arch, so well fit together that Jamie couldn't see any cement. There were number of handsome sculptures adorning the structure. Jamie recognized the bas-relief of fasces, the ancient Roman bundle of rods tied around an ax.

"The Arch of Marcus Aurelius," Jamie said to Simon. "Surely you remember reading about it in our Latin studies."

"So what?" Simon answered. "The Romans are dead. All I care about is my redemption."

A whack from Kemal's cane across Simon's shoulder stopped him from talking.

"At least I know which of you is the smarter. I hope yer French is as good as yer knowledge of antiquities, Sharpe."

Simon rubbed his shoulder, not understanding what Kemal meant by Jamie's knowledge of French.

They walked on in silence. Jamie observing the sights, sounds, and smells of the city. The shops, nothing but stalls actually, sold all types of merchandise: woolens, shoes, weapons, spices, and surprisingly, gold, pearls, and silver. They neared a shop where an old man wearing a black cap was being beaten by a janissary, a Turkish soldier, while another Turk was putting silver vases and ewers in a sack.

The old man cried out in Arabic.

Without being asked, Kemal explained, "The old Jew is pleading for mercy." He gave a little snort.

"Why are they beating him and taking his wares, sir?" Jamie asked.

"Someone at the castle, maybe the bashaw himself, wants silver," Kemal said with a shrug. "It's no concern of mine. Now, enough wasting time. Me house is this way." He pointed to his left.

Jamie shook his head in disgust.

"What's the matter, Sharpe?" Simon said. "It's only a Jew."

"A human being. But I forgot, Cutts, you think everyone's inferior to you. But, of course, you're a slave now, so that makes you no better than those you so easily look down upon."

Simon frowned, but said nothing, fearing to stir Kemal Rais' anger.

❁ ❁ ❁

From the outside, Kemal's house resembled the others Jamie had seen — whitewashed stone and brick, a flat roof, and two stories — but on closer inspection, he noticed the entrance was flanked by marble pillars of Roman design, chipped here and there, but mostly intact. Rich scrollwork adorned the brick. It had a very broad front, larger than other houses he had seen.

Two large Berbers stood guard at the gate, pistols shoved into sashes, holding large scimitars which they raised to salute Kemal.

Kemal didn't acknowledge them as he led his charges into a hall lined with stone benches. They passed a staircase and a courtyard paved with black marble. At its center stood a marble fountain of the same jet color as the floor. The courtyard was surrounded by a cloister supported by curved arches over which a gallery ran, enclosed in a lattice of wood. Jamie could see doors along the cloister and wondered where they led.

Kemal took a seat on several silk cushions and clapped his hands. From one of the doorways, a short, chubby moon-faced European emerged, followed by four slaves, three Europeans and an African.

The slaves ran to attend Kemal, bringing him drink and sweets. Two of them helped him out of his outer garments and boots, replacing them with a white linen caftan and soft slippers. When he was fully refreshed and clothed, Kemal turned to the moon-faced European.

"Tomaso, these two..." He pointed to Jamie and Simon. "...are now part of the household. This one..." He indicated Simon. "This one is to work in the kitchen. Give him to the head cook."

Simon's face fell on hearing his fate.

"*Si*, master. And of the other?"

"He's to be me clerk. He claims to read and write French, Latin, and Greek. When he is not working with me, he will tend the garden." Kemal addressed Jamie and Simon. "Tomaso is my majordomo; in my absence, he runs the house. He is also in charge of the accounts. Obey him as you would me."

Both Jamie and Simon nodded.

"I own you now," Kemal said. "The bashaw has sold you to me. I am your master. I brook no rebellion. At the first sign, it will be the bastinado." He fixed Simon in his gaze. "Simon Cutts, you claim to have a rich father. You will write him and tell him I demand two thousand dollars in gold for your redemption. The details, I will spell out for you. I may be Irish, but I read English, so no tricks, laddie."

Kemal stroked his beard and turned to Jamie. "As for you, Sharpe, Tomaso's cousin Marco told me you also are the son of a rich man. Write your father. Tell him I be askin' three thousand dollars in gold. You are more valuable to me as clerk than a kitchen boy. If your father is so inclined, he can pay a thousand for your big friend and five hundred each for the rest of your crew." Kemal gave a doubtful laugh.

"Until and unless you are redeemed, you will work for me. I will pay you wages, Sharpe, if you prove your worth as my clerk. You will be paid twenty paras a week."

Jamie did a fast calculation in his head. It came to about one shilling, four pence or about 28 cents American. It was better than nothing. He could repay Marco, feed his friends, and save a little for himself.

"And what of me?" Simon asked. "What will I be paid?"

"You?" Kemal gave a dismissive wave. "I don't pay the kitchen boys. You are next to worthless."

"I know mathematics and navigation. I could assist you with that."

"I don't need your help. I can navigate a ship anywhere in the Mediterranean."

"I too read and write French. I clerked for my father. I was supercargo on my ship."

"Do you read and write Spanish? Italian? Turkish? Arabic? Berber?"

"No."

"Well then, I have no use for two French reading clerks. Sharpe applied first."

"You can't trust Sharpe. He's always plotting. He took my ship."

"He doesn't beg. As for plots, he has no chance to escape. Now, I've had enough of your whining." He turned to Tomaso. "Get this sniveler out of here. Put the other one to work in the garden. But first, make sure they bathe and get them some clean clothes. Burn the old ones. They're infested with vermin. I can't have my clerk looking like a beggar, so get him something decent. Any rags for the other as long as they're clean."

Tomaso bowed and hit Jamie and Simon with his cane, telling them to do the same. Simon bowed low. Jamie bowed his head, holding his temper. *There will come a time*, he thought, *when I won't be the one bowing.*

Chapter 8

TOMASO LED JAMIE and Simon through one of the enigmatic doors lining the cloister. They passed through a hallway, out through a garden, and into a hot kitchen. Here, men both Black and white stood over hot stoves and ovens, all under the direction of a large fat Black man of indeterminate age, wearing a grease-splattered apron. He was raging over the supine body of one of the poor Black slaves.

He gesticulated with a large kitchen knife, kicked the pitiable soul mercilessly and yelled, "*Kalb, ruth al'iibil!*" By this time, Jamie had picked up enough Arab curses to understand the man was being called a *dog* and *camel dung*. "*Adhhab lileamal!*" Jamie heard that phrase often enough — the cook had told the man to "get to work."

The injured man cringed as he regained his feet, only to be kicked in the direction of the stove.

"The big man, Badr, is of the Hausa people. They are Muslim." Tomaso said. "He is the *capo*, the chief of the kitchen. The man he is berating is a pagan from the Mossi tribe. Badr hates anyone who is not Muslim." He turned to Simon. "You will work for him. He is a man of evil temper, as you can see. He punished the man for burning meat. I warn you, do what he says or you will suffer."

"I'm to work for him? A Negro?" Simon shuddered.

"Ironic, isn't it, Simon?" Jamie gave a short laugh.

Tomaso said something in Arabic to Badr and pointed to Simon.

The chef growled, turned cold eyes on Simon, and pointed to a pile of wood, indicating he wanted the oven fed.

Tomaso shook his head and spoke to Badr again. The cook nodded.

"I told him you were to bathe. There will be no vermin in his kitchen. Now, both of you follow me."

They walked to a courtyard behind the kitchen where a well stood in the center.

"Here, you will clean yourself. This well is for the servants and slaves. Take off your clothes, use the bucket. There are soap and brushes by the well."

"A razor?" Simon asked, scratching at his blond beard.

"What, so you can slit my throat?" Tomaso scoffed. "Just wash your beard and hair and comb the nits out."

The water was cold, but Jamie was glad to bathe. His body, covered with nit and lice bites, itched terribly. He noticed Simon also suffered from them. Both men had lost weight in the days they had been fed meager rations. Jamie hoped the food was more plentiful under Kemal Rais' roof.

Once they were clean, Tomaso led them through another door. He rummaged through a pile of clothing and tossed a pair of pantaloons and a rough muslin shirt to Simon. For Jamie, he selected a pair of pantaloons, a shirt of cotton, and a gray wool djellaba — a long caftan with a hood. It was a bit threadbare, but serviceable. Neither was offered shoes.

"Wear the djellaba only when you go out," Tomaso said. "And keep it clean."

They returned to the kitchen, where the Sicilian left Simon in the tender care of Badr, who seized him by the scruff of his neck and shoved him to the woodpile.

Tomaso gestured for Jamie to follow, shoving the bundle of old clothes into Jamie's hand.

"Are you going to burn those as Kemal ordered?"

Tomaso gave a wry smile. "No, I'll have them cleaned and sell them. There are merchants who will buy them for a few coppers. Money is a language all here speak. If your family doesn't redeem you, I would advise you save your wages, but I fear it will do no good, for you would be an old man or dead before you could pay the gold ransom our master demands."

Tomaso led Jamie through an arch into garden. Jamie was astounded. Here in the dusty city of Tripoli stood the most beautiful garden he had ever seen. He had expected a vegetable patch as one would have in a yard in Boston. Instead, this was a place of fountains, flowers, date palms, gazebos, fruits, and yes, vegetables.

Along two sides of the garden ran a high wall. The other two sides were enclosed wings of the house. On the second story of the house was a long balcony and behind it, louvered windows and doors. Tomaso saw Jamie looking up at the doors and cuffed him on the side of his head.

"Keep your eyes off that balcony." Tomaso pointed to the garden and gave Jamie a shove. "Here, you will work until Kemal Rais calls for you. There is a gardener here who will show you what to do. He's very strange. If I were you, I'd be wary. Some of the slaves think he's a devil because of his eyes. They call him Al-Ayn, 'The Eye.'"

Tomaso turned and shouted. "Al-Ayn!"

A man rose from behind a tall bush laden with fruit.

The first thing Jamie noticed about the man was that he had one blue and one brown eye in his bronzed, weathered face. His mustache and beard were black with strands of gray, as was the hair that peeked from under his cap. The man stood a good six feet in height in a lanky but well-muscled frame. He looked to Jamie to be a man of forty years or thereabouts. He scowled at Tomaso, then looked Jamie straight in the eyes, seeming to appraise him. Jamie stared back, holding his gaze. Finally, the bronzed man nodded and a suspicion of smile crossed his lips.

Tomaso pointed to Jamie and spoke to the man in Arabic. Jamie followed some of the words, but Tomaso's gestures also helped. He was telling him that Jamie was to work with him and that Al-Ayn was to train Jamie in tending the garden.

The man shrugged.

"I'll leave you now," Tomaso said. "Our master may call you later. Until then, work with this heathen." With that, the Sicilian turned on his heels and walked away.

To break the ice, Jamie pointed to his chest. "Jamie." Then he pointed to the gardener. "Al-Ayn?"

The man shook his head vigorously and pointed to himself. "Shams al-Din Abu'Malik Muhammad ibn Abdallah ibn Muhammad ibn Ibrahim ibn Muhammad ibn Yusuf Zuwarah al-Zuwarah ibn Malik."

"Well," Jamie said with a smile, "that's quite a mouthful."

"Then you may call me Malik." The man returned Jamie's smile.

Jamie was stunned once again. First the garden and now this. "Y-you speak English?"

"Yes, young man. I was for several years the head gardener of the Honorable Richard Tully, counsel to His Britannic Majesty, King George III. Now, may I ask your full name?"

"James Montgomery Sharpe, but my friends call me Jamie."

"Well, perhaps we shall be friends and I will call you Jamie. I've been instructed by that peacock, Tomaso, to teach you how to garden. Have you any experience?"

"I sometimes helped my grandfather on his farm. But he raises sheep mainly, though he grows some Indian corn and wheat and has an apple orchard."

"Good, though you will see what we grow here is different. First, let me show you around the magnificent garden. It is only rivaled by those owned by the bashaw and his family."

"Are you a slave as well?" Jamie asked.

"No, I am a free Muslim man."

"Oh, an Arab. Or are you a Turk?"

"I am neither, my young friend. Some call us Berbers or Moors, but we call ourselves Imaziyen. I am an Amazigh."

"Amazigh?"

"The singular of Imaziyen."

Jamie nodded. "I shall endeavor to learn your language."

"I would be glad to teach you, but you will be better off learning Arabic, which I would also be willing to instruct you in."

"I'd be most grateful."

"Now, we must start your lessons in Arabic and tending the garden." Malik signaled to Jamie to follow him. In Arabic, he said, "*Nadhhab lileamal?*"

This was a phrase Jamie well understood. "Yes, we get to work."

Malik led the way back to the bush he'd been attending. He showed Jamie how to pick the fruit and put in a basket.

Jamie examined the fruit. "Pomegranate."

"*Rumaan*," Malik said.

Jamie repeated, "*Rumaan.*"

Taking a knife, Malik sliced open the leathery skin. They shared the sweet seeds inside. Red juice ran down their faces and collected in their beards. Malik buried the husk under the tree and brought water and gestured for Jamie to wash his face and hands.

"Bastinado," Malik said. "If you are caught eating the fruit, you would have the soles of your feet beaten. Me, they leave alone. Only the bashaw can order my punishment."

"Why is that?" Jamie asked.

"After Mr. Tully returned to England, I worked for Consul Mr. Burghall, then Consul Mr. Lucas, but I was not as happy as I was with Mr. Tully and his family. It was his sister, Miss Tully who taught me English. Then fate, *qadar*, intervened. Kemal Rais was given this house by the bashaw. It once belonged to one of his father's advisors, who commissioned the garden for his favorite wife. When the bashaw gave Kemal Rais this house, he instructed me to become the gardener, for he knew Kemal wouldn't care for it. So here I will stay. It is a wonderful place, despite Kemal Rais and his toady, Tomaso. Here, *I* am in charge." Malik smiled. "Now, my young apprentice, we must get to work."

As they worked around the garden, Malik would say a word or phrase and Jamie would repeat it. Jamie hoped he would soon be able to converse in the language.

Jamie was bending over picking fruit, when suddenly he heard a pianoforte and then a most beautiful soprano voice singing in English. He stood straight up. It was coming from the doors behind the balcony.

> Domestic peace, my soul's desire,
> The dearest bliss fate could bestow,
> At length, to thee I may aspire;
> Misfortune's storms no longer blow.
> Escaped their ire, now safe on shore,
> I listen to the tempest's roar:
> And while the billows, the billows idly foam,
> They more endure my long-lost home.

Jamie stood gape-jawed for a moment. He called out, "Hello. Are you English?"

The singing stopped and the wooden blinds opened a slit. Jamie saw two green eyes staring out.

"Are *you* English?" a woman's voice called out.

"I am an American. Who are you?"

Another women's voice interrupted. "Claire. Who are you talking to? Get away from the window."

The blinds snapped shut.

"Are you still there?" Jamie called.

He started to climb one of the date palms near the balcony when Malik pulled him back.

"*La! La!*" Malik yelled. "No! No! Harem." He made a throat-cutting motion. "You must never talk to the women."

"But she's an English woman. Why is she there? Is she Kemal's wife? Did he bring her from Ireland or England?"

"I know not," Malik said. "There are two women who speak English. I hear them sing, but it is better not to inquire, my young friend. And if the eunuchs come, we must leave the garden, for that is the time the women will be here. They come mostly in the evenings. But I warn you, you must never be seen talking to them."

Jamie nodded. *I'll find another way. Who are those women? Are they prisoners too? I must find out!*

Chapter 9

JAMIE QUESTIONED MALIK about the women again.

The gardener shrugged. "Not now. We must return to work."

Reluctantly, Jamie helped pick fruit and vegetables. Malik named them in Arabic and Jamie repeated the words. They were carrying full baskets toward the kitchen when they heard a scream coming from near the stove.

They rushed to the sound to find one of the slaves prostrate on the floor. A knife lay next to his open hand. Simon Cutts swung a heavy piece of wood at another slave, who was advancing on him with a cleaver. This man went down as well.

Simon was bleeding from the nose and had a cut on his forearm. He was breathing heavily as Badr, the cook, came at him with his large butcher knife.

"*Tawqf!*" Jamie yelled.

Badr looked at him with an evil cast in his cold eyes and started gesturing with his knife.

Malik stepped between Jamie and the chef, pointed his finger at Badr, and stared hard at him. Badr twitched, threw down his knife, covered his face with his hands, and screamed, "Al-Ayn. *Alshaytan!*"

Jamie went over to Simon. "What happened?"

Simon pointed to the first man on the floor. "That one demanded my shirt. I told him no, so he hit me and cut me on the arm with a knife. I knocked him down and when his friend came at me, I laid him out as well."

Jamie remembered Simon was strong and, when cornered, he could be dangerous.

"You're bleeding," Jamie said. "Let me bind the wound."

He took a towel off a table and wrapped the cut.

Simon looked up in surprise. "Why did you stop the cook? Why did you help me?"

"I haven't forgiven you. I need you to return to America and tell the truth. If by any chance you don't, I'll kill you myself. Until then, I'll keep you alive if I can."

Simon shuddered, then seemed to regain his bravado. "I doubt your father returned from China. You'll rot here while I'm redeemed."

"Captain Collins knows my father returned and yours is hiding out in South Carolina. I saw my father's ship, the *Julia Sharpe*, sailing for Boston. We'll see who's redeemed."

Simon scoffed, but before he could say anything, Tomaso came running into the kitchen followed by a tall Berber armed with sword and pistol.

Tomaso questioned Badr in Arabic. The cook answered in an angry voice, pointing to Simon.

The majordomo turned to Simon. Aggravated, he shook his finger in his face. "Badr said you started a fight and injured two of his men. It's the bastinado for you."

Simon, with a look of dismay, pointed to his wound and then to the first slave on the floor. "Look, he punched me and cut me. I was defending myself. He tried to steal my shirt."

Tomaso turned to Jamie. "Badr said you and the devil with the blue eye threatened him."

"No one threatened him. I told him to stop and Malik stared him down."

"Malik? That's his name?"

"Yes. If you had asked, he might have told you."

"Watch your tone with me." Tomaso scowled. "I must tell our master about this. In the meanwhile, the three of you, out into the garden. Tariq will watch you." He pointed to the Berber guard and left the kitchen.

In the garden, Tariq gestured for them to sit on a pair of stone benches.

"What do you think Kemal will do to us?" Simon asked, pressing the bandage to his cut. Apprehension covered his face.

Before Jamie could answer, Kemal came striding into the garden, followed by Tomaso. Kemal's face reddened with anger and the little veins on his nose and cheeks enflamed. Jamie could smell rum on his breath even from several feet away.

"What have ye done?" Kemal boomed, pointing at Simon. "Ye have injured two of me slaves. I should kill you meself, but it's the bastinado for you."

Simon shook with fright and held up his wounded arm. "The first slave tried to steal my shirt. He hit me and cut me. I had no choice. He would have killed me. The other one attacked me as well and I laid him low."

"Bring me the other miserable slaves," he commanded. "And Badr," he added.

Tomaso ordered the Berber guard to get them and, in a minute, the two slaves and Badr were brought into the garden.

Kemal, with the help of Tomaso, questioned the three of them. When finished, he turned to Simon.

"They say ye lie. Ye started the fight. It's the bastinado for you."

"No!" Simon cried.

"Sir," Jamie spoke up. "I wasn't there, but it doesn't sound like something Simon Cutts would do. You see, he's a coward and only starts something when the odds are in his favor. I believe he was fighting for his life. As you can see, he's been cut and punched. I believe the others lied."

"Do I care what ye believe? He will be punished."

"Sir, I hate Simon Cutts. I'd like to see him punished, but he's not guilty of this crime. Ask Malik to question the men. They won't lie to him."

"Malik?" Kemal demanded scratching his chest. "You mean the gardener? The one they call Al-Ayn?"

Jamie nodded.

Kemal beckoned Malik. "Can ye get the truth of this?"

"I can try."

Malik questioned each man in turn.

They all quailed under Malik's interrogation. Jamie watched the fear in their eyes. Badr tried to make a show of standing up to Malik but, sweat appearing on his face, he faltered and could no longer look at the gardener.

Finally, Malik turned to Kemal and said, pointing to each man, "*Hu yakdib,* he lies. *Hu yakdib,* he lies. *Hu yakdib*, he lies."

They are truly afraid of Malik, Jamie thought.

Kemal saw it too. His face turned grim. "Bastinado." He pointed to each man.

They threw themselves at his feet, begging for mercy. He kicked them away and nodded to the guard, who ushered the three miscreants out to meet their fate.

"Damn it," Kemal swore. "Badr won't be able to stand in the kitchen for at least a week. But he lied and must be punished. The others, I don't care about." Kemal pointed to Simon. "I don't suppose ye can cook."

"No."

Kemal slapped his face. "No, *sir*. Useless!" he said in exasperation. He turned to Tomaso. "Until we find a cook, you will be in charge of the kitchen, along with your other duties. Go and take Cutts with you. Clean his wound. He is worth more to me alive and I don't need him dying of the gangrene."

Tomaso left, a sour look on his face. Cutts followed, his head bowed.

Kemal gestured to Malik and said, "*Aleamal, aleawdat, 'ant!*"

He turned to leave, then left the garden.

Malik turned to Jamie and whispered, "Kemal's Arabic is very bad, he just said, 'Work, back, you!'"

Jamie smiled. "I hope I learn to speak it well."

"With practice, you will do well."

They had gotten back to work when Jamie heard the pianoforte and the voices of two women singing. The first voice was a bit more mature. The second, Jamie recognized as the voice he'd heard earlier. He walked toward the sound and looked up at the windows. Malik put his hand on Jamie's shoulder and shook his head.

Jamie ignored him.

The first voice sang, "*Madama brillante*."

The second voice answered, "*Non sono sì ardita, Madama Piccante.*"

They alternated the next two lines.

"*No, prima a lei tocca. No, no, tocca a lei.*"

"*No, prima a lei tocca. No, no, tocca a lei.*"

Then together: "*Io so i dover miei, io so i dover miei, io so i dover miei, non fo inciviltà.*"

"Come away, Jamie!" Malik begged.

"That's Mozart," Jamie said. "'Via Resti Servita' from *The Marriage of Figaro*. Who's singing?"

So enrapt in the singing, Jamie hadn't heard Kemal walking up. Before Malik could warn him, Kemal struck Jamie with a blow to his head that sent him to the ground.

"Never speak of them again or, by my beard, I'll cut out yer liver. Now get up and follow me."

Chapter 10

HIS EARS RINGING from the blow, Jamie slowly regained his feet. Anger burned in him. A few months ago, he would have lashed out, but now, he remembered his grandfather's advice: "A cool head will prevail more than the man who's gone berserk."

As for the singing women, he was more determined than ever to find out who they were. He was shaken from his thoughts by a push from Kemal.

"I *said*, follow me."

Kemal led Jamie from the garden, through the courtyard, and up the stairs to his private chamber.

"This is me own grand apartment." He spread his arms in pride. "It is called the gulphor. I tell ye this so when summoned, ye'll know where to go. Ye may never enter without me own permission."

"Yes, sir," Jamie replied, taking in the large room.

It was richly decorated with Turkish carpets and tapestries of finely woven wool and silk. The apartment was furnished with large brocade cushions and chests handsomely carved in geometric patterns. Two carved wooden screens partitioned off a corner of the room. Wooden jalousies overlooking the street in front of the house let in diffused light. There were two western-style chairs in the room as well as a walnut writing desk. A barrel of rum was set on a low table, its bunghole replaced by a wooden tap. It was one of the barrels salvaged from the *Barbara Allan.*

Kemal's personal items and weapons hung on the walls. Jamie's sword, dirk, and pistols were there.

He took a deep breath. *The damn pirate has no right to the weapons given to me by my grandfather.*

"Stop yer gawking," Kemal said with an impatient grumble. "Take a seat at the desk and be prepared to write in French me words. If you deviate, it'll be the bastinado and then I'll have ye thrown over the walls where you'll hang on hooks 'til ye die. Is that clear?"

A bit of Jamie's self-confidence evaporated under Kemal's malevolence. "Yes, sir. Quite clear."

He tried to regain some composure as he took his seat and arranged the paper and ink. Kemal took a silver cup, tapped the rum keg, and between drinks, began to dictate.

> To His Excellency, Yusuf ibn Ali Karamanli, The Grand Bashaw of Tripoli,
>
> Your servant Kemal ibn Yusuf Ireland most humbly petitions Your Excellency to receive into his possession the remaining prisoners from the schooner *Barbara Allan.* Since the English and Dutch prisoners that had been promised to me have been returned to their governments, I pray Your Excellency will, in his benevolence, hand the others over to me as just compensation. I'm sure Your Excellency remembers the gold, the many slaves, and goods I've brought you since I began in your service. Two of the infidels have decided to join the true faith, Praise Allah! And with men such as those, I will be able to take many more prizes. The others shall be part of my household.
>
> I await Your Excellency's pleasure. I remain your most faithful, obedient, and humble servant.

"Read it back to me," Kemal commanded.

Jamie read it back, slowly so Kemal could follow the gist. Jamie wondered if Kemal could crawl any lower to the bashaw. His faith in himself returned. America had thrown off the tyranny of monarchy, but even George III wasn't as cruel as Yusuf.

"Sounds like ye wrote what I told you to." Kemal nodded in satisfaction. "I'll sign it meself."

He took the pen from the stand, dipped it in the inkwell, and signed his name. After the ink dried, Kemal folded it, lit a piece of sealing wax, dripped the melted wax on the paper, picked up a seal from the desk, and pressed down on the wax.

Kemal rang a bell. After a minute, he cursed and rang it again.

"Where's that damn Tomaso?"

"In the kitchen," Jamie said.

"I need a head cook, damn it."

"If I may, sir, should the bashaw grant your request, Dimas, one of the two Portuguese is cooking in his excellency's kitchen. He was our ship's cook and a good one."

"The one the old marabout claimed? I'll have to bribe the old man. All right, enough. Find Tomaso and bring him to me."

A few minutes later, Jamie returned with Tomaso. The Sicilian was sweating profusely, his hand bandaged.

"What's wrong with yer hand?" Kemal demanded.

"I burned it on the oven, sir." Tomaso was close to tears. "Master, I am no cook."

"Stop," he said impatiently. "I'll find a cook. Now, I need to have a message sent to the castle." He handed the petition over. "See that the bashaw receives it."

Tomaso nodded his understanding and left the room. Kemal waved Jamie away and he followed the majordomo down the stairs.

Jamie called after him. "Tomaso, who are those women — the ones that sing?"

The Sicilian stopped cold and spun on his heels. "Are you mad?" he warned. "The master will not hesitate to kill you."

"I believe they are Englishwomen," Jamie said. "If the British Consul finds out, there will be hell to pay."

Tomaso grabbed Jamie's shirt and pulled him close. "They are not English," he hissed. "I warn you, young man, do not attempt to find out more. The harem is sacred. Should you try to enter that sanctuary, you will die a most painful death."

Jamie shook himself loose. "If you ever put your hands on me again, I'll beat you within an inch of your life. I'll risk the bastinado."

Tomaso backed away, frightened. He tried to regain his composure. "Now get back to the garden," his voice cracked. "I've this missive to bring to the castle."

❁ ❁ ❁

Jamie found Malik high up in a date palm. He was making incisions in the trunk with a sharp knife. He then affixed a stone jar beneath the cut and let the sap drip into it. While aloft, he cut a bunch of dates and lowered them to the ground on a rope.

When finished with his labors, he swiftly climbed down, the jar in hand.

Looking puzzled, Jamie asked, "*Ma hdha?* What is that?" He pointed to the jar.

Malik smiled and indicated with his head for Jamie to follow. He led him to a corner of the garden where several of the stone jars sat covered with muslin. He lifted the cloth off of a jar, dipped a cup in it, and handed it to Jamie.

Jamie took a sip and look of surprise crossed his face. "Wine. No it's stronger."

"Lāgbi." Malik said. "Palm liquor. Kemal *yashrab alkuhul.*" He made a motion with his hands, pantomiming drinking.

Jamie repeated the phrase. "Kemal drinks alcohol."

"Yes, Jamie. You are a fast learner."

"Language has always come easy to me. But I ask you, aren't intoxicating beverages forbidden by your faith?"

"Yes. It is written in the Holy Qur'an. Sura five, verse 90 is very clear." Malik scratched his head. "I will do my best to translate. In Sura five, verse 90, it is written: 'O you who believe, intoxicants, and gambling, and the altars of idols, and the games of chance are abominations of the devil; you shall avoid them that you may succeed.'"

Jamie nodded. "I see. So Kemal disobeys the Muslim holy book."

"He is not alone. Even the bashaw disobeys the words of Allah, the Beneficent, the Merciful, as revealed to the Prophet Muhammad, peace be upon him. For the bashaw killed his own brother, Hassan, the eldest son.

"Their mother, Lilla Halluma, whom we her subjects called Lilla Kebbiera, Queen of Tripoli, brought Hassan and Yusuf to her quarters and sat them on either side of her. She had hoped to settle the animosity between them. Yusuf took out a pistol and shot his brother. His mother, trying to protect Hassan, had her fingers shot off. After he became bashaw, he exiled his other brother, Hamet.

"In Sura 4:93, it is written: 'Anyone who kills a believer on purpose, his retribution is Hell, wherein he abides forever, Allah is angry with him, and condemns him, and has prepared for him a terrible retribution.'

"Remember the son of Adam killed his brother. It is written in Sura 5:30: 'His ego provoked him into killing his brother. He killed him and ended up with the losers'."

"What you are saying," Jamie replied, "is not all Muslims obey the Qur'an."

Malik smiled. "Do all Christians obey your holy book, the Bible?"

"I see your point," Jamie answered.

"Yes, my friend. But we can only *strive* to obey the word of Allah."

They spend the rest of the afternoon weeding the garden, watering the plants, and exchanging language lessons.

After the afternoon call to prayer had passed, Malik said, "We eat."

He left Jamie in the garden and came back with a large steaming bowl.

"Couscous," he said and set it on the ground.

Jamie looked in the bowl to see a fine grain mixed with some vegetables and lamb.

"*Ta'akul*, eat."

Malik dipped his right hand in the bowl, scooped up the couscous, and ate. Jamie did the same.

"Good," Jamie said, smacking his lips.

"Good, *jyid*," Malik replied, smiling.

They finished off their meal with some dates. It was then that he heard the singing again. This time, it was the younger voice he heard and he recognized the tune for it was a favorite of his grandfather's and his mother sang it often.

Of all the money that e'er I spent
I've spent it in good company
And all the harm that ever I did
Alas it was to none but me
And all I've done for want of wit
To memory now I can't recall
So fill to me the parting glass
Good night and joy be with you all

It was "The Parting Glass." His mother had told him it was popular in Scotland, Ireland, and England. He picked up the next verse in a pleasing baritone.

If I had money enough to spend
And leisure to sit awhile
There is a fair maid in the town
That sorely has my heart beguiled
Her rosy cheeks and ruby lips
I own she has my heart enthralled
So fill to me the parting glass
Good night and joy be with you all

The pianoforte and the singer stopped for a moment and then joined Jamie in the final verse.

Oh, all the comrades that e'er I had
They're sorry for my going away
And all the sweethearts that e'er I had
They'd wish me one more day to stay
But since it falls unto my lot
That I should rise and you should not
I'll gently rise and softly call
Good night and joy be with you all

The song over, the female singer rushed to the blinds. She opened the louvers and peered out. This time, Jamie saw not only green eyes but the face of a lovely young girl a year or two younger than he, with a fair complexion and auburn hair.

"You are the American," she called.

"James Montgomery Sharpe at your service," he bowed. "May I have the honor of knowing your name?"

"Claire Andreasson."

"You are Swedish?"

"My father was Swedish. My mother is Anglo-Irish."

"How did you come to be here?"

Malik grabbed Jamie's arm, but Jamie shook it off.

Claire answered. "The beast Kemal captured our ship when Tripoli was at war with Sweden. He killed my father and took my mother and me captive." She broke into tears.

"Dear girl, don't cry," Jamie said with pity.

"Oh, I must go. If they find me talking to you, they will punish me and kill you."

She shut the louvers, but Jamie could still hear her crying.

"Damn," he cursed under his breath. He turned to Malik. "Who is that girl?"

Malik spread his hands. "Do not ask."

"For God's sake, she's English!" Jamie clenched his fists. "Or at least part English or Irish."

"Yes." Malik nodded and looked down. "Woman slave."

"I know she's a slave," Jamie said in frustration. Then, he realized that Malik was afraid to say more. He pointed. "I'm going up there."

Malik tried to dissuade Jamie. But Jamie ran to the hut where the tools were stored and took a knife and a stone jar. He climbed the palm closest to the gallery.

He tied the jar to the tree just above the gallery and made a slash to drain the sap. He was about to call out when he heard a gasp and then the voice of a second woman crying.

"*Mamaí!*" he heard Claire call out. "What happened? Did he beat you again?"

"Nothing, my child," the older woman answered.

"Mamaí, I'm not a child. I shall be fifteen in a month. I know what that means. He will take me into his harem."

"No, darling, he won't. I told him I would kill him if he touched you."

"That's when he hit you?"

"He was drunk. Rum he took from some ship. I told him if he even looked at you in that way, I would never sing for him."

"What did he do?"

"He begged me to sing an old Irish tune, so I sang 'The Dawning of the Day.'"

"Oh, Mamaí, was that not dangerous? Claire asked. "The last line. 'Go away and let me go — you rake! There from the south the light is coming with the dawning of the day.'"

"Hah!" Her mother laughed. "The beast cried, for he was so drunk, he thought it was a tender moment."

"You are the bravest mother in the world," Claire said.

"If it were not for you, my darling, I would have stabbed him to death by now. As long as I live, Claire, he shall not hurt you."

"But Mamaí," the girl said, "Sweden is no longer at war with Tripoli. If we could get word to the Swedish consul..."

"Even if we could reach the Swedish consul, would he find the means to redeem us? Your father was last of his line. There are no other relatives. And remember, your father was out of favor at court. King Gustav Adolph hated your father because of his liberal ideals."

"Maybe with father gone," Claire said, "the British consul could—"

"When I married your father, I lost my British citizenship."

"We are lost then?"

"I don't know what to do," her mother said with resignation.

For the first time, Jamie spoke up. "Ladies, I shall do my utmost to save you."

"Who's there?" the mother asked in alarm.

"He's an American," Claire said. "His name is James Montgomery Sharpe."

"Foolish man," her mother said. "Get away before you're found out. None can save us."

"I shall try, Madame," Jamie answered. "I shall try."

Chapter 11

"*ANZIL!*" SOMEONE YELLED.

Jamie looked down to see standing next to Malik, the Berber guard, Tariq, his pistol drawn, shouting at him.

"*Anzil!*"

Jamie didn't need to understand Arabic to be told to get down. He climbed down as fast as he could.

Tariq grabbed him by his shirt, slammed him against the tree, and waved his pistol in Jamie's face. "*Madha tafealun?*"

Jamie shrugged, not understanding.

Tariq repeated the question in French. "*Que faites-vous là?*"

"Oh," Jamie replied in all innocence. He pointed to the stone jar he had attached to the upper trunk of the palm. "Lāgbi. Wine. *Vin. Pour Kemal.*"

Tariq nodded and then pointed up. "*Harem, non!*"

"*Oui,*" Jamie answered, smiling. "*Je comprends.*"

Malik stepped in front of the Berber. "Lāgbi. *Hal turid sharab ya, akhi?*" He pointed to one of the jugs.

Tariq looked around to see if anyone was watching, nodded, and Malik offered him a cup. Although forbidden, Tariq took a hardy swig, wiped his mouth with his sleeve, and winked.

The guard turned and left the garden.

Malik shook his finger in Jamie's face. "That was dangerous. You are fortunate that Tariq likes lāgbi."

They both burst out laughing, relieved they'd gotten away with it.

"So," Jamie said, "Tariq speaks French."

"Yes, but not as well as you. Though he understands it well enough. I speak some but my Italian is better."

Jamie nodded. "You asked him if he wanted a drink and then you called him *ya 'akhi*. What does that mean?"

"It means 'my brother,'" Malik replied. "He is not my real brother, but a friend. You too are my brother, my *shaqiq*."

Jamie took Malik's hand. "Brother."

❁ ❁ ❁

Just before sunset, Tomaso, followed by two armed Berbers, rounded up Jamie and Simon Cutts.

"You are to be kept in the bagnio at night."

"The bathhouse?" Jamie asked.

"No," Tomaso answered. "This bagnio refers to the prison from whence you came. The bashaw commands it for now. Perhaps in time you may remain in the slave quarters here, but for now, you will be escorted to the prison every night."

"May I get my djellaba?" Jamie asked. "It gets cold in the prison."

"Hurry! You must get to the castle before evening prayer."

Tomaso waved his hands. "After prayers, the eunuchs bring the women from the harem to stroll the garden. No man can be here."

Jamie ran to the little hut where he had stored his caftan. He also picked up a knife and some dates and hid them beneath his clothes.

The prisoners were rushed through the streets as the Berber guards shoved and pushed at the crowds who were trying to get home before the call to prayer. They reached the forbidding crimson pile of stone in record time. Castle janissaries took Jamie and Simon in their charge, bringing them through the twisted passageways of the castle until they reached the cell. They were forced in and the door was slammed.

It was a small, sad lot of exhausted men who greeted them: George, Fenton Webb, Dimas, and Mateus.

George grabbed Jamie's hand. "It's so good to see you. When they took you away this morning, I didn't know if I'd see you again."

Jamie smiled at his friend. "I'm in better condition than any of you." Speaking slowly so the Portuguese sailors could understand, he related the events of the day, all but the story of the singing women.

Through the tale, Simon had sulked in a corner, envious that Jamie had run of the garden. Finally, he spoke up, his voice sullen. "While Sharpe was enjoying the fresh air, I was forced to work in a hot kitchen where I nearly lost my life to Black slaves."

"You may be working in the kitchen," Fenton continued. "But be glad you ain't back repairing the walls or breaking rock." He showed his cracked and bleeding hands.

Mateus nodded in agreement, showing his damaged hands as well.

"Where is McPhee?" Simon demanded, ignoring Fenton and Mateus.

"He turned Turk, like Billy Scars," Fenton said, scratching the fuzz growing on his shaved pate.

"Good," Simon said. "They'll free me. My father will pay them well."

"Don't be too sure," George said. "Those two may well join Kemal or some other captain and enjoy the spoils of piracy."

Simon sat back against the wall, falling back into his gloom.

"Well, George," Jamie asked, "tell me about your day."

"Not much to tell. The Turkish gunsmith had me straighten musket barrels. It wasn't hard work, I must admit. He's a kind old sort. Fed me and paid me, he did. I did pinch a bit more gunpowder. Almost felt guilty stealing from him."

"If the bashaw grants Kemal his request, we all may be under one roof. You may not have many more opportunities to get gunpowder."

"Is there any food?" Simon asked impatiently.

"*Sim*," Dimas said. "We still have goat and fresh carrots and an onion. I also have salt." He sat by the iron pot and stirred. "Throw in your bread and oil."

"I didn't get any."

"Nor I," Jamie said, "But I ate at Kemal's. What of you, Cutts?"

"Scraps, nothing more."

"I doubt the bashaw will feed us now that we belong to Kemal."

"Am I to starve?" Simon whined.

"You work in a kitchen. You won't starve."

"What about Dimas? He works in a kitchen. How come he gets to eat?"

"Because he brought salt," Jamie said, exasperated.

"It isn't fair." Simon pouted.

"Nor is being kidnapped by you," George said, his face in a fierce scowl. "I ain't eating either. The gunsmith fed me. Mateus and Fenton are working at hard labor, they get the food."

Fenton spoke up. "You paid for some of it, George. You get a share."

"No." George stood adamant.

"Here," Jamie said, reaching under his djellaba and bringing out a bunch of dates. "These will be shared by all, including sniveling Simon. Dimas, divide them."

After they ate, Jamie called George and Fenton aside.

"We will have to bide our time. As of now, I see no way to escape. But when our chance comes, we must be ready. Here." He passed the knife to Fenton. "Keep it hidden."

"Aye," Fenton said, hiding the knife in his waistband and pulling his shirt over it.

"George, is there any way you can get us guns?"

"I don't see how. The Turk knows his inventory. Powder is another matter. There is so much, I can take a bit at a time with little danger. However, I might be able to get broken pistol barrels. Filled with powder, they will make fine grenades."

"What of Dimas and Mateus?" Fenton asked. "Do we let them in on our plans?"

"Not yet." Jamie shook his head. "We really don't know them that well. They seem to be fine fellows, but they could give us away to better their lot." Jamie lowered his voice. "There is one more thing I must tell you. There are these two women..." He proceeded to tell them about Claire and her mother. "...and so I wish to liberate them from the harem when we escape."

"You're daft," George said. "How are we going to get two women out of Kemal's house, guarded as they must be?"

"I haven't thought that out yet, but we can't leave them. The girl is nearly fifteen and, despite her mother's warning to Kemal, he'll take her into his harem and we know what that means. We will get them out."

The certitude in Jamie's voice, his convincing tone, and his steadfast manner made George and Fenton nod in agreement.

"Good. Now to sleep, for it gets dark and there is neither warmth nor light in this prison."

They curled up as best they could. Exhausted, they fell into restless sleep.

Chapter 12

IN THE MORNING, Jamie and Simon were brought to Kemal's house. Both were summoned before the renegade, who sprawled by the fountain in the courtyard. Early as it was, he was already drinking rum.

"I want you to write to your families. Tell them you will be redeemed for the sums I spoke of yesterday. No tricks, ye bloody rascals — I read English."

"Tomaso," Kemal bellowed. "Bring writing tools."

The majordomo ran off and returned shortly with paper, pens, and ink. Jamie and Simon wrote their letters.

"Let me see them," Kemal slurred. He read them over. "They'll do. Tomaso, see these get to Malta on the next boat." He waved them away. "Get ye to work, y'lubbers. You'll be me 'guests' for a long time. Tomaso. I'm going up to me gulphor." The more he drank, the thicker his brogue became. "If ye hear from the castle, come at once."

But there was no word from the castle that day or, for that matter, for more than a month. Sometimes there was sound of crying coming from the gallery above the garden, but Jamie couldn't get Claire to answer his calls. Nightly, he returned to the castle prison along with Simon, who did nothing but complain about hunger. But Simon was actually putting on weight.

Badr, the head chef, returned to his duties. Simon's stance against his attackers gave the chef pause to confront him and Simon began to use flattery on him until the chef lightened Simon's duties. Tomaso also began to delegate some of the kitchen accounts to Simon, who proved he knew his mathematics. Jamie saw that Tomaso had also given Simon better clothes and paper and ink. Jamie had heard Tomaso say that when his letter was done, it would be sent to Malta, where it would be forwarded to America. Jamie wondered if Simon had promised the Sicilian money from America. Simon could be charming and was an accomplished liar.

Kemal was almost always drunk. He would brood when no word from the castle came and took it out on the slaves. Several times, he punched Jamie but was so drunk that Jamie was able to roll with the punches. Still, he was often black and blue and, at least once, cut by a cup thrown at his head which had nearly hit his eye.

The rum and wine salvaged from the *Barbara Allan* were running low and Kemal began to demand lāgbi, which Jamie brought from the garden to Kemal's gulphor. On one such occasion, Jamie caught a glimpse of a woman with very light skin being hustled from the apartment by two female slaves heavily covered in blue abayas. The woman was wrapped in a barracan, a large blanket woven of camel hair. But he saw enough of her face to realize she must be Claire's mother.

"What the hell do you want?" Kemal demanded. His face was bloated, his red eyes matched his red-veined nose.

"I've brought you the lāgbi you requested."

"I prefer rum, even that raw poteen that come off yer ship. The palm liquor is too sweet." Nevertheless, he took a swig of the liquor. "As long as you're here, I want you to write a letter to the almighty bashaw. Tell him I'm sick of waiting. I captured more loot than that scoundrel, Lyle. Damn it, I want those men." He swayed and knocked over his screen, exposing a disheveled bed, and proceeded to fall on it and drift off into a drunken slumber.

Jamie looked swiftly around. Was this his chance? He saw his grandfather's Highland dirk hanging on the wall next to his sword. He took it down and approached the sleeping pirate. *One quick thrust through the heart and he'll be dead*, Jamie thought. He raised the knife, ready to plunge it into Kemal, but suddenly stopped. *I can't. I can't kill the man in cold blood. Even if I did, where would I go? The hue and cry will be raised once he's found. Even if I did manage to escape, what of George and the others?*

Dejected, Jamie hung the weapon back on the wall and left the apartment.

☸ ☸ ☸

Back in the garden, Jamie found Malik tending the olive trees.

"I could have killed him," Jamie said, his eyes downcast.

"A coward kills that way. Allah would not approve. The bashaw would have you killed." He put his hand on Jamie's shoulder. "You are no coward. Face to face, you could kill him."

"Thank you, my friend," Jamie said. "Still, I must escape this place and take my friends with me."

"And the women who sing?" Malik pointed to the gallery.

"Aye, the women who sing, too."

"You must be mad. But I will help you if I can."

Chapter 13

Tripoli, Late October, 1803

THE NEXT MORNING, Tariq arrived and pointed to Jamie.

"Master wants you. Get your djellaba."

Jamie pulled on his djellaba and reported to Kemal in his gulphor.

Kemal was formally dressed in his finest silks. He wore Jamie's Highland blade and dagger at his waist. His beard was combed and Jamie could smell perfume wafting from it. Jamie eyed the weapons but held his tongue.

"There you are. You are to accompany me to the castle. I want you to listen carefully to what the bashaw has to say, for he will speak in French. You are to tell me later what he said. I'm sure I'll get the gist of it, but in case I don't, you'll provide me what I miss."

"Yes, sir," Jamie answered.

"Find some damn sandals. I can't have my slave looking like a beggar. Then meet me by the door. Be quick about it."

Jamie returned to the garden. He told Malik was going to the castle and needed sandals. Malik went to his quarters and returned with a pair of fine Moroccan leather sandals.

"These should fit."

"Thank you, brother."

Jamie slipped on the sandals and ran to the front door.

"Come." Kemal motioned to Jamie to join the rest of the escort.

Two were Black slaves from what the Europeans called the Ivory Coast. Jamie had met them both when slaves were fed. Kweku was tall and wiry. He held an umbrella over Kemal's head, shielding him from the sun, while Ekow, also tall but with bulging muscles, carried a large palm fan. Two Berber guards made up the rest of the party. One guard walked ahead, his scimitar drawn, and cleared a path through the crowded streets of Tripoli by shoving aside anyone who blocked the way, threating them with his drawn sword. Jamie and Tariq brought up the rear.

Tariq whispered to Jamie in French that he would like more palm liquor. "Sometimes Kemal Rais can be quite miserly with our rations of lāgbi."

"That will be no problem," Jamie replied, swatting away a fly. "Malik called you *shaqiq*. He calls me brother too."

"Malik is a good and great man. He has traveled far and learned much. He made hajj to Mecca, he is a scholar, and he can recite from the Qur'an every passage. Yet he chooses to work in a garden, saying it brings him closer to Allah. So if he can call a slave 'brother,' he must know you are a good man, even if you are an infidel. So I give you this advice: even if Kemal Rais is often drunk, he is no fool. Cross him at your peril."

Jamie thanked him.

❁ ❁ ❁

Once Kemal and Jamie reached the castle, they were ushered into the throne room. Yusuf Bashaw sat on his cushions, surrounded by his whole inner council, the Divan. Murad Rais, looking even more dissipated than Kemal, paced up and down.

Kemal bowed to the bashaw, who waved him forward.

"Kemal Rais, *il y a des rapports d'une frégate américaine dans nos eaux*." There was worry in the bashaw's voice.

Jamie could hardly repress his glee on hearing that there was an American frigate in the waters off the coast but did his best to translate.

"We must prepare our defenses," Yusuf continued in French. "I've ordered all the forts in the harbor to be on watch and that the guns are to be manned day and night."

"Americans," Kemal said in his bad French, "to be fooled if the port they enter."

Yusuf nodded but didn't bother to correct Kemal. However, Murad snorted.

The bashaw ignored Murad's derision and continued in French, "I want you to command a gunboat division."

Kemal frowned. "Face with my ship the Yankees."

"You're a damn fool, Curran," Murad said in English, using Kemal's Irish name. "Your ship's no match for a frigate."

"At least I would lose me ship fighting, not abandon it like you, then have the nerve to creep back here."

Yusuf didn't understand English, but he understood his captains and their animosity toward one another. "*Arrêter!*" Yusuf shook his fist. "I've had enough of your quarrels."

Both men bowed.

The bashaw told them to prepare the gunboats and make ready in case of attack. Addressing Kemal, he said, "*Vous ne devez pas utiliser votre navire pour attaquer les Américains. Les canonnières suffiront.*"

Kemal turned to Jamie. "What did he say about the gunboats?"

"He said, 'The gunboats will suffice. You are not to use your ship to attack the Americans.'"

"*Oui, mon bashaw.*" Kemal bowed, then beckoned Jamie to follow.

Once outside, Kemal turned to Jamie. "Not to use my ship?" he questioned. He cocked his head. "Are you sure he said that?"

"Yes, sir."

"I was never sure if Murad translated what the bashaw said."

They proceeded to the harbor and, at the wharf, climbed into a small boat. Kemal ordered Jamie to row out to his xebec, the *Aldhib.*

Once on board, Jamie was confronted by his old nemeses, Billy Scars and Bruiser McPhee. Both were dressed in Arab garb and armed with pistol, knife, and scimitar.

"Well, if it ain't Sharpe," McPhee said. "Not so high and mighty now, are you?"

"McPhee, if you and Billy Scars turned Muslim because you believe in the religion, I might respect you. But we both know you did it to save your hides."

"My name ain't McPhee no more," he said proudly. "I'm Al-Thawr. That means *the bull.*"

"I know what it means but, in your case, I think Al-Ijl would be more appropriate."

Kemal roared with laughter. "Sharpe, you have wit, but be careful of insults."

"What did he call me?" McPhee asked.

"He called you *the calf.* It would do you good to learn some Arabic as Sharpe has. Maybe I'll make him your tutor." Kemal laughed again.

The pot calls the kettle black, Jamie mused. *Kemal can barely say a full sentence in Arabic.*

"How about you, Al-Nadba?" Kemal asked Billy Scars. "Should I make Sharpe your tutor as well?"

Jamie knew the Arabic word for scar was *nadba.* Even in Arabic, Billy stuck with his nom de guerre.

"If that's what you want, Kemal Rais," Billy Scars replied. But his eyes narrowed, conveying that was the last thing he wanted.

"Not to worry, Al-Nadba," Kemal said laughing. "Sharpe has other duties. Now, to business. There is an American frigate in the offing. I want you and most of the crew to join me ashore beneath the castle. We are going to man the gunboats. You and Al-Ijl will join me on my gunboat." He laughed at McPhee's expense.

"If it dares to enter the harbor, we are to attack it. I'm putting a great deal of trust in you, Al-Nadba. You and Al-Thawr. If you attempt to join the Yankees, I will cut you down."

"I have no desire to join the American navy," Billy Scars said. "You said there were riches to be made in the service of the bashaw. I'm loyal to you."

"Loyal to gold. But that is good enough for now, since I control the gold." Kemal smiled wickedly. "And what of you, Al-Thawr?"

"I'm loyal to you as well, Kemal Rais."

Kemal nodded. He called his men and gave his orders. With just a skeleton crew left on the xebec, Kemal and the rest rowed to where the gunboats were beached. Jamie was told to help load powder and shot aboard the boats. This job, he did with distaste. But he had no choice.

The shallow draft boats each carried a brass 18- or 24-pound cannon on the prow. Having both sails and oars and manned by a crew of twenty to fifty, they were easily maneuverable in the waters of the harbor.

After the four boats had been prepared, Kemal left Billy Scars in charge of them. Before he returned home, he gave orders that, should the Americans approach, he was to be notified immediately.

"Well," he said to Jamie, as they entered his house, "if yer American brethren dare attack, sure'n we'll blow them to bits."

Jamie didn't answer, worried that the ship in the offing could be the *Constitution*, with his friend Bradley Wells aboard.

"Nothing to say, Sharpe?" Kemal laughed. His mood was brighter than Jamie had ever seen it.

Kemal bellowed in Arabic for the cook. "Badr, get out here." In a few minutes, the cook waddled out of the kitchen.

"Badr, bake loaf of bairín breac."

Badr shrugged and spread his hands. "What is that, master?"

"You stupid man. You bake last year. Never mind. Ask Tomaso."

Badr bowed and went back in the kitichen.

"What is bairín breac, sir?" Jamie asked.

"You're an ignorant idjit." Kemal gave Jamie a superior smile. "Bairín breac is bread made with raisins and other fruits. It tells one's fortune. For in each loaf is placed either a pea, a stick, a piece of cloth, a small coin, or a ring. The pea means no marriage that year. The stick means disputes will happen. The cloth means bad luck. The coin, good fortune and riches. The ring means one would be wed within the year."

Jamie nodded his understanding.

"Tomorrow is Samhain." He pronounced it *Sah-win*. "Some calls it Hallowe'en. I'll be wantin' him to bake me the loaf so I'll know me fortune. Now, get the hell back to work."

Jamie bowed and left. He wondered how Kemal, who professed to be a good Muslim, could still practice a superstition that went back to pagan Celtic religion.

Later, Jamie and Simon were marched back to the castle and locked up for the night. Jamie passed the word that the navy was offshore and gave hope to the men that rescue was at hand.

"As long," Jamie concluded, "as they don't sail too close to the guns and gunboats of Tripoli."

"What kind of captain would be that foolish?" George asked.

Chapter 14

AT DAWN, JAMIE and Simon returned to Kemal's house. Jamie was immediately summoned to Kemal's quarters.

"A letter to the bashaw," Kemal said. "Tell him all my gunboats are ready for action."

Jamie sat down at the desk and wrote the letter in French. Kemal signed and sealed it. He rang for Tomaso, who took the letter and left.

Badr entered carrying the bairín breac. The chef had a big smile on his face. "Here, master, is the special bread you ordered."

Kemal turned to Jamie. "Now, watch as I get me good fortune for the year. It will either be a gold ring and that means I shall marry or it will be the coin and the year will bring me riches." He broke the loaf. "Damn and hell. What is this?"

He withdrew a piece of cloth. Breaking more of the bread, he found it filled with little pieces of cloth.

"You damned *abn eahira*!" he screamed, calling Badr a son of a whore. "You've brought me bad luck."

He drew his dagger and plunged it into the heart of the startled cook. Badr fell to the floor, let out a moan, and died.

Jamie stood in shock. The reaction of Kemal and the swiftness of Badr's death revolted him. The poor man had no chance to explain, never mind protect himself from Kemal's violence.

"You, Sharpe, call the guards and get this offal out of here."

He gave Jamie a shove. Still stunned, Jamie left the gulphor and summoned the Berber guards.

Disgusted by Kemal, Jamie walked to the kitchen, his mind in turmoil. Badr was no special friend, not even a slave, yet his murder shook Jamie to the core. He could be killed just as easily and Kemal would fear no consequences. A slave's life was in the hands of the man who owned him.

In the kitchen, Simon was giving orders to the cooks, using the few Arabic words he had learned. Jamie had watched how, over the months, Tomaso had given over duties to Simon.

"What's the matter, Sharpe?" Simon asked. "Look like you've seen a ghost."

"Badr's dead. Kemal killed him for filling the Hallowe'en bread with bits of cloth."

"That means bad luck for Kemal. It certainly brought bad fortune for that Black devil, Badr." Simon didn't seem surprised at all.

"How did you know about bairín breac? We don't celebrate Hallowe'en in America."

"Perhaps not in New England, but in South Carolina, it's not unheard of. We had several Irishmen working in my father's counting house in Charleston."

It dawned on Jamie. "Did you tell Badr to fill the bread with cloth?"

"Me? Of course not." Simon smiled. "He must have kept the rings and the coins for himself."

"You got him killed. You hated him and hated working for a Black man."

"Prove it, Sharpe. What are you going to do, tell Kemal? When they search Badr's belongings, I'll wager they find the coins and the rings."

"Because you put them there. One day, you shall get your comeuppance and I'll be there when you do."

Jamie turned on his heels and went into the garden.

It was not long before the whole house was in turmoil. Jamie walked back in the kitchen when Tomaso returned from the castle.

"I know I gave Badr the coin." Tomaso said, wringing his hands in despair. "What am I to do?" he wailed. "There is no head cook. I don't want to be in charge of the cooking." He held his hands to his head and cried some more. "The last time, I burned myself. What am I to do?"

Jamie overheard his lament. "Why don't you put Simon Cutts in charge? He does much of the inventory. Make him head cook." He figured one problem could solve another.

"That's the answer. Thank you, Sharpe. I will not forget."

❃ ❃ ❃

Jamie was summoned by Kemal once again. Upon reaching the rais, he found him fully armed, the brace of Jamie's pistols in his sash, Jamie's Highland sword at his side, and a musket in his hands.

"Come, Sharpe. Bring my telescope." He gestured to the brass instrument on a table. "The American frigate has entered the harbor. We shall see if my luck be bad or good this day. Ye'll assist with the launching of the gunboats."

"An American frigate is a powerful ship," Jamie said. He had toured the *Constitution* when the frigate had been in Boston. Commodore Preble was known to be a fine example of the American Navy, as well as a fighting man.

"We shall see, once it comes under our guns." Kemal laughed.

On his way out, Kemal called for Tomaso. "Give Simon Cutts the bastinado. Twenty on his feet, forty on his back. He burned my couscous."

"Master, if I have him beaten, then no one in the kitchen will know what to do. The other cooks need constant overseeing."

"Very well, give his forty on his back. But warn him if he burns my food again, I will not spare his feet."

It's little enough punishment for what he did to Badr, Jamie thought.

❃ ❃ ❃

Down at the harbor, Jamie caught a glimpse of a large ship about four or five miles offshore. By her rigging, he could tell she was defiantly a frigate. She was sailing before the wind on the heels of a Barbary cruiser.

Kemal used his telescope to watch the chase.

"I see the United States flag on the frigate. She doesn't know it, but if she keeps to that course, she'll be in trouble." Kamal sounded downright gleeful.

"Here, Sharpe." Kamal handed the glass to Jamie. "See if ye can make her out."

Jamie took the glass and focused on the frigate. She was a bit smaller than the *Constitution*. She had to be the *Philadelphia*.

Chapter 15

Aboard the USS *Philadelphia*
Dawn to Sunset

"SAIL HO!" THE lookout called from his perch high in the riggings. "Off the port bow."

Captain William Bainbridge was notified and came on deck. Looking through his telescope, he saw the other ship raise her flag.

"Damn me if she ain't flying the yellow and red stripes of Tripoli. Give chase, all possible speed."

Heeling first to larboard and then to port, the *Philadelphia* chased the corsair. After three hours, the enemy was in range of the bow chasers.

"Fire!" First Lieutenant Porter ordered.

The shots sailed over the water and splashed harmlessly in the sea, missing their mark.

"Damn and hell," Porter said. "Gun captains take better aim."

The Tripolitan ship hugged the shore and was headed for safety of the harbor, out of gun range.

"Cut her off from the town," Captain Bainbridge ordered. "Raise all sails."

"We shall get a taste of fighting now, Horace," Geoffrey told his friend. "We'll show those heathens what for."

Both midshipmen stood at the larboard rail in the frigate's waist, in command of the marines stationed there.

The crossing from America and learning the ways of the ship hadn't erased Horne's permanent sneer. A bully who was not averse to using his fists or a rope end on seamen who didn't jump fast enough when he gave an order, he'd earned the enmity of nearly every sailor and marine aboard.

He'd learned well from his captain, William Bainbridge, a martinet in his own right and not above punishing a subordinate with his fists.

Horace Long followed wherever Horne led and did whatever Horne did. Long was stocky though not fat. He could use painful punishment on a subordinate, but often held back. While a follower, he was not innately a bully like his friend or that matter like their true leader, Simon Cutts.

They watched as the distance between the *Philadelphia* and its prey closed.

"Look there, Geoff," Long said. "We're really closing in to shore." He pointed.

"I'm more interested in the corsair," Horne replied, pointing at the enemy ship. "We shall blow her out of the water. We're closing on her now."

On the quarterdeck, Captain Bainbridge called to Lieutenant Porter, "We are getting too close. We will be under the shore batteries soon."

"Sir," Porter pleaded, "just a few more shots."

"Very well," the captain agreed. "Then out to sea. I do not like the wind."

Porter ordered cannon fire. More than a few shots were fired, but none of them ever struck their target. After the last salvo, Porter reluctantly relayed the captain's order to turn the ship out to sea.

As the ship was hauling about, the captain said, "Mr. Porter, climb the mizzenmast and appraise what vessels lay in the harbor."

Porter jumped to. Halfway up the mast, he was violently flung back and forth and only a strong grip on the rigging prevented him from falling.

On deck, Geoffrey Horne was slammed hard against the rail, while Horace Long was thrown to the deck.

"We've struck!" Horne wailed.

"Belay that, Mr. Horne," second officer Lieutenant Jones shouted.

"Full sail ahead," Bainbridge ordered. "We will force our way over the reef."

The *Philadelphia*, the wind at her back, slammed forward and caught hard on the reef, then rose up and struck again. A full third of the ship was caught hard on the rocks.

"Set sails aback," Captain Bainbridge ordered, hoping to back off the reef.

Instead, the ship tilted so far over to larboard, her cannon on that side pointed down and the cannon on the starboard pointed to the sky. Worse, the *Philadelphia* was still trapped hard on the reef.

At the same time, the blockade runner they had been pursuing took a few shots at the stranded ship. With the guns in the position of pointing up and down, there was no way to return fire.

Bainbridge called a meeting of the officers.

"Gentlemen, the situation is desperate — our cannon are useless, the enemy is launching gunboats. We must lighten ship."

The officers knew there was no other alternative. The enemy just sat out of gunnery range.

All afternoon, the men worked to lighten the ship. On the spar deck, cannons weighing two thousand pounds each were hoisted and tossed overboard, along with shot and anything else heavy. Then the cannons on the gun deck were lifted out with great strain on the men. All in all, twenty-eight long guns and sixteen carronades were thrown into the harbor of Tripoli. Then the freshwater casks were removed from the hold and tossed overboard. Next, the heavy anchors were cut and fell away. Finally, the foremast and its rigging was chopped down, but the ship remained stuck.

The enemy gunboats finally began to fire on the stricken ship. Most shots fell short or flew through the rigging. Not one cannonball struck the ship.

Most of the crew held steady. A few threw epithets and taunts at the enemy. "Them lubbers couldn't hit a hob with a quoit if it were a foot in front of them."

"Shut your holes, you louts, and get to clearing the deck," a bosun's mate yelled.

On the quarterdeck, Captain Bainbridge called the officers for a second meeting.

"The ship is doomed," Bainbridge said with a heavy heart. "There is nothing for it, gentlemen. I will scuttle the ship and surrender. We can't blow her up. I will not be responsible for the death of three hundred and six souls."

"You've done what you could, sir," Lieutenant Porter said.

The other officers agreed.

"Strike the colors," Bainbridge ordered.

"No, sir," the man at the ensign halyard said. "We cannot surrender to be slaves. The men will fight."

"Damn you, seaman!" Geoffrey Horne drew his dirk. "I'll run you through."

"Do what you must, sir." The man refused to budge. "But I will not lower my country's flag."

Horne turned red with anger, cursed, shouldered the man aside, and lowered the ensign.

"Captain," one of the men yelled, "we'll fight. Raise the flag."

A marine stepped forward. He was a small man, standing no more than five feet, four inches. "We don't wish to be slaves," he shouted. "We will fight." With tears in his eyes, he pleaded, "I beg of you, sir, raise the flag."

He was joined with a chorus of "Ayes!"

Bainbridge ignored their pleas. He called to the bosun, "Take a party and bore holes in the hold and flood the powder magazine."

Then, Bainbridge proceeded to destroy the code books.

After the holes were drilled in the hold, water poured in, but after all that effort, the ship didn't sink. It was stuck too hard on the reef and remained helpless where she lay.

Still, the enemy didn't close in.

"Have they not seen we've surrendered?" Bainbridge asked Lieutenant Porter. "What do you suggest?"

"Sir, with your permission, I'll take a boat under a flag of truce and try to tell them we've surrendered."

A dejected Bainbridge waved his hand in consent.

Chapter 16

The Harbor at Tripoli
October 31, 1803

"HA, WE HAVE HER NOW!" Kemal danced a little jig. "You see, Sharpe? The mighty American frigate is caught upon Kaliusa Reef. She won't get off so easy." He clapped his hands in delight.

"Shall we attack?" Billy Scars called from his gunboat.

"We must be cautious," Kemal said. "They may free themselves from the reef."

They waited most of the day, watching the Americans lighten the ship. Even as the guns were hoisted overboard, Kemal refused to attack. "It has to be a trick. The Americans are just trying to lure us in."

Finally, after hours of waiting, Kemal called to Billy Scars, "Al-Nadba! Take your gunboat and see how badly the American is stuck. Beware, her guns are still on board." He pointed to Jamie. "Take Sharpe with ye and chain him to an oar. Let him see up close how his countrymen fare."

Billy Scars grabbed Jamie and dragged him to a waiting gunboat. He threw him in and chained him to an oar.

Billy Scars had a cruel smile on his lips. "Pull hard, Sharpe, or I'll beat you within an inch of your life," he said.

Jamie picked up the oar and bent to rowing.

Billy Scars steered the gunboat closer, staying downwind of the frigate. He ordered the cannon in the bow to fire on the frigate's rigging. The eighteen-pound ball landed short. Billy Scars cursed and ordered the crew to fire again. The ball fell short once more.

Other gunboats fired as well, but they had no better luck than the one Billy Scars commanded. Cannonballs hit the water all around the ship, sending up violent fountains. None struck.

Jamie had watched in consternation as the crew of the *Philadelphia* began to hoist the large cannon overboard. He knew they were trying to lighten the ship, but also knew the bashaw would try and recover those guns.

Now, as they neared the frigate, he saw for the first time that the way the ship was tilted, the big guns couldn't be brought to bear.

More of the bashaw's gunboats launched and joined Billy Scars' boat. Soon, nine gunboats opened fire on the stricken ship. They fired shot after shot, but the aim was poor and most sailed clear over the frigate or landed short. None struck the hull.

Then late in the afternoon, Jamie clenched his jaw and felt a pain in the pit of his stomach as he saw the flag of the United States being struck. Bainbridge had surrendered without firing a shot.

Still, the corsairs didn't approach the *Philadelphia*. Kemal Rais had pulled his gunboat alongside Billy Scars' boat. Other captains joined them. They argued back and forth in Arabic as Jamie listened. Some wanted to attack and board the frigate; others believed it to be a trick.

"No captain of such a ship would surrender without a fight," one gunboat commander said. "They will wait until we approach and open up with small arms and the remaining cannon."

Jamie wasn't so sure. He knew that Bainbridge had surrendered his command before — the *Retaliation*, to the French during the undeclared war with France in 1798. He also was aware that after Bainbridge had delivered tribute in 1800 to the Dey of Algiers in the frigate *George Washington*, the Dey threatened war unless Bainbridge brought gifts to the Turkish sultan at Constantinople. Adding insult to injury, Bainbridge was forced to fly the Algerian flag above the main topgallant royal sail of the *George Washington*.

But to give Bainbridge the benefit of the doubt, he didn't know the condition of the ship.

By late afternoon, a boat put out from the frigate, carrying a white flag. The tall, handsome lieutenant in the stern sheets hailed the gunboats.

"I am First Lieutenant David Porter of the United States Frigate *Philadelphia*. We have surrendered and wish to discuss terms."

Jamie could hear sadness or even a hint of anger in the lieutenant's voice.

"Is this some sort of Yankee trick?" Kemal shouted. "Do ye plan to have us board and then blow up the ship?"

"I assure you, sir, if we had wanted to blow up the ship, we would have done so. We are trying to save the lives of our crew and your men."

"Return to your ship," Kemal ordered. "We will discuss it."

Rather than discuss, they argued.

"It must be a ruse."

"You heard the American officer. They wish to surrender."

"Don't be a fool. They will kill us if we come aboard."

The arguments went on for hours until, just before sunset, they came to a decision and Barbary pirates swarmed aboard the *Philadelphia*.

From his vantage point aboard the gunboat, Jamie watched nearly a repeat of the boarding of the *Barbara Allan*. The corsairs fought among themselves over the belongings of the crew. Billy Scars was ruthless, stripping the seamen of their possessions without hesitating to beat any reluctant sailor.

Kemal and the other captains separated the *Philadelphia*'s officers from the crew and piled them into the longboats. But the officers weren't spared the robbery of their personal items. They were roughly handled as watches, coats, epaulets, swords, and money were snatched from them. Kemal ordered Billy Scars to command the longboat with the officers.

Before he sent the boat the three miles to shore, Kemal said to him, "We will reap rewards for this. The bashaw will honor me, and I will honor you as I saw you on deck of the frigate. You are a mighty fighting man."

Not much of a fighting man when he had the prisoners under the gun as he beat them, Jamie thought.

As they neared shore, Billy Scars grabbed a midshipman by his collar and threw him into the cold surf. The young man came up sputtering and crying.

"Billy Scars! I knew it was you. It's me, Geoff Horne. How is it that you are here? Save me from these barbarians."

"Shut your gob!" Billy Scars cuffed Horne across the face.

"Billy Scars, that's Geoff Horne, stop!" Horace Long shouted.

Billy Scars smiled and reached out for Long. He threw him in the water as well and watched him struggle through the surf. "Another strutting peacock," he said. He pushed Long under and held him there.

"Belay that, Al-Nadba," Kemal ordered, drawing alongside. "They're officers and the bashaw will want them in one piece."

Billy Scars lifted Long by his hair. "The little bastards will live. I just remember how he and the other one used to swagger about, thinking they was better than the likes of me."

"Well, get them on shore," Kemal said, pointing to the beach. "Time enough for revenge."

Billy Scars tossed them on shore to the waiting janissaries, where they were subjected to running a gauntlet of kicks and punches.

Only then, did Kemal Rais unlock Jamie from the oar. "Come Sharpe, let us see the bashaw's justice on these dogs."

Chapter 17

THE OFFICERS WERE separated from the crew and brought before the bashaw. Jamie, standing next to Kemal, was amazed to see the officers fed a meal in the European style. Then, the officers and their servants were escorted to the house once occupied by the American consul.

The bashaw told Kemal to stay, speaking in French. Jamie translated.

"Kemal Rais, due to your bravery in taking the infidel's ship, I grant you the other slaves you captured. I also present you with one hundred gold coins."

Murad Rais face turned red as his hair. He pulled himself up to full stature but still didn't reach the bashaw's chin. "What of me? Did I not command gunboats? Where is my reward?"

"Husband of my daughter, have I not honored you with many tokens of esteem?" The bashaw sighed. "You did not board the enemy ship. But I will bestow upon you fifty Venetian gold sequins."

Murad Rais could do nothing more than bow. Kemal could barely hide his mirth.

After being dismissed, Kemal was in a jolly mood as he told Jamie of his plans for him and his crew.

"Now, go tell your comrades," Kemal said, turning Jamie over to his jailer.

As Jamie was ushered to his cell, he saw the crew of the *Philadelphia* herded into an open courtyard where, wet and cold, they were subject to the night chills. Jamie heard some cry out for food or blankets, but for their troubles, they were slapped and punched. He recalled that he and his men had received similar treatment.

Back in his cell, Jamie woke the others and told them what had happened.

"My God!" George exclaimed. "They surrendered without a fight?"

Jamie nodded.

"And to think, I was to sail with Captain Bainbridge." George shook his head. "The shame of it all."

Simon lay in his corner, moaning.

"What's wrong with him?" Jamie asked.

"Kemal ordered him beaten," George said.

"Ah. Now I recall." Jamie hid his smile. "He burned Kemal's breakfast."

"I'm no cook," Simon groaned. "I told them I was no cook."

"Well, you're in luck, Simon. A new cook will start tomorrow."

Simon sat up. "Really?"

"The bashaw is giving the rest of you to Kemal Rais. This will be our last night in the castle. Tomorrow, we will all be transferred to Kemal's slave quarters. Dimas, you will become head cook. I warn you to do nothing to make Kemal angry. If he orders cow guts, serve him cow guts. As for you, George, I'm sure you will have to return to your old profession and be a blacksmith and farrier. Fenton and Mateus, you may have the best jobs. You are to be fishermen. Kemal has a fleet of small fishing vessels, which go out daily. You will crew on them." Jamie lowered his voice so Simon couldn't overhear. "Take note of every shoal, rock, and gun emplacement in the harbor. Count the gunboats and other vessels. If we are to escape, we must know the harbor. If we can relay the information to Bainbridge, perhaps he will find a way to send it to Commodore Preble."

"It seems your fates are sealed," Simon said. "The lot of you will be in service to Kemal for the rest of your lives. I will be redeemed. My father will send the money."

"Your father might be in prison or dead by now. Captain Collins told me that Nehemiah Cutts is a wanted man in Massachusetts."

"But not in South Carolina," Simon retorted. "He has powerful friends and influence there and in Washington City."

"Your father's influence doesn't always work out for the best, Simon," Jamie said. "I saw your comrades, Horne and Long.

They were taken prisoner along with the rest of the crew of the *Philadelphia*. Your good friend Billy Scars beat and nearly drowned Long."

"Billy Scars is just biding his time," Simon insisted. "He's loyal to the House of Cutts, but must make a show."

"Believe it if you will, but Billy Scars is a renegade and has abandoned you for the gold he will win as a pirate."

Simon retreated to his corner and curled up.

Chapter 18

THE NEXT MORNING, Jamie and the men from the *Barbara Allan* gathered up their meager belongings. George hid the gunpowder and the pistol barrels he had taken from the gunsmith under his shirt. Dimas carried the iron pot used for cooking, hoping that he would be able to sell it.

They were ushered out of the castle by the bashaw's guards and found themselves on the street. To their surprise, no one from Kemal's household was there to escort them.

"I suppose he knows we can't escape and expects us to find our way back," Jamie said. "Follow me."

They started walking toward Kemal's villa. They passed the Arch of Marcus Aurelius, where fruit and vegetable vendors had set up stalls.

"I'm hungry," George said. "I've a few coins. I'll buy us some oranges."

After he did, he passed out the fruit. They ate as they walked, grateful for something other than oil, bread, and goat leg. Suddenly, they were confronted by several sailors from the *Philadelphia*.

"You there!" One of them pointed to Fenton. "I see by the tattoos that you're a sailorman. Where can a mariner get something to drink around here?"

"I thought you men were prisoners," Jamie said.

"Huh? A Turk what talks like an American? You a renegade?"

"I'm a prisoner like you. What made you think I was a Turk?"

"Well, you be dressed as one, with that wool nightgown you be wearing." He pointed to Jamie's djellaba. "You be burned dark like one. Now that I know you to be a Yankee, can you tell us where we can get something to drink stronger than water? We hid a few coins from them heathens."

"Christian and Jewish merchants have a palm liquor called lāgbi. However, you'll be better off buying food. It will be mighty scarce in prison."

"Captain Bainbridge said the Turks will feed us."

"He doesn't know the bashaw," Jamie said without irony.

"Why aren't you in the prison?" George asked.

"We have to get back afore sundown. No work for us." He laughed and turned to his comrades. "Let's find some drink."

"Wait," Jamie said. "Dimas, give them the cooking pot."

"I thought we were going to sell it," Fenton said.

"They're Americans," Jamie said. He gestured to the sailors. "It's the least we can do."

Dimas handed the pot to the sailor doing all the talking.

"You can use this pot for cooking," Jamie said.

"Why, thankee. Maybe we can trade this for some drink." They wandered off.

"Sometimes, fools have to learn the hard way." Jamie shook his head. "And if they don't get back to the prison by sunset, it will the bastinado for them."

"Who cares?" Simon said. "I got whipped on the back for nothing. Those louts are scum, like all common sailors."

"Scum?" Fenton replied. "They may be stupid, but to call them scum..." He punched Simon in the face, knocking him down. "I've been waiting to do that for a long time."

Simon lay stunned by the pain. Through the blood filling his mouth, he said, "I'll get you for that, Webb."

"Your personal dog Billy Scars don't work for you no more," Fenton retorted. "You'll have to do your own fighting from now on."

"I'm not afraid of you, Webb. One day..."

"All right, enough," Jamie said.

Simon climbed to his feet and trailed the others back to Kemal's villa, muttering "I'll get you all. I'll see you hung yet."

Chapter 19

TOMASO MET THE AMERICAN CAPTIVES when they reached the villa.

"You, Sharpe, show them the well where they are to wash. Have them turn in their rags. I've had clean clothes laid out for them."

The new garments were only a little better than their old ones, but at least they were vermin-free.

Once the men had dressed, Tomaso said, "Follow me."

They entered the kitchen and waited while Tomaso showed Dimas around.

Dimas looked about at the stout wood tables and high cabinets filled with silver and brass. The food, the jars, the spices.

Giving a quick, sharp nod, he said, "I will have not trouble with this place."

"Good. Here are menus for Kemal, the harem, the staff, and the slaves." Tomasos said. "Can you read the Italian?"

"*Sim.* The Italian is close to Portuguese."

"If you don't understand, come to me," Tomaso said. Turning to Fenton Webb and Mateus, he said, "Since the fishing fleet has departed, you will help in the kitchen today."

"Now, listen, all of you. Simon Cutts is the head steward. He is second to me and will keep the kitchen books. If you need something, see him."

Simon gave a triumphant smile.

What the hell did Simon promise Tomaso? Jamie wondered.

Tomaso took Simon away from the others to an alcove off the kitchen.

"This is your office. You will be paid as much as Sharpe." And then in a conspiratorial whisper, he added, "I expect a cut of your profits, for you are smart enough to make them if you order right and keep the books. Also, your promise that I will be paid in gold when your father redeems you."

"I promise. Don't worry."

"Break it and you will die."

"I'll keep my word."

Tomaso walked out of the alcove and pointed to George.

"Sharpe, show *that one* the stables."

George moved to within six inches of Tomaso. George's great size gave Tomaso a start and he stepped back.

In a rumbling voice, he said, "My name is George Washington Walling, little man — I'll thank you not to forget it."

Trying to regain his composure, Tomaso replied, "I am the majordomo of this house. I'm in charge of all the slaves."

"If you say so." George smiled disarmingly.

"I do," Tomaso said, his face turning red, but challenging George no more.

George followed Jamie to the stables.

"The Sicilian," Jamie said, once out of earshot of Tomaso, "can be dangerous. Show him a little deference."

George nodded and took in the stable. There were four Arabian horses in stalls and two camels tethered outside.

"Thank God camels don't wear shoes. I'd hate to tangle with one of those beasts. The horses are real beauties."

A groom came up and introduced himself in passable French. "I am Usem, the head groom in charge of the stables. I welcome you. We have need of a blacksmith." He pointed up. "Your quarters are in the loft above."

Usem showed George the blacksmith shop and the tools.

"It will do," George proclaimed.

Jamie left his friend with a squeeze of the arm and returned to the kitchen.

Dimas had taken charge. The slaves, weary of the late Badr's bullying, were pleased with Dimas' easy commands.

"They not such good cooks, but they do what I tell them," he said in an undertone to Jamie. "In a few days, I make kitchen work well. Food for slaves are not so fine, but I can give it taste. There are many spices and I saw the garden. A little mutton, some fish, the slaves will eat good. As for the master, Tomaso say he like food plenty but plain. Lamb, fish, beef, couscous, fruit, some vegetables. Mostly stews. There are five women in the harem. Three get mutton, fish, fruit, and vegetables. Two of them are special, Tomaso say. They get better food. Lamb, not mutton, also fish and fruit and vegetables, but with more flavor. For the young girl, a sweet called pistachio baklawa. One of the cooks know how to make it. The older woman, she like almond baklawa. I'll learn to make both. Oh, and both women get lemon juice with honey for the throat."

Jamie nodded. "Good. If the ladies are in good spirits, that will make Kemal a happy man and make it easier on all of us. But watch out for Simon. He now is in charge of buying for the kitchen. He doesn't know enough Arabic to bargain with the vendors, but they are too frightened of Kemal to charge too much. He'll probably start hiding some coins for himself. So make sure he doesn't short you on provisions. And don't let him bully you. Tell me if he does."

"Capitão Jamie, when you get a ship, I will sail with you."

"First, we have to get out of here."

Dimas shook his head. "You might have to escape alone."

"We all go together."

"You're a man of your word," Dimas said, and turned back to cooking.

Jamie left for the garden, passing two eunuchs who had come for food for the harem, and an idea struck him. First, he would have to obtain paper, pen, and ink.

Lost in thought, he hadn't noticed Malik. He jumped at his voice.

"Daydreaming, my friend is fine, for those who have leisure, but alas, we who must work have not time. So dream at night when there is not work to do."

He handed Jamie a bucket and told him to water the herbs.

"Sorry," Jamie said, taking the bucket.

It was two days later when Kemal called him to write some letters. As the rais paced about his gulphor, dictating, Jamie hid some sheets of foolscap under his shirt.

Kemal finished and told Jamie, "Sharpe, put on yer djellaba. We are going out. Meet me at the door."

Jamie retrieved his garment, hid the paper, and ran to the front of the house.

Kemal came down dressed in fine red and blue silks and armed with the Highland sword, dirk, and pistols. *Someday, I'll get them back*, Jamie vowed.

Followed by Kweku and Ekow and several Berber guards, they walked to a coffee shop overlooking the harbor.

In the shop's courtyard shaded by date palms, Arab, Turk, and Berber men lay or sat on well-appointed couches, drinking coffee, smoking water pipes, or idling over games of chess.

Several of the men greeted Kemal with deference, for he was the hero of the day, the man who captured the American frigate. The owner of the shop bowed and led Kemal to a couch, where he lit a water pipe for him. Kweku went into the smoky shop and returned with coffee and a plate of figs. Ekow stood over Kemal, holding an umbrella to shade him from the sun. Two guards stood next to Kemal, keeping hands on their pistols. Jamie stood at attention, sweating, his eyes half-closed against the sun.

"Sharpe," Kemal said, "look ye at the frigate."

Reluctantly, Jamie opened his eyes in the midday glare and saw the *Philadelphia* anchored in the inner harbor. "A storm the other night floated her off the reef. If only Bainbridge had waited, he would have got clear! Now, the ship is ours. The bashaw calls her *The Gift of Allah*. As ye can see, we are refitting her."

Jamie watched as the captured crew of the frigate was now forced to repair the damaged ship. He felt for those men. *Poor wretches surrendered without a fight, now this ignoble work.*

"Here," Kemal said, handing his telescope to Jamie. "Look out at the reef where the ship went aground. See those lighters out there? Men are divin' from them and retrievin' the cannon Bainbridge tossed overboard. Once the ship is fitted out, it'll become the flagship of the bashaw's fleet. If I'm lucky, it will be mine and I will destroy any Yankee warship that nears this shore."

Jamie bit his lip, trying not to utter his thoughts. He was sad and angry at the same time.

"I wanted ye to see this," Kemal continued. "Though ye be young, ye be the undoubted leader of them from the schooner. Ye can see there is no escape from here. Tell that to yer men. Do what I say and ye'll survive, perhaps ye'll be redeemed. Plot against me and ye'll face me wrath. I can be a good or bad master, it is up to you. Ye be smart enough to know what I'm sayin' is true, so tell yer friends to do their work and they will live better being a slave to the bashaw than sold to traders from Algiers."

For the moment, Jamie thought. Better the Devil you know, than the Devil you don't.

"Train the glass on the men repairing the seawall." Kemal's voice was solicitous. "They are part of the American crew that has felt the bashaw's justice. They didn't return to the prison when told to and it was the bastinado for them."

Jamie looked at the men and recognized two as the sailors who had been looking for liquor the other day. Not only were they limping, but they were each dragging a ball and chains that must have weighted at least twenty pounds. He could imagine how that felt in the punishing heat.

Kemal took back his telescope. He lay back on his couch, took several puffs from his hookah, and then sipped coffee.

Jamie had a lot to think about. The odds of escaping were worse now that the bashaw had the frigate. He could wait to be redeemed, if his family had received his letter and if they could raise the money, but even if they did, it would take months, maybe even years. And if he were redeemed, what about his crew? And of course, there was the promise he'd made to the women. He couldn't leave them to Kemal's tender mercies.

Chapter 20

THE NEXT DAY, Jamie took his purloined paper, a pen from a feather he found, and ink he made from berry juice. He sat down and wrote a note to Claire.

> Dear Miss Andreasson,
>
> It has been six days since we met. I have not forgotten my promise to you and your mother. I will do my best to liberate you both from the clutches of the Kemal Rais and this nest of evil pirates. It is no place for you ladies.
>
> I hope you don't think me a Don Quixote tilting at windmills, but rather as a man of determination. I beg you to take heart. Somehow, I will succeed.
>
> The American Navy is in these waters and, though they lost a frigate, they will surely strike again. When they do, I will also strike.
>
> I will try and talk to you when your mother is not about and the garden is clear of guards. Please keep faith.
>
> Your Obedient Servant,
> James Montgomery Sharpe
> (P.S. Destroy this note, lest it fall into the wrong hands.)

Reading the letter over, Jamie wondered if he really was a Don Quixote. What right did he have to make promises, to give false hope? How could he liberate the women when he hadn't a plan to liberate himself? Still, he had to try.

He folded the note and entered the kitchen. Dimas was preparing food for the harem.

"Dimas," he whispered. "Hide this note in the food for the young girl."

"She's the one I make the pistachio baklawa?"

Jamie nodded. Dimas took the note, put it on a plate, and placed the sweets over it. The eunuchs came for the food and Jamie prayed Claire would get the note.

❁ ❁ ❁

For days, Jamie had no chance to talk to Claire. The garden was busy nearly all the time. Some days, Kemal took his ease near the fountain or under a palm tree. Other times, Berber guards came seeking lāgbi. Or Claire's mother was with her as they played the piano and sang duets.

Perhaps she didn't get my note or her mother found it, he worried. Maybe when he was away, she'd come to the window and couldn't see him.

Finally, on a late November morning, while working alone in the garden, he heard Claire singing "The Parting Glass." He whistled the tune and she threw open the louvers. For the first time, he had a good look at her face. It was framed in the light of the eastern sun. Her dark auburn hair cascaded around a face with nearly perfect features. Her green eyes were large with long lashes, her nose straight, and her lips full and red. Here was a young girl destined for classic beauty. Her eyes darted about, perhaps in fear of being caught, yet he thought there was a hint of boldness in them.

"James," she whispered, "it is dangerous for you to talk to me."

"And what of the danger to you?" he asked.

"I fear not for myself, for none dare lay a hand on me. If Kemal hurts me, he knows my mother will never sing for him again. He also knows she will find a way to kill him."

His heart skipped a beat. The fear in her eyes was for him.

"You must not think of trying to help us escape, there is no way," Claire pleaded. "Though mother and I have private quarters, the harem is guarded day and night. And even if I were to climb down from here, the villa is surrounded by a wall. The gates are always guarded."

"I have more freedom now," Jamie said. "I could get word to the British consul."

"We are not British subjects. Though my mother was born in Ireland, my father was Swedish and so then are we."

"I will still try."

Claire suddenly turned. "I must go, someone is coming."

She closed the shutters. Jamie stood in the garden looking up, thoughts racing through his head. *I have got to save her.* There was no doubt he was smitten.

For more than a week, he tried to get Claire to come to the window by whistling "The Parting Glass," but she did not come. *She fears for me.* He smiled. *She must care for me a little.*

Jamie confided in George his frustration in not having a plan.

George replied, "Even if we get out the villa, where will we go? The desert? The harbor? It is as Marco told us, there is nowhere to go. We are blocked everywhere. Fenton and Mateus confirmed the harbor is too well-guarded to steal a boat."

"The next time Kemal sends me on an errand by myself, I will notify the British consul. He may be gentleman enough to demand the women be turned over to him."

"I wish you luck, my friend." George shook his head. "If you plan an escape, I'm with you. I have gunpowder and can make more. The charcoal I need comes from the forge. I can recover saltpeter from horse piss and manure. I need sulfur. Perhaps you can find some for me. I'll forge us some nice grenades."

"We use sulfur in the garden to fertilize and also to kill insects. I can get it, but what good will it do to make gunpowder if we have no way to escape?"

It was rare for Jamie to be so downhearted. George put his hand on his friend's shoulder.

"Jamie, don't let the girl cloud your mind. We may need the weapons to assist the navy when they attack. At any rate, it will give me something to do."

"Stout fellow," Jamie said. "We will do something. Make the powder and grenades. I must get Claire free of Kemal before she is inducted into his harem."

Chapter 21

THE FOLLOWING WEEK, Kemal called for Jamie.

"Sharpe, I want you to go to the Jew, Ephraim de Aragon, and buy some whiskey. Tomaso is on another errand and Cutts'll get lost in the mellah, the Jewish quarter. He couldn't find his arse with both hands. De Aragon's residence is near the Bab il Giadid, the New Gate. Ye'll see a synagogue. Go past it and turn left. Ye'll find de Aragon's place there. Ask if ye get lost. The Jews speak Arabic. De Aragon has a shipment of spirits from England. Buy as much as he has. For sure, I'm sick of the palm liquor." He handed Jamie a purse. "There should be enough. Get a receipt."

It was what Jamie hoped for, a chance to get out and perhaps see the British consul.

Jamie went to the consulate first, but the Turkish guards blocked him.

Standing tall, looking officious as possible, Jamie addressed the guard. "I, Hamid ibn Kalil, bring a message to the consul from my master," he lied.

A guard conferred with an official inside. A few minutes later, Jamie was ushered into a reception area where he was met by a stout British naval officer. He looked at Jamie as if he were a piece of debris that blew in from the street.

"I am Lieutenant Ewell," he said, "naval attaché."

"I've a message for the consul from my master, esteemed officer," Jamie said, trying to sound like an Arab speaking English.

"His Excellency Mr. Langford is not available. Give me the message."

"In the household of Kemal Rais are two captive Anglo-Irish women."

"I know of whom you speak," Ewell interrupted. "*Baroness* Andreasson and her daughter. I'm well aware of their fate. But it is out of my hands. After the former Miss Catriona Tyrrell chose to marry the Swedish Baron Andreasson, she ceased to be a British subject. She and her child are Swedish. It is out of the hands of his majesty's government." Ewell waved his hand as if shooing a fly.

"How did you come by this information?" he demanded.

"Ai, sir, it is a long story. My master was once done a service by a Swedish merchant who wrote him to intercede. My master, he sent me. For I, Hamid ibn Kalil, speak the language of the great king of the British."

"Who is your master?"

"Ai, great sir, that I cannot reveal, for my master does not want his name involved."

"*Ha.* What does he expect the consul to do?"

"Pay their ransom. My master's friend, the Swedish merchant, fears for the ladies. The daughter will be taken into the harem of Kemal Rais."

"The *woman,*" Ewell replied with haughty distain, "was a singer of opera in Ireland and England. A woman of the theater. Actresses are not known for their chastity. She is by law tied to her husband's nationality. We can do nothing." He turned away.

Jamie's eyes turned menacing. He nearly grabbed Ewell by the throat, but quickly regained as much composure as he could. The lieutenant called for his guards and told them to show Jamie out.

When you press our sailors, you claim once a subject of King George, always a subject of King George. But when two of your countrywomen are in jeopardy, you say they are not British subjects. Jamie cursed the lieutenant and himself both for his failure.

Jamie stood in the street, jostled by the crowd, until he remembered he had an errand to run for Kemal Rais. He had to find a Jewish merchant and buy alcoholic spirits. He shook himself from his self-recriminations and started walking toward the Bab il Giadid and the Jewish quarter.

He walked the twisting streets, looking for the landmark synagogue Kemal had mentioned and found a building with a Star of David over the doorway. He walked past the building and onto a bustling street to his left. Here, Jews dressed in black with black head coverings and slippered feet conducted business. The Jewish women were dressed similar to the Arab and Berber women in black abayas, but some had one and some two eyes uncovered.

He searched for the shop of Ephraim de Aragon, but all the buildings looked the same. A few shops had lettered signs above their doors. He had briefly studied Hebrew as part of his classical education and was able to make out names, but none mentioned de Aragon. Finally, he stopped by a man sitting in front of a shop repairing copperware.

Jamie asked the smith in Arabic, "*'Ayn hu bayt Afrayim di 'Araghun?*"

The man pointed down the narrow street to a building on the corner. "*Hnak*," he replied.

Jamie thanked him and walked to the building. It was more substantial than most of the structures in the neighborhood, walled, with thick doors heavily studded with brass ornaments. There was no sign over it, nor did it look like the typical tavern run by the Jews or Christians that Jamie had seen outside the mellah. It looked like a house belonging to someone of importance. Jamie wondered if this was indeed the right place and the coppermonger had misunderstood him or purposely sent him to the wrong house.

He raised the brass knocker and let it fall. A wicket opened in the larger double doors and a face peered out.

"*Madha turid?*" he asked. *What do you want?*

"Excuse me," Jamie replied in Arabic. "I am looking for Ephraim de Aragon. I was sent by Kemal Rais to buy liquor."

The man said, "*Tafaddal*," gesturing for Jamie to enter.

The gatekeeper stepped aside and Jamie passed into a small courtyard. Jamie eyed the gatekeeper, who turned out to be very tall and well-armed Black man. He asked Jamie to wait as he went off to notify his master.

While he waited, Jamie looked around. The courtyard was paved with white marble, with a fountain bubbling in the center. Behind him was a high wall and the doors he had come through. A two-story house of white limestone stood beyond the courtyard. The limestone was accented with arches and tiles in blue, white, and gold. Carved wooden balconies and lattice windows painted in blue and white ran the length of the second floor. Worked into the design of some of tiles were Stars of David, candelabras, and tablets that Jamie recognized as the Ten Commandments.

As swiftly as he disappeared, the guard reappeared at Jamie's elbow and beckoned him to follow. The man led Jamie through the house into an interior garden courtyard — while not as large as the one he tended with Malik, it was as elegant.

A woman wearing a beautiful silk head covering sat on a bench by a fountain, talking to a little boy of about six or seven who was holding a book. The woman, perhaps in her thirties, was attractive, with a round face, very bright blue eyes, and a welcoming smile. She stood as Jamie approached.

There was something in her manner that made Jamie give her a little bow. In excellent but French-accented English, she welcomed him.

"You are the American captive of Kemal Rais." It was a statement rather than a question.

Taken by surprise that she knew who he was, Jamie stumbled in his reply. "Ah, yes, I've been sent to buy alcohol from..."

"My husband." She finished the sentence for him. "Please sit." She indicated a bench across from her. "I am Garvriella, wife of Doctor Ephraim de Aragon. I will send for him."

She motioned to the guard. "Abdullah, ask the master to join us here."

The man nodded and left.

Jamie was stunned that she treated him with respect. Wasn't he a lowly slave in her eyes?

Remembering his manners, he said, "It is a pleasure to meet you, but how did you know who I am?"

"In Tripoli, there are very few secrets," she said with a wise look. "Some of our servants have seen you about. And even here in the mellah, we have heard of the capture of the American schooner and the men taken."

"This is our son, Eitan." She touched the boy on his shoulder. "He is studying French." She pointed to the primer in his hands.

"*Bonjour, Monsieur Américain*," the boy said, bowing his head.

"*Bonjour, Eitan*," Jamie replied. "Eitan? Ethan? *Le nom de mon père est Ethan.*"

"Your father has a good name," Madame de Aragon said. "It means strong or enduring. But I am a poor hostess."

She rang a bell, a servant appeared, and she spoke to him in Hebrew. He nodded and left.

"I've sent for my husband. While we wait, tell me something of yourself and of America."

He related his history, how he was raised in Boston, and how he came to be captured.

In the middle of his narrative, the refreshments were served — iced sherbet, dates, figs, and nuts. Jamie marveled at the food. Even Dimas couldn't offer such a delicacy as cold sherbet. He ate with delight.

After finishing the refreshments, Jamie thanked Madame de Aragon.

"Please continue your story, young man," the lady requested.

"There is not much left to tell. I hope my family can redeem me and my friends."

"If they can't?" she asked.

"I don't plan to be a slave the rest of my life" was all he said.

She nodded. "I see."

"Madame de Aragon, may I ask why you are treating me as a guest instead of a slave?"

She smiled. "We are commanded by God, Blessed be He, to show hospitality. Just as Abraham did to the strangers that appeared at his tent. You may be a slave to Kemal, but before that, you are one of God's creatures."

"I thank you, Madame."

She smiled once again. "I understand there are Jews in America. Are they a free people?"

"Yes, George Washington, wrote a letter to the Jewish people in the state of Rhode Island. I remember my mother making me learn it. 'All possess alike liberty of conscience and immunities of citizenship. ... For happily the Government of the United States, which gives to bigotry no sanction, to persecution no assistance requires only that they who live under its protection should demean themselves as good citizens. ... May the Children of the Stock of Abraham, who dwell in this land, continue to merit and enjoy the good will of the other Inhabitants; while every one shall sit in safety under his own vine and figtree, and there shall be none to make him afraid.'"

She nodded. "So, there is no bigotry in America?"

"I wish that were true, Madame de Aragon, but alas it exists. Slavery as well."

Just at that moment, a man entered the garden. His robe was blue, not black, and trimmed in gold. He wore a black cap on his head. He was about forty and gray flecks appeared in his dark beard. He was a well set-up man, strong in appearance with long fingers and delicate hands.

"So," he said in English, his accent heavier than his wife's. "This is the slave of Kemal Rais who sits with my wife and takes refreshments as an honored guest."

Chapter 22

JAMIE ROSE, WORRIED he had offended de Aragon by sitting with his wife. "I- I meant no disrespect, sir. I'm James Sharpe, send by Kemal Rais to buy alcohol."

"Sit, sit, young man," de Aragon said. "I jest with you! My wife is an enlightened woman. If she invited you to join her, who am I to deny her?"

He turned to his son and said something in Hebrew. The boy smiled, picked up his book, and turned to Jamie.

"*Au revoir, Monsieur Américain,*" he said. "*C'était un plaisir de vous rencontrer.*"

"*Au revoir, Eitan.* It was a pleasure meeting you as well."

Eitan kissed his mother and father, then left the garden. Jamie was touched and realized how much he missed his own parents and his sister.

"Now, young man, down to business," de Aragon said. "Kemal Rais sent you here to buy spirits. He must have heard from his informants in the customs house of a shipment I received. The bulk of it I use in my practice of medicine. I am the physician to many prominent Arab and Berber families, as well as my own people. I have treated the bashaw and his family, including his mother and late father. Now, the bashaw prefers the American doctor from the captured frigate."

"I was told to buy it all," Jamie said. "I have the money."

"I will sell only one quarter of it. I shall keep the rest to be divided between my elder brother who resides in the city of Derne and myself."

Jamie nodded and paid a quarter of the money from the purse.

"Kemal will not be happy for he knows exactly how much I have," the doctor said. "He may take it out on you. So tell him I shall treat his illnesses for a lesser fee. And I have sent for another shipment. It should arrive within the month. That, I will sell to him. I hope he will be satisfied. He may go after some of the Jews of the city. I pray he will not."

He bowed his head. "We Jews are in a precarious position here. Most are poor and often put upon by the Muslims, but a few of us are fortunate to have some wealth and provide the bashaw and others with banking, one of the few occupations open to us, or in my case, medicine."

"Why do you stay?"

"I stay to serve my people. We were driven from Spain in 1492 along with the Muslims. My wife's family immigrated to France and then to Holland. Some of our people went to the new world and others to Turkey. Even *Eretz Israel*, the Land of Israel — it is in the hands of the Turks. Yet someday, I hope to take my family there, for the Turks let us practice our religion." He looked up, as if hoping for an answer from above.

"I'm sure you will be missed, knowing Kemal Rais' impatience. Tell him the spirits will be delivered this afternoon. I hope he will not be too hard on you."

"I thank you for your hospitality. I haven't seen much kindness since I was taken. I wish someday I might return the favor."

"You are welcome here whenever you can get away," Doctor de Aragon said. "Despite the wealth you see, we know what it is to be considered a lesser people in this society."

Jamie felt heartened by this invitation. "I'm not sure it will be very often that I can come."

"I wish you the best, young man, and hope that you will see your homeland soon," Garvriella de Aragon said kindly.

"And I," Jamie said, "that you might see the Land of Israel soon."

Jamie left the mellah with mixed emotions. He had been treated well by the de Aragons, but his heart was still heavy over the fate of Claire and her mother. It had come as a shock that Claire was the daughter of a Swedish nobleman. He was infatuated with her, but would she even consider him? *But why not? I'm an American. I come from good stock. Even my grandfather gave up the chance to be a baronet after his brother died. I've nothing to be ashamed of. Yet I feel I've failed her and her mother. I don't know what I can do. If the navy would come and put down this nest of thieves...*

He saw a troop of American sailors being sent to the harbor to work on the *Philadelphia*. As they passed, they were spat upon and small stones were hurled at them along with curses and epithets.

What a sad lot they seemed. At least now I'm well-fed, have clothes on my back, and no more forced heavy labor as these men have to endure.

He made his way back to the villa to face the wrath of Kemal Rais.

Chapter 23

JAMIE WAS GREETED by Tomaso as he entered the villa. "Where have you been, Sharpe?"

"Buying spirits for Kemal Rais."

"Did it take all morning and half the afternoon?"

"I had to find the house of de Aragon," Jamie answered, "and also had to bargain with him."

"Report to the master." Tomaso gave Jamie an evil smile as if to tell him he was in for it. "He's been waiting for you."

Jamie went up to Kemal's quarters.

"Well, what the hell have ye been doin' all day?" Kemal asked.

"Buying your alcohol, sir."

"How much did you get?"

Jamie stood up straight; he knew he was in for a tongue lashing or, worse, a real lashing.

"Two kegs of five gallons each."

"What? de Aragon was shipped four times as much. I told you to buy it all."

"He would only sell me one quarter of his shipment. He said the rest was for medicinal purposes. I've brought the extra money back. And a receipt."

"Damn you, I wanted it all." Kemal raised his hand to strike.

"Doctor de Aragon said he's ordered another shipment that he will sell to you," Jamie said, standing still in expectation of the blow, "and that any medical needs you may have he will treat at a reduced fee."

Kemal dropped his hand. "I'll not strike you, for Ramadan starts tonight and I wish the favor of Allah. It wouldn't be right on this night. But mark you, I'll not always be so easy, should ye try to cross me." Kemal groaned. "Fifteen measly gallons. I'll have to suffer through until de Aragon gets a new shipment. With the month of Ramadan, I must fast all day but can feast at night. Fifteen gallons might last — what kind of whiskey did ye say ye bought?"

"I believe it is grain alcohol, sir."

"Neutral spirits. Well, it ain't rum and it ain't poteen, nor even gin, but it will do. Now get yerself from me. I must prepare for Ramadan."

Jamie left, wondering how Kemal, who wished to be seen with favor by Allah, still consumed forbidden drink.

In the garden, he found Malik carrying a fine white djellaba and a green turban.

"This is the most holy of months," Malik said, "for it is the month that Allah, blessed be he, revealed the Qur'an to the Prophet. I will bathe at the hamam and go to the mosque. Tonight, I shall eat with friends from the city. I will leave the garden in your care, Jamie. I trust you to tend the plants. Tomorrow, I will work with you only during the day. It will be a great temptation to work among the fruits and vegetables, but I will refrain from food or drink."

"May I ask you a question?" Jamie inquired.

"Of course." Malik smiled.

"Today, when I was in the house of Doctor de Aragon, I saw he was wearing a blue robe. Are the Jews the Blue Men who run the slave caravans? I was told that Blue Men have no faces, but the doctor had a face."

Malik roared with laughter. "Jamie, the Blue Men are a Berber tribe to the south called the Tuareg. They wear blue robes dyed with indigo. The dye colors their skin, so they appear blue."

"But they have faces, don't they?"

"Yes, Jamie. They have faces. Though they are Muslims, the men cover their faces and women go uncovered."

"And they are the ones that control the slave trade from the south?"

Malik nodded, "Yes.

Jamie thanked him as Malik left to prepare himself.

Jamie went into the kitchen, where Dimas was preparing a feast for the night.

"Can you make cold sherbet?" he asked Dimas, remembering the wonderful treat.

"One need ice or extremely cold water." He shrugged. "Very difficult without. There is a sherbet that is a sweet drink made from fruit. That I can do."

"Make some for the women. They need some sort of treats."

Dimas nodded.

Simon was in his alcove, enjoying a cup of coffee, the kitchen books opened before him, but he paid them little attention.

"I see you're hard at work, Cutts," Jamie said.

"I've been in this hot kitchen all day, whilst you were running an errand in the city," Simon huffed. "The books need going over and I had to confer with that stupid Portuguese cook about ordering food. His English is dreadful."

"I'm sure it's better than your Portuguese."

"Don't be smart with me, Sharpe. If I asked, Tomaso would order you to receive the bastinado." Cutts said. "In fact, I might just ask him to do it on general principle."

"Stop with the empty threats, Cutts. Tomaso will do nothing to me. As Kemal's translator and secretary, I hold a higher position. I warn you not to create mischief for me or my friends, for the beating you receive would not be from the bastinado, but from me personally. You know by now that is not an idle threat."

Simon's handsome face turned white as Jamie stood over him. "You can't talk to me like that," he said, regaining his composure. "I'm just as valuable to Kemal as you are."

"Still the blowhard," Jamie said, and walked away.

He sought out George, who was at his forge, making shoeing nails.

"Give the bellows a pump, Jamie," George said.

Jamie obliged, pumping the bellows and watching the fire in the forge rise. George heated twisted wire, then pounded it into one long piece. He cut and hammered each nail into shape.

"Tedious is what this is," George complained. "At home, we had a machine to cut nails and shape them."

After a while, George stepped away from the forge and anvil. He washed off the grime, using a handy bucket.

"Do you realize that it is only ten days 'til Christmas? I never thought I'd be sweating over a forge, let alone as a slave. I don't want to spend the next Christmas here."

"Now, George," Jamie laughed, "you know very well Christmas celebrations are frowned upon in Boston."

"Just because the Puritan fathers said no holy days except the Sabbath were sanctioned in Scripture doesn't mean I want to be here next December." He sat down on a stool. "Besides you know as well as I do we both belong to the Episcopal Church, where no such prohibitions were preached."

"I was only jesting, friend."

George nodded. "Dimas and the other Catholics here in Muslim Tripoli are allowed to celebrate Christmas. The irony would be lost on those Puritans."

Jamie laughed.

"Usem, the groom, is off to prayer. I'll be making some gunpowder this evening. The sulfur you brought will do the trick just fine. We can use our grenades to escape. That is, if the navy returns," George said, doubt creeping into his voice.

"They know they must free the men from the *Philadelphia*. But with winter upon us and the winds being what they are, it might not be until spring or even summer."

"That's not encouraging, but if they don't attack and just ransom the sailors, where will that put us? We won't be part of the transaction."

"If my family provides the money for ransom, we'll be free," Jamie said. "If not, then we will find another way. Because, as you said, we won't be spending a second Christmas as slaves. We will escape."

"I'm with you, my friend," George said.

Chapter 24

DURING THE MONTH of Ramadan, according to religious custom, Kemal and the other Muslims in the household refrained from food and drink. At night, replenishment was allowed and Kemal ate and drank to excess.

Jamie insisted Malik rest most of the day and only consulted him when he had a question about the garden. Jamie weeded, watered, and harvested. Though it was now winter, the garden still bloomed.

Life went on for the captives — Ramadan made no difference to most of them. It was work from sunup to sundown and sometimes into the night. Mateus and Fenton Webb went fishing every day. George studied the way the Berbers and Arabs made horseshoes, different from the kind he made in Boston. For Dimas and the cooks the only difference was they had to work harder preparing the evening feasts. The dinners were served in the garden or, if the weather was bad, in the inner court.

Claire and her mother could be heard singing nearly every day and, as they did, Jamie's heart ached. Claire couldn't be kept from Kemal much after Ramadan. Jamie still had no plan to free her.

Soon after Christmas, Jamie was sent on errand for Kemal. He stopped to watch as men from the frigate were forced into the freezing water up to their armpits, digging an old wreck out of the sand beneath the water. The men had no change of clothes and were shaking with the cold. One man crawled to the beach, his legs no longer working. The overseers drove the others even harder.

As before, Jamie was able to pass for an Arab or Berber and, in his Muslim clothes, managed to get close enough to one of the men to hand him a small copper coin. "It's all I have, brother," he whispered.

One of the overseers shooed him away.

On New Year's Day, Jamie saw his old schoolmates and enemies, Horace Long and Geoffrey Horne, strolling about the city. He knew the officers had been given their parole and were free to go about. Both men were dressed rather shabbily. Their clothes had been taken when they were captured and replaced by whatever odds and ends they could muster. Horne limped a bit, but otherwise seemed well-fed and in good condition. Long also looked well.

As Jamie approached them, Horne said in English, "Get away from me, you filthy Turk."

Jamie laughed. "Now, *Geoff*, is that any way to treat a fellow from home?"

"What? Who?"

"My God!" Long exclaimed. "It's Jamie Sharpe. How did you come to be here? Last we heard, you were on your way to the Slave Coast."

"A long story, Horace. Let's just say your old friend Simon had much to do with it. After he kidnapped George and me."

"Simon Cutts?"

"Oh, he's here too. A slave of Kemal Rais, the man that led the raid on the *Philadelphia*."

"Simon here, a slave! I'll notify Captain Bainbridge at once," Horne said. "He'll try to arrange his parole."

"Don't count on it. Kemal Rais awaits payment from Captain Cutts for Simon's redemption. The bashaw will not interfere."

"His father has the money. He'll redeem him," Horne said.

"Captain Cutts is a fugitive, hiding out in South Carolina for what he did to George and me," Jamie said, remembering what Captain Collins had told him when they first met in Malta. "Not to mention stealing from my family."

"Even if that were true," Horne crowed, "Captain Cutts still has influence in Charleston and has his assets there."

"My father will deal with him if he hasn't already. I know he's back in Boston." Jamie looked Horne up and down. "But tell me, Horne, why are you limping?"

Horne looked down at his left leg. "An accident."

"He was injured in a duel," Horace volunteered. "Shot in the hip."

"Shut up, Horace."

"Shut up yourself, Geoffrey. He was shot in a duel with your friend Bradford Welles when our squadron stopped at Gibraltar."

Jamie's heart lit up. *Good old Brad.*

"He cheated," Horne said. "He fired before the signal was given. He could have killed me."

"Brad wouldn't cheat," Jamie answered. "If he wanted to kill you, you'd be dead. He's a crack shot."

"Go to hell, Sharpe."

"Tripoli is pretty close to it. But if you want to know about hell, look toward your ship's enlisted men toiling around the corner. The bashaw treats them abysmally."

"They are not our concern. Captain Bainbridge has made arrangements for them. They are fed and given shelter. These are men used to hardship. Dregs of the earth."

"Fed and given shelter," Jamie muttered. "Two loaves of coarse bread, a little oil, a dank prison. Dregs of the earth. I wish Brad had killed you. You aren't fit to be called a man, let alone a ship's officer."

Horne raised his hand to strike.

"Don't think about it," Jamie warned. "I'll break every bone in your body."

"He means it, Geoff," Long said. "Leave off."

"I'm not afraid of him."

"You should be," Long said. "He beat Simon in a duel and Simon is stronger than you are. Don't forget you've been wounded."

Horace dragged the red-faced and angry Horne off.

"I'll see if I can get the captain to get the men some help," Long called to Jamie.

Jamie walked off. *Horace seems to have grown a bit*, he mused. *Geoff is still the same small tyrant he's always been.*

❁ ❁ ❁

Whenever Jamie was sent on an errand, he tried to talk to the sailors of the *Philadelphia*. He sought them out during the midday Islamic prayers, when their overseers were otherwise occupied. One day, he succeeded in engaging in conversation with a small American who seem to be better educated than some of the other seamen.

"My name's William Ray," he said. "I came to these unhappy circumstances when I joined the marines. I had fallen on hard times and, seeing our country's flag, I signed on, much to my great regret. The cruelty aboard the frigate whilst I was sailing and the way our American ships' officers walked away from us and left us to cruelty at the hands of the Turk has made me bitter. We've been beaten, flogged, and ill-used. Yet every man jack of us would rather have fought to the death than surrender to the heathen."

Jamie felt for the fellow, but suspected he was a bitter man before he enlisted.

"Cruel is what the officers are," Ray continued. "Oh, not all. Mr. Jones, the second lieutenant, is a fair and decent man. Commodore Preble, Mr. Decatur of the *Enterprise*, and Midshipman Welles of the *Constitution*, are said to be fine officers. But so many are not." Like a dam bursting, Ray ruptured with a flood of rage. "The great fault, the chief cause of so much tyranny, of so many just complaints of cruel officers is the practice of giving warrants to boys — to the upstarts; the fops; the base, unprincipled, inexperienced idols of licentiousness who are trained to exercise undue authority over men whose shoes they are not worthy to unloose." His fury couldn't be contained. "What necessity, what propriety, what justice is there in giving a boy of eleven or twelve years of age a warrant, with liberty to command, to insult, to strike in the face men old enough to be their great-grandfathers? How can human nature brook such abuse?"

Ray gave a great sigh, his anger finally abated.

Jamie remembered his own cockiness just six months past. Could he have been one of those cruel boys lording it over ordinary sailors? He hoped not, for beneath his brashness, there was a sense of fair play.

Ray continued with his narrative. "One of the worst villains is Mr. Horne. Crueler than the younger boys. He'd beat a man at the slightest error. After he was wounded at Gibraltar, he was worse, taking it out on the men."

"I'm appalled at your treatment," Jamie said. "I've seen what the Turks, as you call them, have done to you and the others, but for our navy to treat men in such a manner is disgusting."

"Look you there, Mr. Sharpe." Ray pointed to a man in western clothes, carrying a staff. "That is the frigate's carpenter, Mr. Gobey. He has built gunboats for the bashaw. He oversees us most cruelly. He is as cruel as the other drivers. He does not have to do this work — he is a petty officer and they are not forced to work for the Turks. He does it for money and he brags of it. Our sergeant, David Irving, beat him for it and, in turn, was beaten and bastinadoed on his feet and buttocks, most unmercifully."

"It is cruel, Mr. Ray." Jamie knew that men like Gobey and Billy Scars could be crueler than some of those born Muslim. But unlike them, the turncoats were in it for themselves and their conversions were a sham just as changing their names."

"The men yet keep their spirits, for they are a hardy lot. Though some men have died, most survive. The officers fare better." There was that bitter tone in Ray's voice again. "The Danish consul, Mr. Nissen, arranged credit for Captain Bainbridge and the officers. They eat well, are on parole, occupy the abandoned American consulate, but for us, we are at the mercy of the bashaw."

"So I've heard. I'm so sorry for your plight." Jamie said.

"It is you, Mr. Sharpe, and your companions I think of. We sailors and marines will be ransomed one day or saved by the squadron, but how will you be saved?"

Reluctant to reveal his hopes for redemption or plans of escape, Jamie simply said, "I thank you for your concern, Mr. Ray."

Chapter 25

RAMADAN ENDED ON January 15, 1804 and the Muslims of Tripoli celebrated with a holiday they called Bayram, the sugar feast. Kemal, dressed in his best attire, held a feast in the garden. Jamie was pressed into service as a translator.

The festivities went on for three nights, ending each night with a salute by cannons and fireworks.

Kemal became too drunk each night to visit the harem, making the Andreasson women safe from his attentions, at least for the time being.

Kemal was called to the palace soon after the end of Bayram. Jamie translated as the bashaw said, "The American ships have been seen offshore. You will take your vessel and patrol. Keep them from Tripoli."

When they left the bashaw, Kemal said to Jamie, "I'll hunt down the damn Yankees and send them to hell."

Kemal left the next day, and Jamie waited until morning prayer to take a chance. He climbed the palm closest to the women's rooms. He could hear them singing. He leaped from the tree to the small balcony and knocked on the wooden blinds.

There was a startled gasp from inside.

"Who is there?" the older woman called, panic in her voice.

"James Sharpe, Baroness."

"Young man, are you quite mad? If you are caught, you will be killed."

"My lady, I want you to know that I am still working on a plan. You and your daughter must be ready to flee at a moment's notice.

Kemal is patrolling out to sea, which means the Americans are in the vicinity. If they attack, I will do what I can to rescue you and Claire."

"Oh, you foolish lad. I honor you, but it will be to no avail. Where would you take us?"

"The Swedish consul."

"He will not have us. My husband was *persona non grata* at court. Now go, before you are found out."

"Do not give up hope," Jamie said as he jumped back to the tree.

Yet was there hope? If the British and the Swedes wouldn't take the women in, who would? Certainly not the French, nor any of the smaller countries that had diplomats at Tripoli.

Then Jamie had a thought. Perhaps the Danish consul. Although Sweden and Denmark were at odds, the Danish consul, Mr. Nissen, might help. He was said to be a good man and had helped the American officers.

At the next opportunity, I shall approach him.

No opportunity arose until Kemal returned from the sea and called Jamie to his chambers.

"Sharpe," he said, "de Aragon has the shipment of spirits he promised. Take this purse and buy it all. I want it delivered no later than tomorrow."

Jamie took the money and gladly left the villa. First, he went to the Danish consulate, hoping he would be better received than he had been at the British consulate. As was common in Muslim countries, Greeks acted as dragomen, or interpreters, who served the consulate as go-betweens of the consuls and the courts.

Jamie asked in Greek to see the consul. Jamie's Greek was classical, the dragoman's was not, but he was impressed that the young man spoke his language.

Jamie waited but a few minutes before the dragoman ushered him into the book-lined office of the consul, Nicholas Nissen. Mr. Nissen was a kindly looking man who greeted Jamie with a smile.

"You are an American," he said as a statement. "What is it I may do for you?"

Jamie explained about the Andreasson women.

"I know of their plight, but what is that you think I can do?"

"Could you purchase their freedom?"

"I'm afraid your master, Kemal Rais, wouldn't part with them for any amount of money. When the Swedish captives were freed after they were ransomed and Sweden paid tribute, the bashaw allowed Kemal to keep the women."

"If I could arrange their escape, could you get them on a ship out of Tripoli?"

"Young man, what you propose is impossible. How would you get them out of Kemal's villa? It is guarded by Berbers, Arabs, Turks, and renegades."

"I'm working on a plan," Jamie said. "When our navy returns, I will free them."

"*If* your navy should return and you can liberate them and bring them to me," Nissen said with much sympathy, "I will do my utmost to get them free of Tripoli. However, it is nearly impossible for you to free them. You will need more than courage, young man. You will need money. Money for passage, money for bribes. Where would you get it?"

"I will write a promissory note, guaranteeing to pay you. I will write my father and ask him to honor the note."

"I see," Nissen replied with some skepticism.

"My father made a fortune in the China trade and he will honor any amount."

The consul thought for a moment. "For some reason, I believe you. Perhaps because I like Americans and because the former American consul at Tunis brokered the return of six Danish ships captured there a few years ago."

"Do you mean Mr. Eaton? I know him — his stepsons are friends of mine."

Nissen smiled. "That will seal the deal. But I warn you, it could be months before your navy returns or peace is brokered. Even if they attack, your odds of getting the ladies free are nearly impossible."

"I must try, sir," Jamie said, adding, "I know our navy is close."

"I can see you are an honorable and brave young man. Please wait here." Mr. Nissen left the room, returning shortly with a purse. "Here is the money. It comes to five hundred English pounds. Guard it well."

"Sir, you are too generous." *That is over two thousand dollars,* Jamie thought.

"Your Mr. Eaton saved Demark more than that. You must take it."

Jamie took the purse. "Thank you for your kindness, sir."

Mr. Nissen offered his hand and Jamie took it.

"The best of luck, young man, for you will need it. And may God go with you."

Chapter 26

JAMIE TUCKED THE purse into his belt alongside the money Kemal Rais gave him for buying liquor. He walked to the mellah and, this time, found the de Aragon house without a problem.

Abdullah, the same servant who had guarded the door the previous time, bade him enter and took him straight to the garden. An elderly Arab man, his eyes wrapped in bandages, was being led through the garden by a younger Arab and Doctor de Aragon. The younger man was thanking the doctor and pressing money into his hand.

"You have restored my father's sight. I am in your debt."

"Just wash the eyes with the solution I've given you," de Aragon said. "Remember, three times a day and his sight should improve in a week."

After the men left the garden, the doctor turned to Jamie.

"Jamie, I see you have come to pay for the alcohol."

"What was wrong with the Arab gentleman?" Jamie asked.

"His eyes were cut by sand," he explained. "His son feared it was trachoma — that's the name for an eye disease given by the Greek physician Dioscorides, nearly eighteen hundred years ago in his work, *De Materia Medica* — a disease that causes blindness and for which we have no real cure. It is a terrible scourge. Some say cutting near the eye to cause bleeding may help, but I doubt it will work. Some of my fellow physicians have observed that keeping clean will help prevent the disease. As to its cause, we know not. Many of Napoleon's army had come down with it when they invaded Egypt. Stay clean, wash regularly, and avoid sharing towels, Jamie, and you should be safe. I gave the old man sassolite, a crystal that comes from the volcanic islands off of Italy. When mixed with warm water, it cleans the eyes." He smiled at Jamie. "But you did not come to discuss medicine. Come, sit. My wife will join us, as she is fascinated by your stories of America. In the meantime, I will send for refreshments."

Garvriella de Aragon arrived, followed by a servant carrying a tray of dates and figs and a pot of tea. Jamie stood.

"Jamie Sharpe, it is nice to see you. Please sit. I long for you to tell me of America."

Jamie related tales his grandfather had told of fighting in the Revolution and of his father, who at sixteen joined the fight for independence. He talked of his twin sister, Maisie, and of his mother. And finally, of how he came to be a slave.

Doctor de Aragon held up a finger and turned to his wife. "Poor Jamie has not had time to eat, nor drink his tea. Give the young man a chance to breathe."

Madame de Aragon laughed. "I'm sorry, but your stories of America are fascinating. A young country of much promise. Now please, eat, have some tea. It's mint and quite refreshing."

She poured him a cup.

After a while, Doctor de Aragon told Jamie he would have the liquor delivered the next day, a full shipment of forty gallons.

"It should last him a very long time."

"If it doesn't kill him first," Jamie muttered.

"In time, it will," Doctor de Aragon said. "Between him and Murad Rais, it is a contest to see which will succumb to death by alcohol first. Both men became Muslims because piracy suited them, but they don't obey the Qur'an's stricture against intoxicating beverages."

"They hate each other," Jamie said.

"Murad Rais, he who was once Peter Lyle, is still the favorite of the bashaw. He gave his daughter to Murad in marriage."

"I know," Jamie said. "Kemal Rais often broods on it."

A servant approached and said something to the doctor.

"James, I must leave you. I have a patient waiting."

"I must be going. They will wonder where I've been."

"I will see you out," the doctor said.

Jamie bid adieu to Garvriella de Aragon and followed the doctor to the gate.

An elderly Jewish man, his garments torn and his face a mass of contusions, sat on a bench in the courtyard. He spoke to the doctor in a language that sounded like Spanish but wasn't.

"What happen to the poor man?" Jamie asked.

"He was set upon by some thieves who robbed him of his last sequins. All the money he had in the world. I must tend to his injuries."

"What language were you two speaking?"

"Sephardi, the language of my people when they lived in Spain."

Jamie looked at the man, who was moaning in pain. "I have some money. I could pay for his treatment." He fingered the purse the Danish consul gave him.

"I don't charge the poor," Doctor de Aragon said. "If this man was a Christian, Arab, Turk, or Berber and poor, I would not charge him. I have enough rich patients to cover his medical costs."

"I meant no disrespect," Jamie said.

"I know you didn't, James. You are a kind young man. Come to my house if ever you are in need."

"Thank you, Doctor. Your hospitality is overwhelming."

Jamie walked back to Kemal's villa, feeling better than he had for a long time. He began to formulate a plan to free Claire and her mother. Now, if only the navy would attack.

Chapter 27

THE NEXT DAY, February 7th, started out clear with a light breeze. Jamie went to work in the garden, hoping to see Claire, but the louvers were tightly closed. He worked hard weeding, just to keep his mind off plans for escape.

By late afternoon, the wind had picked up. Soon, a gale blew in from the Mediterranean. Working in the garden became impossible and Jamie slipped into the stables to see George.

"I've seen the Danish consul, Mr. Nissen, and he's agreed to help. We must be ready at any time to act. When our navy attacks, we'll use the grenades to blow a hole in the back wall. During the chaos, I'll escort the women to the Danish consulate. Mr. Nissen will hide them until he can get them on a ship."

"Risky," George said. "So many things can go wrong. But if it works, you go with the women on the ship."

"No. I will not leave you or the others. We all go."

"There's no arguing with you, is there?" George asked.

"No."

One of the Arab guards ducked into the stables, out of the rain. He told Jamie that Kemal Rais wanted to see him in his gulphor.

Now what am I in for? Jamie wondered as he followed the guard out and into the villa.

Kemal was in a terrible mood, his face red with anger. He tossed a chair and kicked over a table. He saw Jamie and rushed to him, grabbing him by the front of his djellaba.

"Where is my liquor?" he raved, spittle coming from his mouth. "It was supposed to be here by now. Did ye even pay the Jew? Did ye steal the money?" He shook Jamie.

"I- I paid him," Jamie stammered. "I gave you the receipt yesterday."

"If that Jew cheated me, I'll have him hung on hooks. I'll sell his household into slavery."

"I'm sure there is an explanation," Jamie reasoned. "Doctor de Aragon is not a man to cheat one such as you. Perhaps the gale blowing outside has delayed the shipment."

"Damn it. Come. We go to find out. And if you had anything to do with this, it will be the bastinado for you and it will be you hung on hooks."

Kemal grabbed an oilcloth coat and shoved Jamie in front of him. Four of Kemal's guards fell in and they left the villa in the pouring rain. Jamie was immediately soaked to the skin.

The streets were nearly empty as they made their way. Just beyond Bab il Giadid, they came across a scene of carnage. Seven men lay in the street. Even the rain couldn't wash away the enormous amount of blood from their wounds as it ran in the gutters. Jamie recognized Abdullah, the servant and guard of Ephraim de Aragon. He was barely alive, his normally healthy skin was ashen. Jamie knelt by him.

In Arabic, he asked, "Abdullah, what happened?"

"We were attacked," he whispered. "They hacked down the others. I killed two, but I was overwhelmed. There were five of them. Tell my master I am sorry. They took the shipment I was to deliver to Kemal Rais."

"Send for Doctor de Aragon," Jamie pleaded. "The man's still alive."

"Aye," Kemal Rais said. "He might tell me who did this."

He dispatched one of his guards.

Jamie removed Abdullah's sash and used it to staunch a wound on his head. Then he took off his own djellaba and used it to stop the bleeding from a deep cut on Abdullah's chest.

Abdullah's breathing was shallow, but steady. It seemed to Jamie that it was taking forever for the doctor to arrive, but it was only a matter of a few minutes before the doctor came running to the scene; his house was only a street away.

Doctor de Aragon, slightly out of breath, dropped next to Abdullah and checked his wounds.

"We must get him to my house," de Aragon said. "I can do little for him in this filthy wet street."

Jamie and two of Kemal's guards carried the man home. The doctor directed them to his surgery. Doctor de Aragon brought out an opiate and was about to give it to the wounded man when Kemal stopped him.

"I want to know who did this. I want to know who stole me liquor."

He bent over Abdullah and asked him. The man, in obvious pain, whispered something to Kemal, too quiet for Jamie to hear.

Kemal threw back his head and roared, "I will kill him!"

Doctor de Aragon shouldered Kemal aside and tended to his patient.

Jamie watched as the doctor cleaned the wounds with alcohol and checked for any debris left in them. He then began to stitch the more serious ones. Finally, he applied bandages over the wounds.

While the doctor worked, Kemal paced back and forth, cursing in English, Irish, and Arabic.

"He can tell you no more," Doctor de Aragon said wearily. "He will be unconscious for some time. I've done what I can. Now, only time will tell."

Kemal Rais grunted and turned to Jamie.

"Come! We go to the castle. I will lay me grievance before the bashaw! That bastard Murad stole me liquor. I'll demand his head!"

As they left, a servant handed Jamie his bloody djellaba and a finer one of rich wool with a hood. He thanked the man and put it on.

Kemal grabbed Jamie by the arm and marched to the castle.

Kemal was forced to wait for an audience with the bashaw. He paced back and forth, his face turning red. He clenched and unclenched his fists repeatedly. Finally, he was granted audience.

The bashaw was sitting on his cushions, enjoying coffee. He waved a jeweled finger, beckoning Kemal Rais forward, and nodded, allowing the renegade to speak.

Still red-faced, Kemal began in a mix of English and broken Arabic, which Jamie translated into French.

"...it was none other than Murad that stole my purchase and killed the servant of Doctor de Aragon."

"A cargo I must remind you that a devout Muslim should not be indulging in," the bashaw pointed out.

"It was," Jamie translated for Kemal, "for medicinal purposes, Majesty. I ask for justice." Kemal hadn't said *ask*, he'd said *demand*, but Jamie thought it wise not to antagonize the bashaw.

Yusuf nodded and stroked his beard. "So you would have me punish Murad Rais, my son-in-law, on the word of a servant?"

"The man is a Muslim, sire," Jamie added, making it clear. He repeated Kemal's accusation. "Murad is a thief. Abdullah recognized Murad's majordomo."

The bashaw nodded. He turned to a retainer and told him to send for Murad Rais. It was but a few minutes later when the diminutive Scotsman came in and made his obeisance to the bashaw.

Yusuf told his grand admiral why he had summoned him.

"Your Majesty, I took the liquor to prevent this drunk from breaking the laws of Islam," Murad said in French, pointing to Kemal.

Yusuf choked down a laugh. He knew his son-in-law was also a hard drinker. He sat for a moment, looking at the two men.

"Murad Rais, you will pay Kemal Rais for the items. You will compensate Ephraim de Aragon for the death of his servants and return his mules."

"The Jew?"

"He saved my father's life many years ago and attended to my mother after her accident with a pistol."

You mean, Jamie thought, *when you shot your brother and your mother tried to stop you and lost her fingers.* He saw the same idea cross the faces of the two renegades.

Then Kemal gave a winning smile and sniffed.

Jamie carefully translated the next series of conversations.

"As for you, Kemal Rais, I can no longer tolerate this feud between my captains. Therefore, I'm sending you to Derne, where you will be in charge of a fleet. I will make you Admiral of the Barqa. You will leave for the Barqa within a fortnight. I will send a message to the governor, my brother-in-law, Mustapha Bey, to prepare a suitable palace for you and your household. I shall also give you gold to go with your new rank. But refrain from excess in liquor. And that goes for you as well, Murad Rais."

"Am I to take the American frigate?" Kemal asked hopefully, nudging Jamie to translate.

"No, I will sell the ship to the Dey of Algiers, who will pay me well for it," Yusuf said. "Now, both of you leave. I've work to do and you've interrupted my day."

He waved them out.

"Exile," Kemal mumbled angrily, leaving the castle after Jamie repeated what the bashaw said. "No frigate and I'm the one that captured it." He spit. "Damn and hell. Well, from Derne, I'll attack the vessels of the United States, be they merchant or warship. Those of Naples and Sicily as well. Sure'n the name of Kemal Rais will strike fear into all those that cross his path."

Two weeks! Jamie despaired. *If he takes the Andreasson women to Derne, I'll never free them.*

Chapter 28

THE RAIN AND HIGH SEAS continued. When Kemal wasn't drunk, he was planning his move to Derne. He sent many of the household goods by caravan, but he planned to go by sea.

Jamie was at a loss. His whole plan was based on if and when the American Navy might attack Tripoli. But with winter upon the Mediterranean, he wasn't sure they would come until spring or summer. He was going to have to do something drastic. As soon as the weather cleared and neutral ships could sail, he would get the women out, even if it meant his own life.

Kemal called for Jamie.

"I'm taking you and the others of yer crew with me to Derne. Unfortunately, I will not be able to sail me xebec, for she's too large. But I've a galliot — fast, with a shallow draft. Yer navy will not catch her, for they can't enter the shallow waters." He rubbed his hands with glee. "Ye and yer other friends will be rowing her. I hope ye ain't got too soft." He laughed. "But because ye be smart, ye'll be my secretary when we reach Derne. Once there, a fleet of swift xebecs awaits me."

He smiled in anticipation.

"Now, listen well, Sharpe. Ye may be redeemed someday, but as long as we're at war, ye belong to me. So make yer peace with it and obey me, and there will be no trouble."

Jamie nodded but, underneath, he seethed. He was sure Kemal had no intention of letting him go or, for that matter, the others. Just as he kept the Swedish women, he would find some cunning way to keep his new captives.

Jamie met with George that evening.

"If the navy won't come before we leave, I'm getting the women out. Kemal has no plans to ever release us."

"We can't escape from Tripoli," George said. "It's too well-guarded. We'll have to wait until Derne to try."

"Agreed, but the women are our first priority."

"If only our navy would come."

Chapter 29

Aboard the USS *Intrepid*, February 16, 1804

"THIS IS A FOUL VESSEL," Midshipman Brad Welles said to his fellow midshipmen as he scratched at the flea bites on his arm.

"It is indeed," Midshipman Ralph Izard replied, stabbing a rat with his cutlass and tossing it overboard. "If I get my hands on the crew that allegedly fumigated this floating trash scow, I'll disembowel them."

"Ah, Ralph, just think, we have such wonderful ship's biscuits to eat and water to drink," Brad said with dark humor. "And don't forget the beautiful weather and fine sea air."

"Ha! Since the meat was packed in unclean barrels, what else could we eat or drink?" Ralph said, spitting over the lee side of the boat as if he could taste the foul meat.

"Then a week of gales driving us from Tripoli," Brad said, "just when our goal was so close. Sleeping on that makeshift platform atop the water casks, with not enough headroom to even sit up." Then shaking his head, he remembered the crew. "Well, in truth the crew had it worse, confined below decks amid rolling cargo, and when on deck, they were soaked by high seas."

"Don't forget the hours at the pumps to keep us from foundering. Add to that the meager rations and the men are near exhaustion," Midshipman Charles Morris said, joining the conversation.

"At least, Charles," Brad said with envy, "you had a chance to see the *Philadelphia* when you and Mr. Catalano surveyed the harbor." Brad was referring to the Sicilian pilot hired by Commodore Preble, to guide his ships into Tripoli's harbor.

"Don't be jealous, Brad, for a sad sight she was," Charles Morris replied. "It was my sad duty to inform the captain that Mr. Catalano was right. With the wind rising, we couldn't enter the harbor. Thank God the seas are calm now."

"If all goes well, then the attack will happen tonight," Brad said. "Now, we best stop carping. If the captain hears us, he will be none too pleased."

The others nodded.

"Look, you there!" John Rowe, another midshipman, spoke up. "The *Siren* has moved off, so the Turks won't see her. I just hope her boats will be here in time to haul us out if needs be." He was referring to the brig that accompanied them.

"Captain Decatur has confidence in Captain Stewart and that's good enough for me," Brad said. He, along with most of the fleet, held the dashing twenty-five-year-old lieutenant in high regard. Now in command of the boat, he was addressed with the honorific "captain."

To them, Stephen Decatur was already a hero. He had captured this Tripolitan ketch, the *Mastico*, and re-christened her the *Intrepid*.

Captain Decatur ordered drags over the side to slow the ketch so it wouldn't reach the harbor until after dark. From the shore, it would look like the vessel was a slow sailer so as not to arouse suspicion.

As darkness descended, Brad took a position aft. Several minutes later, he called in a low voice, "Boats approaching."

The men's nerves were on end, but as the boats neared, they saw they were from the *Siren*. Decatur allowed thirty men to board the already-crowded *Intrepid*. He ordered the others from the *Siren* to row to the rendezvous point outside the harbor.

"To your hiding places, lads," Decatur said. "From now on, utter silence." He turned to the Sicilian pilot. "Take us in, Mr. Catalano."

As the ketch made its way through the tricky entrance of the outer and inner harbors, the time ticked by slowly. By nine, those on deck could see the dark outline of the *Philadelphia* silhouetted against the lights from shore.

As the *Intrepid* sailed closer to the frigate, Brad was probably not alone in thinking his heartbeat could be heard aboard the man-of-war.

Finally, by nine-thirty, the *Intrepid* was under the guns of the *Philadelphia*, the gun ports were open, and the cannon appeared to be pointing at the frail ketch.

Turbaned heads appeared along the high rail of the *Philadelphia* and hailed the ketch, telling them to bear off.

Decatur nodded to Mr. Catalano, who explained to the men aboard the *Philadelphia* the ketch was a Maltese trader that lost its anchor in the storm and wondered if they might tie up for the night. After a few minutes, they were told they could. A boat from the *Philadelphia* was lowered with a line and Decatur ordered a boat from the *Intrepid* to meet her with a line from the ketch. He didn't want the enemy boat to get too close. The boats met, the lines were spliced, and men on the *Intrepid*, dressed in Maltese garb, began to haul the ketch toward the frigate. As the vessels closed, a stern line was tossed to the *Philadelphia*, where it was made fast.

Nice of them to be so accommodating, Brad thought. But before he could even smile at the notion, someone on the frigate shouted "Americani!"

Catalano shouted, "Board, Captain, board!"

But Decatur called, "No order to be obeyed but that of the commanding officer!"

The men pulled faster until the *Intrepid* bumped up against the *Philadelphia* and Decatur yelled "Board!" The lieutenant jumped first but missed his footing and nearly fell, so it was Midshipman Charles Morris who boarded first. Decatur regained his balance and climbed aboard, nearly running Morris through until the midshipman called out the password, "Philadelphia!"

The men of the *Intrepid* surged aboard the *Philadelphia*, slashing and cutting their way down the deck. Brad was confronted by a large Arab wielding a scimitar. The turbaned foe brought up his sword and slashed. Brad parried the attack with a powerful stroke of his cutlass. This was no fencing lesson, but hand-to-hand fighting where it would end in death for the loser. Brad followed the parry with a killing blow to the man's throat. In a matter of minutes, the ship was taken. The surviving crew of the frigate jumped overboard or took to their boats, leaving their dead comrades behind.

The men aboard the *Intrepid* passed up tinder, boxes of tar, and powder to the deck and through the gun ports. Those on the frigate carried the incendiaries to their assigned stations and, on Decatur's word, lit sperm oil candles and tossed them into the debris. All the fires went up at once.

Brad had joined Charles Morris and his crew on the orlop, the frigate's lowest deck, which was below the waterline. After lighting their fires, they realized they were trapped by fires and smoke from the deck above.

Lieutenant Decatur counted each man as they jumped from the burning frigate to the *Intrepid*. There was no sign of Brad, Charles, or their squad.

Below, the smoke was thicker and flames closer as Brad pointed forward.

"That way!" he shouted, hoping it was the way out.

Charles nodded and led the way along the orlop deck, crowded as it was with coils of rope and barrels. The men weaved their way desperately forward, with Brad taking up the rear to make sure all were accounted for. Finally, they reached the forward ladder, climbed to the hatch, and made it to the deck. Brad exited last, breathing hard, the fire nipping at his heels.

"Over you go!" Decatur commanded and the squad quickly obeyed.

When all were on board the *Intrepid*, he jumped as well, nearly falling again. He caught the ketch's rigging and slid to the deck. The whole adventure took but a scant 25 minutes.

The burning frigate so visibly lit up the *Intrepid* that the Tripolitan batteries began to fire at the ketch. Most shots were well wide of the mark. One shell passed through the ketch's topsail just as Decatur ordered the stern line cut. The bowline had already burned away. But the ketch was not out of danger. Her long boom caught on the *Philadelphia*'s stern. Her cotton sails were scorched by the burning ship and threatened to ignite the volatile explosives still on board. The fire on the frigate was so powerful, it created a backdraft that threatened to draw the ketch into the flaming inferno.

The crew finally freed the boom. Decatur called out over the chaos, "Sweeps out and row for your lives!"

The cannon of the frigate, loaded with double shot by the Tripolitans, began to go off, sending cannonballs into the town. The guns pointed at the *Intrepid* missed their mark as a breeze came up and the ketch sailed out of gun range, entering the outer harbor. The flames of the fire finally reached the *Philadelphia*'s powder magazine. A tremendous roar went up and the frigate rose out of the water and exploded into a thousand fireballs.

The crew of the *Intrepid* was struck with awe at the stunning result of their endeavor. As the boats from the *Siren* pulled up, Charles Morris turned to Brad.

"My God, what a sight! And we haven't lost a man!"

"That should have shaken the bashaw from his bed and awakened the town. Better fireworks than on the Fourth of July," Brad said.

Suddenly, his thoughts turned to his friend Jamie, remembering his birthday was also on Independence Day. *Poor Jamie and George — are they marooned on some African shore to the south or are those brave lads dead?*

Chapter 30

THAT SAME NIGHT, a thundering boom woke Jamie from his troubled sleep.

At first he thought it was a storm, but when the roar was followed by another, he realized he was hearing cannon fire.

"The navy's here! Tripoli is under attack!"

He rolled from his pallet in the garden shed and flung the door open. He heard screams of women and shouts of men from both inside the villa and over the walls in the town. The bombardment continued as he ran to find George.

George was already awake and coming into the garden, calling to Jamie, "The navy!"

Jamie returned to the shed and grabbed the ladder. He and George set it against the balcony and Jamie climbed up.

Just as he reached the top, a cannonball tore a hole through the garden wall and brought down a date palm. The palm fell across the balcony, nearly knocking Jamie off the ladder, which wobbled dangerously. Jamie clung to the balcony rail and flung himself over as the ladder fell, barely missing George, who dodged just in time. He recovered quickly and reset the ladder.

Jamie pounded on the closed louvers. "Baroness, Claire, open the windows!" he shouted over the sounds of the explosions.

Claire, dressed only in a robe, threw open the louvers. "Jamie!"

"Aye, I've come to get you out. Get your mother."

Baroness Andreasson arrived at the window in a quick sprint. "What is going on? What are you doing here, Mr. Sharpe?"

"Get dressed. We're getting you out of here."

"Are you mad? We will all be killed."

"No, we won't. The United States Navy is here. I will get you to the Danish consul. Mr. Nissen will get you out of Tripoli. Now hurry, we've no time to lose. Dress as a devout Muslim woman would. Cover yourself from head to toe."

The baroness hesitated.

"Mamaí, we must go," Claire insisted. "I'd rather take my chances with Jamie than end up in Kemal's harem."

Baroness Andreasson shook her head as if to clear the cobwebs of sleep. "Yes, my sweet daughter, you're right. I'd rather risk my life to see you free than be his slave."

"Hurry," Jamie urged. "If they catch us now, it will mean death for us all."

The women needed no more prodding. They ran inside and slipped into Arab garb which covered them completely.

George called, "Someone's coming."

Malik had entered the garden. At first, his attention was drawn to the destruction, but he looked over and saw George holding the ladder, then up at Jamie.

"What are you doing?"

"I'm helping the ladies escape. Please don't try and stop us, my friend."

Malik stroked his beard and shook his head. "Jamie, that is foolish! You hear the naqqāra, the kettle drums calling out the guards? You will be caught and killed. The women will be horribly punished if not also killed. I beg of you, don't do it."

"Malik, it is better to be free."

"I will not try and stop you, Jamie, but it is dangerous. I will leave now. Your fate is in the hands of Allah, but I will pray for your safety and your success. Go with God."

With that, Malik turned away and left the garden.

The women were ready. Jamie assisted the baroness down the ladder, then Claire.

George handed Jamie the cloak with the hood that Doctor de Aragon had given him.

"Put the hood up. You'll blend in better."

"George," Jamie said, "Put the ladder back and return to the stables. I hope to be back before dawn, but if I shouldn't return..." His voice failed.

"You will, lad, you will. And when you do, we'll find our own way out of this hell." He clasped Jamie's hand.

"Jamie, you're not going to escape with us?" Claire wondered.

"I can't leave my friends and crew. They would be killed. Now, we must hurry. If we're stopped, I'll do the talking."

He stepped through the hole in the wall and helped the women over the rubble.

Out in the narrow streets, there was nothing but chaos. Cannonballs slammed into buildings and people were running in a panic, not knowing which way to turn. Janissaries, trying to reach the harbor, pushed their way through the frightened crowd. Jamie heard someone say the Americans had set the *Philadelphia* on fire and that had set the frigate's cannons to shelling the town.

Jamie led the women into the mass of panicked people, where they blended in with the turmoil. No one paid any undue attention to them as they were dressed in local clothing. Jamie looked like an ordinary Arab or Berber trying to lead female family members to safety.

"This way," he whispered, as they neared the Danish consulate.

When they reached the building, instead of the Greek dragoman, the gate was guarded by two armed janissaries.

"Go from here," one of the janissaries said, waving his scimitar. "No one is to enter."

There was no way they could enter the safety of the consulate and yet they couldn't return to Kemal's villa.

"Jamie!" Claire cried out in despair, but her exclamation was drowned out by a terrible explosion.

Chapter 31

ALL EYES TURNED seaward. The *Philadelphia* had blown up, the fire finally having reached her powder magazine. Debris flew in all directions. While the crowd stood stunned, Jamie thought fast. He led the women through the New Gate and into the Jewish quarter. The devastation here was worse than in the other parts of the city, for many of the doubled-shotted guns of the *Philadelphia* were facing the direction of the mellah. Jamie prayed the home of Ephraim de Aragon had been spared.

It was just as chaotic in the Jewish quarter as it was in the rest of the city. People were out in the streets trying to make sense of it all. Some crying, some cursing, some stunned into silence. A number of people ran to the synagogue, others to wells, filling buckets to douse fires. Still others were digging through rubble.

Adding to the cacophony was the boom of guns from the castle and the forts trying to destroy the raiders.

A few people gave Jamie and the women wondering looks, for it was unusual for an Arab man and two women to be in the ghetto this time of the night, but this was not a usual night.

Jamie and the women turned a corner. He was relieved to see the de Aragon house was still standing and appeared undamaged. The building across the street had a large hole in it where an errant cannonball had struck.

Jamie pounded on the doctor's gate, until a slot opened in the door and part of a face looked out. The door was quickly opened. There stood Abdullah, his head bandaged but otherwise seeming unharmed.

"*Eajal!*" Abdullah urged. *Hurry!*

Once the three were inside, Abdullah slammed the door and threw the bolt.

"Sir," he said in Arabic, "it was you who sent for Doctor de Aragon and helped to carry me to his surgery. The doctor told me by stopping the bleeding on my chest, you saved my life. I am in your debt."

"I am happy to see you are healing, Abdullah," Jamie answered in the same language. "Now I must see your master."

Abdullah nodded and led the way. They hadn't gone far when they were met by Doctor de Aragon, his wife, and son, followed by servants crowded in around them.

"Jamie," the doctor asked in French, "What is this? Why are you here?"

Jamie quickly explained, "Doctor, I had no other place to turn. I beg you to hide the ladies until such a time as I can get them to Mr. Nissen and out of Tripoli."

"Jamie, what you ask of me is dangerous. Kemal will tear the town upside-down to find these ladies."

"I care not so much for myself," the baroness pleaded. "But I can't let my daughter fall into the hands of that beast." Tears flowed from her eyes yet did not diminish her great beauty.

Garvriella de Aragon stepped up to her husband and put her hand on his arm. No words were spoken, but they looked at each other and the doctor nodded.

"Of course we will hide them" he said.

Jamie gave a sigh of relief. Baroness Andreasson removed her head covering and said, "*Merci, Madame. Merci, Monsieur Docteur.*"

Garvriella took her hand to comfort her. "You will be safe," she said in English. "We have hidden others here, mostly Jewish, fugitives from the bashaw and his minions. Come with me. I will get you some refreshments and show you and your daughter to your quarters."

Claire removed her headscarf. "Jamie, you must hide here as well."

"Claire, I can't. It's my duty to return to George and my crew. I best not linger, lest Kemal finds I have gone."

Claire threw her arms around Jamie and kissed him on the lips.

"Jamie, will I ever see you again?"

Stunned and pleased by the kiss, it took Jamie a moment to regain his composure.

"When it's safe, I'll see you to Mr. Nissen's house." He turned away to start out, when the doctor pulled him aside. "Jamie, worry not about the ladies. I will see to their passage, whether to Malta, Sicily, or Gibraltar."

"Mr. Nissen has advanced me some money to pay passage to Malta."

"The ladies will also need money to live on and to take passage from Malta. I will give them the money."

"Sir, I will pay you back with interest when I am free. I promise."

"This is not a loan. I give the money freely. Our Hebrew scriptures teach the obligation to aid those in need. It is called *tzedakah*, meaning righteousness and justice. Abdullah will see you safely back to Kemal's house. Go with God."

Jamie thanked the de Aragons once again, then followed Abdullah out to the street.

"This way," Abdullah said.

He led Jamie through the crooked streets of the Jewish quarter. It was a different way than he had come. Abdullah explained it was safer. Jamie would never have found this way by himself.

They moved swiftly until they were nearly at Kemal's villa, when a corner of a building they were standing near collapsed. They dodged the falling debris as best they could, but a piece of masonry caught Jamie above his right eye, slashing his forehead and knocking him to the ground.

Chapter 32

"*YA SIDI!*" Abdullah yelled, bending down to help Jamie. *Sir!* He cleared away the plaster and helped Jamie to his feet. "Are you badly hurt?"

"I don't think so. Just stunned." Jamie wiped away the blood from his eye. "More blood than I expected." Jamie sounded a little surprised.

"With head wounds, there is often much blood," Abdullah said. He used a cloth to wipe away more blood. "There is a gash, rather deep, but not to the bone." Abdullah removed his sash and bound Jamie's head. He smiled and pointed to his own head. "We both have bandages upon our heads."

"Thank you for the use of your sash." Jamie reached up and touched his head. He flinched. It hurt more than he let on.

"It is but a small gesture. Hardly worthy of thanks, for as I have said, 'I'm in your debt.'" Abdullah said. "I have assisted the doctor in his surgery. I believe you will heal but have a small scar. When you get to your quarters, apply alum mixed with water as a poultice. It will halt the bleeding."

"Thank you, I will."

A small crowd had gathered when the plaster had fallen. They started to question if the young man was all right.

This was no time for the curious to halt Jamie's return to the villa. A fierce look from Abdullah gave them pause. They couldn't help but notice his fine livery and how he was bristling with weapons; he could be none other than a bodyguard to an important person. Jamie's new wool djellaba was of fine material. The onlookers knew to give Abdullah and his charge a wide berth.

"Nearly there, *ya sidi*."

Abdullah led Jamie down the lane and, in a few minutes, they arrived at the rear of the house. The hole in the wall was still open and Jamie climbed through.

He turned to thank Abdullah, but the man had already disappeared down the alley.

Jamie started toward his shed, when Malik greeted him.

"Praise Allah, you are back." Then he saw the bandage on Jamie's head, leaking blood. "You are hurt!"

"Aye, a gash. I need alum and water."

"Go to your shed, I will get alum from the kitchen."

When Malik returned, he removed Abdullah's sash, applied the alum poultice to Jamie's cut, and rebandaged his head.

"I just saw your countryman, Simon Cutts, cowering under his desk."

Jamie gave a little chuckle. "I believe the shooting has stopped. But Simon is a cautious lad." Then he turned serious. "Where is Kemal? Has he discovered the women missing?"

"No. He has been summoned to the castle. I assume the bashaw will be raving."

"I hope," Jamie said, "he doesn't take out his rage on the Americans."

"He will punish them. But he won't kill them. There are a number of important Tripolitan prisoners held by the Americans at Syracuse in Sicily," Malik said. "I worry what Kemal will do to you and your friends when he finds his women missing."

Jamie thought for a moment. "He won't be able to prove a thing."

"He won't need proof. He will rage and take it out on you." Suddenly, Malik's eyes lit up. "I have an idea. That wound is fortuitous. I will tell Kemal I found you unconscious under a pile of debris. You will not be implicated."

"Malik, why would you do that? If he finds out you're lying, he'll have you killed."

"There are times when one does the wrong thing for the right reasons. Imam al-Nawawi, a great scholar of the law wrote, 'A Muslim is permitted, indeed, required, to hide an innocent or wrongly persecuted person from oppressors, and if he must lie in this pursuit, he can. But even in such cases, lying should be avoided if possible.'"

Malik stroked his beard.

"In this instance, I see no alternative. True, I should not have an unbeliever for a friend, but you are a Christian and therefore a person of the Book. Kemal is a Muslim in name only, but it is Allah who will decide his fate and mine as well. So I will lie to protect you and your friends if I must. For there is another principle written in the hadith, the great collection of the teachings of Muhammad, the Messenger of Allah, may peace be upon him. Administering justice between two men is a *sadaqh*, a form of charity."

"Sadaqh?" Jamie repeated the word slowly. "Why, it means the same as the Hebrew tzedakah. A charity or act of justice!"

"You are correct, my friend," Malik said. "I see you are a scholar in more than one tradition."

"Hardly that, but Hebrew was one of the languages I was taught in school. And I've been the recipient of tzedakah, and now, sadaqh."

Malik nodded. "I think we've had enough philosophy for one night. You return to your shed. I will inform Tomaso that you've been injured and that the garden has been damaged."

"Tariq once told me that you are more than a gardener, Malik. I see it now."

Malik gave Jamie an enigmatic smile. "Go, my friend, get your rest. You will need it when Kemal finds out what has happened."

Jamie went into his shed and lay down on his mat. He was tired and dirty from his night's work and his head ached. It was not long before he drifted off into uneasy sleep.

He wasn't sure how long he slept, but he was awakened by a violent shaking. He sat up and rubbed the sleep from his eyes.

"Get up! Get up!" Tomaso was yelling in his ear. "The master is calling for you. Oh, what a calamity, the Swedish women are missing from the harem! The master is fit to kill! Report now!"

Chapter 33

THE FEAR JAMIE FELT as he entered Kemal's gulphor was like a punch to the gut.

His fear increased when the pirate captain turned and looked at him. Kemal's eyes were wild with anger. In his hand was his yatagan, a Turkish curved blade without a guard. He laid the tip on Jamie's throat and drew blood.

"Where are they? Where are me women?" He foamed. "I'll kill you, but first you'll tell me what you did with them!"

"Master, I have no idea where they are. I didn't know they were missing until Tomaso told me a few minutes ago. I've been unconscious for hours." He pointed to the bandage on his head. "The last thing I remember was an explosion and then all went black," Jamie managed to croak out as Kemal pressed the blade harder.

"If you're lying to me, I'll cut yer head from your body!" Kemal spat. "Remove that covering so I may see this so-called wound."

Jamie reached up and undid the bandage. As he did, the blood began to flow from the cut. Kemal took a deep breath and removed the yatagan from Jamie's throat.

"Cover your wound," Kemal commanded. "I should still kill you. Your countrymen had the impudence to enter our harbor in the guise of honest mariners and burn the frigate. Many of the bashaw's subjects were murdered by them. And their reckless act set off the cannon on the frigate, which damaged the town and, in the course of this action, blew a hole in me wall and me women escaped." Suddenly, Kemal broke down in tears. "What will I do without me Irish singers?" His brogue thickened. "Only they could soothe me. I can't stand what they call music in Tripoli. The songs from Ireland remind of that green land. Here, all I see is sand. I must have them back. And when I do, I'll make the young one my..."

Before he could finish, Jamie interrupted. "They couldn't have gone far," he said, playing to Kemal's emotions. "I'm sure you will find them."

Jamie's own emotions were churning. The thought of Claire in Kemal's harem made him want to kill the man on the spot. But he couldn't if he wanted the women out of Tripoli and his own crew safe.

"I will tear this town apart until I do find them." Kemal's melancholy left him as his anger returned. "Whoever is hiding them will feel me wrath. The vultures will feast on them."

Kemal would have continued his raving if he hadn't been interrupted by a guard with a message from the castle. The bashaw demanded his presence immediately.

"Again?" Kemal said. "The last time I was there, he tore at his beard and cursed and demanded to know how this catastrophe happened. He sent Murad Rais to find out, and me, he dismissed without any orders." He pointed at Jamie. "You come with me, Sharpe. Wound or not, I'll need you to translate so I can understand the bashaw through his ravin'."

On their way out, Kemal bellowed to Tomaso, "Get that damn wall repaired."

It was late morning as they approached the castle. The city still in turmoil, many people had gathered at the harbor to see for themselves the destruction caused by the cannons and the exploded frigate.

Kemal looked around the crowd, but since all the women were covered from head to toe in abayas, robes like dresses, and all wearing the niqab, a veil that covered their faces, he couldn't tell if they were his women or not. And he couldn't very well lift their veils without bringing down the wrath of law, not to say an irate husband or father. It just made him angrier. He took out his resentment on Jamie by giving him a shove. Jamie felt it was a small price to pay for knowing the women were safe.

The bashaw, yelling in Arabic, was berating Murad Rais when Kemal and Jamie were admitted to his throne room.

"How could your cannon miss? They fired shot after shot and only hit a topsail! I should have you and all of your captains bastinadoed and ridden through town backwards on an ass, as I did to your predecessor, he who had his ship dismasted and lost sixty men to the Americans."

Jamie recalled reading about the incident two years before when Lieutenant Andrew Sterrett, in the schooner *Enterprise*, fought a Tripolitan warship and nearly sank her. Now he had heard how the Tripolitan admiral had been punished. He covered his mouth with his hand so none could see his smile. He hoped Kemal and Murad would receive the same treatment.

Yusuf noticed Kemal for the first time and addressed him in French, which Jamie translated. "You will assemble your crew and patrol our coast. Watch for the Americans and Allah help you if you let them attack again without warning."

"Majesty, what of my posting to Derne? I've sent my household goods there. And during the attack, two of my women have disappeared. I must find them." Jamie was respectful in his translation, not wanting to upset the bashaw.

Too angry to pay attention to Jamie's tone, the bashaw turned red.

"As far as Derne is concerned, you will go there when this crisis is over. The women? Have someone in your household search for them. But you will not search for them yourself. You will follow my orders. See my secretary — you will be given documents so whomever you have searching for your lost women will not be molested by janissaries. I'll assign one of my men to enforce the search. However, you do not have carte blanche. No laws must be broken in the search and your people will not enter women's quarters. That is the best I will do for you and no more." He waved them off. "Now, all of you get yourselves from my sight. I must now attend to the American prisoners. The officers will be confined to the castle, the crew will work twice as hard."

Murad Rais was first to leave. He wanted no more of his father-in-law's belittling. Kemal and Jamie bowed and soon followed.

Outside, Kemal cursed. "I must find those women. You will aid in the search while I'm gone. I will give you guards to help."

"Me?" Jamie was stunned. Nothing could be better, but he had to pretend to protest. "Sir, I don't know what they look like. I don't know city that well. If they are hidden, I can't very search every house."

"You are clever, Sharpe. Smarter than many I've known. You'll ferret out the information. If you can't get it by cunning, then the janissary will persuade the reluctant. As to how the women look, they have red hair and green eyes. How many women in Tripoli fit that description?"

Kemal pointed at Jamie and said, "Find them and I will cut your ransom by a quarter. Don't and I will double it."

Jamie didn't care about the ransom. He could now keep the women safe until he could get them out of the country. He was elated but dared not show it. Instead, he said, "I will search diligently, master."

"You will, indeed. Get to it. I must prepare my crew."

Chapter 34

THE BASHAW ASSIGNED a janissary to assist Jamie in his search. The man was squat, wide-shouldered, and quite ugly. He was armed to the teeth with scimitar, yatagan, two pistols, and a musket. He wore loose pantaloons, a blue shirt, and a short red jacket. On his rather square head sat a tall hat with an ostrich plume. Despite his short stature, he looked like he could scare the dead. In heavily accented Arabic, he introduced himself as Asci Bulut. Asci was a Turkish rank similar to a sergeant. Malik later told Jamie the word was Turkish for cook. All janissary ranks were the same as kitchen help, going back centuries to when janissaries were originally assigned to the kitchen.

Bulut told Jamie in no uncertain words that he resented being assigned to a slave and, after a week, he would be relieved of this unpleasant duty.

"We both have an unpleasant duty, Asci," Jamie said. "I must do as my master commands as you do. When this is over, I hope you will return to your duties in the castle."

"When this is over, I'll leave this desert and join my fellows in Albania, where I was born, and help rule that place. Now, let us get on with this task. I have my orders: you are to lead and I am to make sure we search and to enforce the bashaw's command that no one is to stand in our way."

Jamie stayed away from the mellah and confined his search to Kemal's neighborhood. They searched the house across the alley. It had been badly damaged from cannonballs, but it was empty.

If Bulut resented Jamie, the neighbors resented even more the intrusion into their homes. However, they feared the soldier and the bashaw's edicts.

As the week progressed and the women were nowhere to be found, Bulut became more impatient.

"These women wouldn't hide in a Muslim house. Only a few Christians would dare hide them. The women are not of the Catholic or Orthodox faith, so they wouldn't receive sanctuary in the churches."

Jamie worried. Next were the Jews. If they searched the Jewish quarter, it was possible someone might remember the night of the burning of the frigate and a Muslim man with two women seen in the mellah.

Jamie was relieved when, instead of the Jewish quarter, Bulut said they should inquire at the foreign embassies. "If the women are hiding in one of them, the servants will know."

Jamie shrugged and suggested the Danish consulate first.

When they reached the consulate, the dragoman recognized Jamie.

Jamie quickly said, in Greek, "Pretend you don't know me."

The dragoman replied with a nod, "What can I do for you, stranger?"

Jamie asked the man in Greek if there were European women held inside.

The dragoman shifted to Arabic. "No, there are no foreign women here."

Bulut stepped forward. "Are you sure?" he demanded, his hand on the hilt of his scimitar.

The dragoman showed no fear. "There are no foreign women here. Do you wish me to call the consul?"

"No, that will not be necessary." Bulut backed down.

They went from consulate to consulate with the same question and received the same answer.

Finally, they arrived at the British consulate. Jamie was really worried here. He had lied to the guard to gain entrance when he sought sanctuary for Claire and her mother. He hoped the man wouldn't remember him, for Jamie doubted he would be as friendly as the man at the Danish consulate. He pulled his hood tighter and lowered his head. Bulut prodded him with the heel of his hand, shoving harder than necessary.

Jamie coughed, lowered his voice, and asked about the women.

The man looked at Jamie, trying to place him. He stared for a moment until Bulut shouted at him. “Well, are you struck dumb? Answer!”

“No, no, Asci. Do you mean the consul’s wife?”

“Idiot! No, a young woman and an older woman with hair of red.”

“No, there is no one here like that.”

“Fool!” Bulut said, then walked away.

“Slave,” Bulut said, “we can search for a year and never find the women. My orders from the bashaw were clear. One week and then I am done. Tomorrow, the time is up.”

Jamie had to suppress a smile, although Kemal wouldn’t be pleased.

Chapter 35

"BLAST YE TO HELL!" Kemal cursed. "What do you mean you couldn't find them?"

"Master, we searched for a week. They were nowhere to be found," Jamie replied.

"You," Kemal addressed Bulut in English. "The bashaw ordered you to help find the women. What good are you?"

The janissary couldn't understand the words, but understood the tone. His face reddened as he grasped the hilt of his scimitar. "*Benimle nasıl konuştuğunu izle!*" he yelled back in Turkish. Neither Kemal nor Jamie could understand Bulut.

Bulut repeated it, this time in Arabic, "*Shahid kayf tatahadath maei!*"

Both Jamie and Kemal understood this time. The Turk had said "Watch how you speak to me!"

Kemal didn't dare attack the man who was in the employ of the bashaw. "*Akhraj!* Get out! The crow's curse on ye, ye stinkin' bastard."

Bulut left not knowing he'd been cursed.

Kemal picked up a bottle of spirits and took a dram. He sat down and put his head in his hands. "You say you searched everywhere?"

"Yes," Jamie said, "except the women's baths and the castle itself. We searched houses, shops, churches, even the mosques. Master, I would have kept searching but Bulut said he was through, and I can't enter the houses without him."

"Some scoundrel of a Turk or Arab has taken them into his own harem. Should I ever find the bag o' snot, I'll gut him from gullet to crotch." He took another drink. "For all I know, it was that damn Bulut himself. He could 'ave steered ye off course. He's a shifty one."

Picking up on Kemal's wild thought, Jamie said, "He may have hidden them in the castle. He told me we couldn't search there. And the place is so large, there must be hundreds of hiding places. He leaves for Albania soon — perhaps he will take them with him."

"They are lost to me." Kemal actually broke down and cried. "Get out Sharpe, before I beat ye for the hell of it."

Jamie retreated hastily.

❁ ❁ ❁

The next morning, Kemal sailed out of the harbor in a galliot, a smaller shallow draft vessel with oars as well as sails. The crew were for the most part Kemal's own sailors, but a few slaves were added to row. Among the slaves on the oars were George, Mateus, and Fenton Webb. This worried Jamie. If the galliot were to be attacked by the Americans blockading the harbor, his good friends could be killed.

Jamie itched to get out of the villa and see what progress was being made on getting the Andreasson women out of Tripoli. But Tomaso kept him busy in the garden.

Malik, noticing Jamie's agitation, explained there was very little traffic coming into port because of the American blockade. "Soon, my friend, the Europeans will come in. The Americans will not prevent their commerce."

Malik was right. British, French, Dutch and Maltese vessels soon appeared in the harbor, but not for commerce. They were allowed in for diplomatic business and bringing supplies to the consulates.

Two weeks later, Kemal returned from his patrol. Jamie was anxious to hear the news from George.

"I saw several American vessels, two schooners, and a brig. One of the schooners chased us, but Kemal ran inshore and hid among some small islands and rocks. I was hoping they would sink us if it meant the end of Kemal and Billy Scars."

"Aye," Jamie replied. "But it would mean the end of you, Fenton, and Mateus."

"It might have been worth it," George said, half in jest. "Kemal was in a foul mood the whole voyage. The man was a worse tyrant than ever. He even took a whip to Bruiser McPhee, for not pulling his oar hard enough."

"What about our friends and you, George?"

"No, Jamie, he never struck us, however Billy Scars kicked me a few times, just on general principles. He's a vindictive brute. I will kill him one day."

Jamie nodded. George was not one to make empty threats.

"I had good chance to look over the harbor and fortifications," George said. "There are batteries covering both the northeastern and western entrances to the harbor. I estimated well over a hundred heavy cannon. There are so many rocks, shoals, and reefs, our large ships will be hard-pressed to enter the harbor should they get by the batteries. And if they do, they'll face the bashaw's gunboats and other small craft."

"A daunting task." Jamie agreed. "I hope Commodore Preble is up to it. I remember Mr. Eaton, the Danielson boy's stepfather, saying Preble was real fighting man."

"The one time I met the commodore, he had a strong presence about him," George said. "I remember Brad's brother, Frank, said he was hard as steel and a strict captain. Still, I've seen what he's up against.

"And what of you, Jamie?" George asked.

"I missed your steady presence these two weeks. I've heard nothing of the Andreassons. I must see them and the Danish consul."

"I'm sure they are well. You would have heard by now if they were found. Kemal is bound to send you on some errand soon."

Chapter 36

TWO DAYS AFTER George's prediction, it was Tomaso rather than Kemal sending Jamie on an errand.

"Sharpe, I want you to take these copper pots to Issachar ben Yoel, the coppersmith in the mellah. His shop is not far from the house of Doctor de Aragon. Have the coppersmith re-tin them. Your blacksmith friend, Walling, doesn't have the right metals to fix them. There are six pots. Tell the man who they are for and to send the bill here."

"How am I supposed to carry six pots?"

"Take that ox of a blacksmith with you," Tomaso said in exasperation. "He might learn something from the Jewish smith."

Jamie was overjoyed, but tried not to show it.

He found George in the stables helping Usem, the groom, saddle the Arabian horses.

"Kemal's going riding," George said. "Usem tells me the horses need exercise."

Kemal came striding in, followed by two of his Berber guards. "Sharpe," he asked, irritated as usual, "why are you here?"

"I've come to fetch George. We're taking some pots to be re-tinned."

"Get going then." He smacked Jamie across the shoulder with his riding crop.

Jamie tried not to flinch.

Once out of earshot, George said, "What foul temper that bastard has." He clenched his fists as if he wanted to smash Kemal. Then he noticed blood on Jamie's shirt.

"How's your shoulder?"

"I've been struck worse. But I'll get some alum from the kitchen."

"I'll fetch a cart we can pull."

George turned back to the stables. Jamie went into the kitchen, removed his shirt, and asked Dimas for the alum.

"Are you hurt, Capitão Jamie?"

"Just a whip cut from our benign master."

"Benign?" Dimas asked as he applied the alum to the cut. "Ah, *benigno*! You make joke."

"Not a very good one, I'm afraid," Jamie replied as he slipped his shirt back on.

"Not a very good strike, if Kemal only gave you that little cut." Simon emerged from his cubby off the kitchen.

"At least it wasn't the bastinado," Jamie said, reminding Simon of his own punishment.

"You have pots to get mended." Simon puffed up. "I want them done as soon as possible. I don't need you around my kitchen, taking up the time of my cooks."

"You don't run the kitchen. Dimas does. He tells you what he needs, you follow his orders and obtain what he needs."

Simon sneered and went back to his desk.

George returned with a small handcart and he and Jamie loaded the huge pots. Three were at least ten gallons each. George and Jamie hauled the cart out through the back gate and pulled toward the Jewish quarter.

"The coppersmith is near the de Aragon house," Jamie said. "You stay with the smith. I'll go talk to the doctor."

The young men hauled the cart through the twisted streets, past the New Gate, and into the mellah. The place was busy as masons, carpenters, and other artisans were repairing the damage done by the guns of the *Philadelphia*. Jamie knew where the coppersmith had his stall, for when he had first entered the Jewish quarter, he'd asked the man for directions to Doctor de Aragon's house.

The smith was pounding out a pot when George and Jamie arrived. When Issachar ben Yoel heard the name Kemal Rais, he gave a sour look.

"*Ben kelev*," he said in Hebrew.

Jamie realized the coppersmith was calling Kemal a "son of a dog." Jamie smiled and nodded his agreement. George picked up on it as well and laughed out loud.

This time, Issachar threw back his head and joined George in a hearty laugh of his own. George sat down next to Issachar and, in fair Arabic, asked if he could watch. He explained he was also a smith, who worked in iron and steel. Issachar nodded and tended his small forge.

Jamie left George and Issachar and walked down the street to the doctor's house.

Abdullah answered his knock.

"*Sayidi*, Jamie! How glad I am to see you. We have not heard from you in many days. All in this house were worried. And I am still in your debt, sir, for you saved me from certain death."

"There is no debt between friends and no need to address me as 'my lord.'"

Abdullah nodded and smiled. He led Jamie to the garden.

"Please wait. I will fetch the doctor."

Doctor de Aragon and his wife soon appeared, followed by a servant with a tray of food and drink.

"Jamie," Garvriella de Aragon called in greeting. "We are pleased you are here. We've all been worried. We didn't know if Kemal Rais had punished or, God forbid, killed you."

"He didn't suspect me." Jamie pointed to the scar on his head and explained how he used it to fool Kemal.

"I suppose," Doctor de Aragon said, "a small scar is worth the sacrifice if it removed you from suspicion."

The doctor noticed the blood on Jamie's garment. "What is this?" He pulled back the shirt. "A cut. You treated it with alum. How did it happen?"

"Kemal was in his usual foul mood and struck me with his crop." Jamie waved it off. "It will heal."

The doctor nodded.

"Now, please enjoy your refreshment." He passed Jamie a plate of figs.

"You must," the doctor said, "be here because of the good news from Mr. Nissin."

"What good news?" Jamie said with surprise. "I had no way of hearing from Mr. Nissin."

"Mr. Nissin and I have been in contact. I heard from him yesterday that a Maltese vessel has arrived and the captain is ready to risk taking them away. He wants a hundred English pounds or its equivalent and he will get them to Malta. From there, they can arrange passage to Ireland or even America if they so choose. Do not worry, Jamie, I will pay the money."

"I have the money to pay their passage to Malta."

"You will need the money should you find the means of escape."

"Sir, I'm forever in your debt."

Doctor de Aragon demurred.

Jamie was humbled. "When can we get the women out?"

"Tomorrow night, I will have them escorted to the Maltese ship. Mr. Nissin will finalize the arrangements." The doctor paused for a moment and consulted a piece of paper. "The ladies will be escorted to the customs house at ten-thirty by the clock. Forged papers will say they are to be sent to Constantinople for the harem of an Ottoman admiral. The customs agent will not look closely at them for fear of offending the admiral. Abdullah will pretend to be a eunuch guard. He thinks it is a big joke, since he has six children and two wives."

Sure enough, at hearing the word 'eunuch', Abdullah burst into laughter and waddled around the garden imitating a fat eunuch.

The thought made Jamie cringe. He couldn't smile at Abdullah's antics.

"The Maltese captain," the doctor continued, "will bring them aboard. The Maltese ship will sail on the tide at eleven-thirty. Once in the harbor, Abdullah will be picked up in a boat by another servant and they will return here."

Jamie nodded. He was anxious to see Claire. It might be the last time they would ever meet.

Chapter 37

JAMIE JUMPED TO his feet when Claire and her mother came into the garden. Both women were wearing caftans. Claire's was dark green, which highlighted her auburn hair. Her mother was dressed in blue. Neither woman had their hair covered, but each had a short khimar, a headscarf, draped around their shoulders.

Claire's eyes lit up and a charming smile crossed her face when she saw Jamie. Jamie in turn smiled back, his heart pumping with joy at the sight of her. The baroness, on the other hand, gave a little smile, but the sadness in her eyes betrayed a woman suffering from grief. Jamie, usually so perceptive, didn't notice it, but Garvriella was well aware of it. Understanding what was troubling Catriona Andreasson, she took her hand.

Jamie, in the meantime, shyly took Claire's hand. "Miss Andreasson, Claire, I'm sure you heard the good news. You will be escaping Tripoli and be on your way to freedom on tomorrow's evening tide."

Claire gave Jamie's hand a squeeze. "Thanks to you, Jamie, and the de Aragons. But what of you? Jamie, please come with us."

"I can't. I will not abandon my friends." As much as he wanted to go, he knew his duty and loyalty was to his friends.

"I may never see you again."

Jamie knew Claire was probably right. His heart sank, but he gave her a bright smile. "We will meet again. I'll be redeemed. My family will send the money. Have faith."

"I will," she said.

Jamie turned to Claire's mother. "Baroness, have you made plans as to where you will go once you reach Malta?"

"I...I..." She sobbed and put her head in her hands.

Claire rushed to her side and threw her arms around her.

Jamie stood dumbfounded. "What is it?"

Garvriella took Jamie aside. "Jamie, you are young and may not understand these things. I will try to explain. The Baroness is afraid of what people will say and how she will be treated once she returns to Europe. You see, she will be judged as a soiled woman, a woman who was used in the worst way. And many people will think she should have killed herself rather than be ravaged."

"That's ridiculous. She submitted to keep her daughter safe. People must understand that. Should I or Captain Bainbridge kill ourselves because we were captured?"

"Unfortunately, that is not how the world works. She will be judged. I fear once she's sure Claire is safe, she'll take her own life."

Jamie was aghast. "That can't happen." He thought for few moments then said, "I have an idea."

He went over to the Andreassons. Claire was trying to comfort her mother.

"Please, Baroness," Jamie entreated, "take heart."

She looked at Jamie with red-rimmed eyes and tried to smile. "I am sorry to be so weak."

"Weak?" Jamie questioned. "You are a strong woman. You've survived this ordeal, you protected Claire. In many ways, Kemal was afraid of you. Afraid you might kill him. Afraid you would stop singing. You should know he is in a most miserable state, and in his case, that is a good thing."

"Jamie, you don't understand what I will face on my return to Europe. I'll be an outcast. Society will shun me. And Claire as well."

"Then you shan't go to Europe. You will go to America. You can change your name and your story. I will write to my family in Boston. Believe me when I say my mother and father will protect you. Let me write them and tell them your story."

"Jamie, I'm not sure that's the best idea. What if someone in Boston recognizes me? Someone who saw me in Europe."

"If anyone should question what happened to you, face them and tell them you were able to escape. My family will protect you."

Catriona thought for a moment. "You have done right by us. I will trust you."

Jamie asked for pen and paper and wrote a long letter to his family, explaining everything about the ladies. He included that he and George were alive and well, but anxious to be free. He gave it to Catriona.

"I must say goodbye now. My friend George awaits and we have to return soon. But I will be at the customs house tomorrow night."

"Jamie, that's dangerous," Doctor De Aragon said. "If you are caught..."

"I shall be careful."

Claire took Jamie by the hand and led him to a corner of the garden. "Jamie, as the good doctor said, it is dangerous for you to be there at the customs house."

"I must see you off, I won't feel relived until the Maltese ship sails."

She sighed. "I shall have faith, but I will worry. Until then, be safe."

She put her arms around his neck and they kissed. It wasn't a mere peck either. Both young people knew they were in love.

Chapter 38

JAMIE FOUND GEORGE at the coppersmith's.

"He's very good at his profession," George said. "I could do the work with the proper materials, but let's not tell Tomaso. I hate to take work away from this man."

"We won't," Jamie said. "I've a great deal to tell you, but we should start back. Are the pots ready?"

"Just two. We can get the others in two days."

On their way back to the villa, Jamie told George all that had transpired and the plans for tomorrow night.

"That's excellent news," George said. "Once the ladies are free, we can plan our own escape."

"Yes, however, we'll never get out of Tripoli. Hopefully, it will be easier to escape from Derne. We'll have to wait and see. Now, I'll have to sneak out tomorrow night. I want to make sure all goes as planned."

"Jamie," George said, his brow wrinkled with worry. "If you are caught, it could mean the bastinado or, worse, your death."

"I'll be careful."

George shook his head, knowing he could not dissuade his friend from his dangerous venture.

Kemal did not return that day, nor the next. Tomaso announced "the master" was visiting a marabout in the desert.

In Arabic, Malik told Jamie that the bashaw ordered Kemal to seek out the marabout, who would cure him of his melancholy over the loss of his women.

"Could the holy man cure him?" Jamie asked.

Malik looked around to make sure no one was listening and, to be safe, he switched from Arabic to English. "The bashaw relies on this marabout for advice and guidance. The marabout claimed he put a spell on the American frigate so it ran aground and could be captured."

"You sound skeptical."

"Several years ago, this same marabout told the bashaw that adding pig manure to horses feed would cure them of distemper."

"Where did the bashaw get pig manure?" Jamie asked. "I should think pigs are scarce in this city."

Malik laughed. "From the American consul."

"What happed to the horses?"

"They died. But the marabout insisted the pig manure was poisoned. This added to the bashaw's distrust of the Americans. However, he never told the consul why he needed the manure. It never occurred to him that feeding manure to horses would kill them."

"So you don't think the marabout is really a holy man?"

Malik spread his hands and shrugged. "I think he and the bashaw think he is a holy man."

Jamie said nothing to Malik about leaving the villa later. He didn't want his friend implicated if he should be caught. As night approached, he met with George in the garden to go over his plans.

"The back wall is patrolled by several of Kemal's guards, as is the rear gate," George pointed out. "Nor is the front any safer – it too is guarded."

Jamie nodded. "I've been mulling it over all day. I can climb to the top of the wall at the northeast corner. From there, I can jump to the roof of the house across the back passage. The house is empty. It was damaged by the cannon fire from the *Philadelphia*. From there, I can make it to the street."

George rubbed his beard. "I don't know. It's a good eight feet from the wall to the roof. You can't even take a running jump."

"I can do it."

"Jamie, why must you go?" George asked. "The ladies will be safe under Abdullah's protection. You told me he's a formidable fellow."

"Aye, he is. But I must see them off. They're my responsibility."

"Then go with them," George insisted.

"I can't leave you or the others to suffer the wrath of Kemal."

George shook his head. "You are a stubborn fellow, my friend. But I shan't sleep a wink whilst you're gone."

"I'll be back before dawn."

Chapter 39

AT SUNSET, THE muezzins throughout the city called the faithful to Maghrib, the evening prayer.

"I should go now," Jamie said. "The guards should be at prayer."

He wrapped his jellabiya, turban, and knife in a bundle, added rocks for weight, and was ready to go.

George watched as Jamie climbed a palm tree in the northeast corner of the garden. The wall was three feet or so from the top of the tree.

Jamie swayed back and forth, moving the treetop closer, then jumped, grabbed the top of the wall, and pulled himself up. He waved to George and turned to face the roof of the damaged building across the way. Like all of the houses in Tripoli, the roof was flat with a narrow masonry railing at the edge.

The gap between his perch on the wall and roof looked wider than eight feet. With the setting sun at his back, Jamie could see the white building in the fading light. He heaved his bundle of clothes across and it landed on the roof.

He looked down, estimating it was at least twenty-five feet to the ground. The passageway was strewn with litter, smashed masonry, shards of glass, broken timbers — all remnants from the destruction of the frigate.

He remembered an old sailor, a topman on his father's ship, telling him as they stood on a footrope high above the deck, "It ain't the fall that'll kill ye, it be the landing!" The old salt had laughed hard, showing yellow and missing teeth.

With that macabre thought in mind, Jamie decided it was time to jump, before he lost what little light there was left.

Looking at the roof, Jamie stood with his feet slightly apart, rocked his arms back and forth, bent his knees, took a deep breath, swung his arms forward as if he were going to dive, and launched himself up.

Below, George, his heart rapidly breathing, couldn't stand it any longer and climbed up the palm tree. He looked across to the roof next door and saw Jamie clinging to the masonry railing with one hand as he attempted to scramble up and over.

George was about to call out when a guard came walking down the passageway. The guard stopped just below Jamie to urinate.

George hissed to warn Jamie, hoping the guard wouldn't hear him. Jamie looked over at his friend and George pointed down. Jamie looked. Hanging by one hand, he dared not move lest the guard hear him.

Jamie was in pain, his arm and hand strained to the limit. Any moment, he'd weaken and fall. If he wasn't killed outright, the guard would surely do the job.

It seemed to take forever for the guard to finish. Finally, he adjusted his pantaloons and marched off.

Jamie took a mighty swing with all he had left. He reached out, grabbed the railing, and heaved himself up and onto the roof. He lay panting, trying to catch his breath.

Finally, Jamie stood up and waved to George, who breathed a sigh of relief.

It suddenly occurred to Jamie he couldn't jump back across, there was nothing to grab on to should he not land squarely on the top of the wall. *Well*, he thought, *I'll worry about that later.*

Jamie surveyed his surroundings. A large hole in the roof where a cannonball had struck made the opposite corner unsafe. He dressed in his Arab garb and wound the turban around his head. He had passed for an Arab or Berber before and hoped he could do it again.

A stairway leading down to the courtyard was partially destroyed at the top. It was about five feet to where the undemolished stairs still stood. Rather than jump, he lowered himself down to the steps and proceeded to the courtyard.

Mosaic tiles had been removed from part of the courtyard. Jamie was sure the house had been looted at one point. Despite city watchmen, the narrow streets and alleys allowed gangs of thieves to roam at night and he had heard they were not above killing.

An abandoned house was a perfect hiding place. He made sure his dagger was in easy reach and searched among the debris for another weapon. He found an iron poker in the kitchen fireplace. It was long enough to double as a staff.

A lanthorn lay near the fireplace. He picked it up. The glass was broken but it still had a candle stub inside. A tinderbox hung from a chain near the fireplace. He removed it, struck the flint a few times, and the tinder flamed. He lit his candle.

He heard a rustling behind him, raised the poker, and turned quickly to see a large cat with a rat in its mouth. The cat looked at him and hissed.

"Enjoy your dinner, Puss."

Jamie walked out of the kitchen, leaving the cat to its repast.

He searched the lower level and found it empty of people but with signs of looting. He walked out to the garden to see it was overgrown with weeds and dates had dropped from the palms to rot on the ground or be eaten by birds, rats, or other vermin. One tree still held a cluster of dates, so he climbed it and loaded his pockets with the fruit.

He searched the rest of the house and, besides the cat and the vermin, it was empty. The former owner's gulphor faced the street and harbor. He blew out the candles and opened the windows. He heard the bells from the Catholic Church and figured he had a little over an hour to wait before the ladies would be brought to the customs house. The less time he was on the streets after dark, the less chance he would have of being stopped by the watch. He made himself as comfortable as he could, dragging over some torn cushions to sit on.

He was joined by the cat, which laid part of the rat at Jamie's feet. The cat then made itself comfortable on his lap. Jamie stroked the cat and it purred.

"Well, my fine furry friend, you wish to join me on my vigil? I welcome the company."

He stroked the cat while he waited.

Outside, there were some people moving about. A man came along — an Arab by his dress — weaving as he walked, probably drunk despite the prohibition against alcohol. Suddenly, three men stepped out of a doorway and attacked him. The man didn't have time to even cry out before one of the assailants slashed his throat. One of the thieves picked up the man's purse, looked in it, cursed, and said, "His purse is empty!" But that didn't stop them from stripping the man naked, taking his clothes and sandals.

Jamie was appalled. They didn't even give the poor soul a chance. He was glad he had taken the iron poker. Death could come in an instant.

The thieves rolled the naked man into the doorway of the house and disappeared into the dark and twisted streets.

"Puss," he said, "if the watch comes by and sees the body, they'll enter the house to investigate."

He lifted the cat from his lap, got to his feet, and went downstairs. The cat meowed and padded down after him.

Downstairs, he cautiously opened the door and started to drag the dead man in when he heard footsteps. It was either the watch or the thieves returning.

Chapter 40

JAMIE DUCKED BACK in the doorway, hid in the shadows, and put his knife in his left hand and the iron poker in his right. The footsteps approached and he recognized the voice of the man who killed the drunk.

"The watch! Into this house, it is empty." They dragged the body in, leaving a trail of blood, and hid it behind a bench.

Jamie wasn't sure he could defend himself against three men, so he retreated to the garden. Fog had descended and helped hide him among the overgrown plants and weeds. He waited, not moving. Then he heard someone yell "Stop!" in Arabic.

The thieves ran into the garden. Close on their heels was an Arab watchman armed with a heavy club. A brave man, Jamie thought, to face down three armed men.

The watchman ordered the three to drop their knives, but the murderer, obviously the leader, just laughed.

"We will kill you, fool," he said in Arabic.

He and his cohorts advanced on the lone man.

The watchman shifted his stance and raised his club. The thieves surrounded him and lashed out with their knives, but the watchman swung his heavy club and struck one on his forearm. The man let out a terrible scream. The blow must have shattered the bones in his arm.

The other two stepped back and kept out of reach of the club. One of the thieves feinted an attack and the watchman raised his club. That's when another man got behind him and stabbed him in the shoulder.

The watchman staggered, but swung his club and hit the man in front with a blow to the head. The thief went down like a felled ox. Now the loss of blood from the stab wound hindered the watchman from defending himself. The head thief, alone, took advantage, and raised his knife to strike a killing blow.

Jamie leaped from his hiding place and yelled in his harshest voice, "*Lisun waqatila. Abn alshaytan!*" *Thief and murderer. Son of Satan!*

The man looked up, startled at the menace stepping out of the fog. Before the thief could recover, Jamie struck with his iron poker, breaking his shoulder. The man went down screaming. Jamie had drawn the end of his turban over his face so he couldn't be identified, picked up the man's knife and went to the watchman,

The watchman looked at Jamie with disbelief. "*Hal 'ant aljinn?*"

Jamie didn't answer. He smiled under his mask. Malik had once told him a jinn was an Arab mythological being that could be either good or bad. Apparently, the watchman thought Jamie was a good jinn.

Jamie examined the cut. It wasn't deep. He pressed some spider webs into the wound and the bleeding stopped.

"*Shukraan lak bark Allah fik.*" The watchman thanked Jamie and asked Allah to bless him.

Jamie helped the watchman to his feet and handed him his club. The two wounded thieves moaned and begged for help and mercy.

"Those two are in no condition to put up a fight," Jamie said. He pointed to the man on the ground. "That one's dead. They murdered a man and robbed him. His body is behind a bench near the door. I must go now."

Jamie turned and disappeared into the fog. It was at that moment the cat appeared, looked at the watchman and his prisoners, mewed loudly, and followed Jamie into the mist.

"Ai! He *is* a jinn. He turned into a cat!"

The two thieves moaned even louder, this time with fear.

Jamie smiled.

He turned to the cat and whispered, "Well, Puss, it's not safe for me here any longer. I must be on my way. Good hunting, my friend."

That cat rubbed up against Jamie's leg, meowed a farewell, and moved deeper into the garden.

Chapter 41

JAMIE WAITED UNTIL the watchman was far enough away to safely leave without detection. He made his way along the waterfront, avoiding anyone out at this late hour.

He approached the customs house and ducked behind a small dhow, which was pulled up on shore. He saw a vessel tied up alongside the customs house pier. Several men were standing on the pier talking — two dressed in the Turkish style, one in seafaring garb. He recognized Mr. Nissin and his dragoman.

Mr. Nissin approached the seafarer and shook his hand. "Hello, Captain," he said.

Jamie figured he must be the Maltese captain Mr. Nissin had hired to bring the women to Malta.

"Your passengers haven't arrived, Captain," one of the Turks said to the seafarer.

"I shall wait until the tide turns," the captain answered.

His voice was familiar, but before Jamie could place it.

A large man leading three donkeys towards the pier neared Jamie's hiding place. Two of the animals were carrying veiled women, the third donkey carried baggage.

Jamie recognized Abdullah, looking ridiculous as he waddled toward the pier in an imitation of a eunuch. Jamie adjusted his turban, stood up, and faced the little caravan.

Abdullah drew a huge scimitar. It took him a minute to recognize Jamie in his disguise, then he smiled, sheathing his weapon.

"Come," he said. "Take the lead and present yourself as Kadeem ibn Omar, secretary to Ali ibn Hassan."

"Who is that?"

Abdullah smiled. "An Arab friend of the doctor's. He's the one presenting these women to the Turkish admiral."

"Of course," Jamie said, amused. It was all part of the deception.

They climbed the pier and walked toward the men waiting by the boat.

The captain turned to the official. "Here are my passengers, effendi."

Jamie stepped forward and introduced himself as secretary to Ali ibn Hassan.

Then, the customs official asked for the papers. Suddenly, Jamie panicked. He didn't have papers. Abdullah tapped him on the shoulder and handed him a packet.

Jamie breathed a sigh of relief and handed the packet to the customs officer. While he waited for the papers to be checked, he looked around, but not daring to catch Claire's eye. Instead, he saw Consul Nissin and his dragoman handing papers to the captain.

"Please make sure you get these documents to the Danish consul at Malta."

The captain nodded and turned around. To Jamie's astonishment, before him stood Captain Sabatier, the man who had rescued him and the survivors of the *Beneficence.*

Sabatier looked at the newcomers and, as the moon came out from behind a cloud, his sharp eyes penetrated the Arab garb. "Jamie Sharpe!"

The customs officer turned his head abruptly and looked at Jamie. "*Jamie Sharpe nedir?*"

No one spoke. The only sound heard was the slapping of the waves against the ship's hull. Once again, the official asked, "*Jamie Sharpe nedir?*" *What is Jamie Sharpe?*

Jamie reached inside his jellabiya for his knife. But before he could draw it, Captain Sabatier spoke up.

"He's a Maltese patron saint. I call on him for a safe voyage."

The official nodded. Jamie let go of his knife and Jamie choked down a laugh. *A saint!* He didn't think he was any kind of saint.

The customs official said everything was in order and the women could board. Abdullah escorted them up a gangplank.

"I must give orders to the eunuch," Jamie said.

The official gave him permission to go aboard. "Just return before they sail."

Jamie nodded and boarded. He followed the women to the captain's tiny cabin.

Inside, both women removed their heavy veils. Claire rushed to Jamie and threw her arms around him.

"Jamie, I wish you were going with us."

"Claire," he said, his heart breaking, "you know I can't."

Catriona took Jamie's hand. "I'll never forget you. And I'll never be able to thank you."

Jamie smiled. "Baroness, go to America. Seek out my family in Boston and give them the letter I wrote. They will watch over you and Claire."

Catriona smiled through tears. "No more 'baroness,' just Catriona Tyrrell Andreasson. I understand, in America, nobility is frowned upon."

"Perhaps," Jamie said, "but not noble people."

"The good doctor and his wife gave us enough money."

Captain Sabatier coughed. "Ladies, I'm sorry the accommodations are so small, but once we are away from Tripoli, you may come on deck to get some air. Mr. Nissin has provided some European clothes for you." He pointed to a bundle on the bunk. "Jamie," the captain said, "I must prepare to sail, but we should talk."

Jamie nodded and bade the women farewell. With much sorrow, he finally joined Sabatier on deck.

"How are you here, Jamie?"

Jamie quickly related his story.

"My God," Sabatier said. "You would have been better off facing the British in Malta. You and your friend George were cleared of charges."

Jamie was stunned. "What?" How?"

A man by the name of Lucius Bent, or Bentley, said you would never participate in putting the British sailors and marines in a boat. This was confirmed by Master's Mate Griffith and Bosun's Mate Milburn, as well as the marines and British sailors who were put overboard."

"Did they hang Bentley?"

Sabatier shook his head. "It turns out he had told the truth. It was his twin brother who wrecked the British ship. At the court-martial, a naval captain who came from the same town as the brothers and knew them well as young men, testified that Bentley was indeed Lucius. Although they were identical twins, Lucas had a small birthmark on his neck. Lucius didn't. That is the only way the captain said he could tell them apart."

"Scoundrel's luck." Jamie said. "Someday, I hope to meet Mr. Lucius Bent or Bentley again."

"Don't you see, Jamie? You are not wanted by the English. I could take you with me to Malta."

"I can't. I will not abandon my men. However, I will be ransomed as well as my men. I've written to my father. He will honor my request to pay their ransom. My father is not one to let seamen be slaves. The letter was sent to America via the United States consul at Malta. I'm sure the money is on its way."

"No, it's not on the way." Sabatier shook his head. "When your Commodore Preble arrived at Malta, he discovered that the American consul at Malta, Joseph Pulis — a countryman of mine, I'm ashamed to say — let letters pile up. He can neither read nor write English. They sat on his desk, often unopened. The commodore has sent them on, but it could be months before the ransom is paid."

Jamie stood for a moment, dumbstruck. Although he and George had seriously planned to escape, they had hoped it wouldn't be necessary and that they and the others would be ransomed. How much longer would they have to endure? With Kemal's temper, they could be killed, maimed.

"Now, you must come, Jamie," Captain Sabatier said, putting his hand on Jamie's shoulder.

Jamie was tempted but would regret it the rest of his life if he took Sabatier's offer. "No," he said. "My duty lies here."

"You are a man of honor, James Sharpe, and it is my honor to call you friend." Sabatier offered his hand and Jamie gripped it in his. Then, Sabatier handed Jamie a purse. "I shall not charge for this voyage. Return the money to Mr. Nissin."

"Thank you, Captain."

Sabatier waved his hands. "No need for thanks. Do you wish to say goodbye to the ladies once more before I sail?"

"No. If I see Claire again, I might change my mind."

"Then farewell, friend," Captain Sabatier said.

Jamie left the ship. He kept a brave face, but sadness permeated his very soul.

Chapter 42

JAMIE WATCHED AS Captain Sabatier's ship, *Falkun*, raised sail and headed out into the harbor, toward freedom for Claire and Catriona. When he could no longer see the ship's stern lantern, he turned and walked away.

"What of the donkeys?" the customs officials asked.

"Someone will be here soon," Jamie said.

The official nodded.

Mr. Nissin waited at the end of the long pier for Jamie. "They are safe, Jamie."

"They won't be truly safe until they reach America, but I'm grateful for all you have done. By the way, Captain Sabatier returned the money you paid him." Jamie handed the Danish consul the purse. "I still owe you and Doctor De Aragon more, but it will take longer."

Jamie explained about the American consul at Malta not forwarding the mail.

"I know, Jamie," Nissin said. "I've been the go-between for Captain Bainbridge and Commodore Preble. When the commodore found out that Mr. Pulis wasn't sending him the correspondence, he hired a new agent."

"Then you knew it would be some time before you were reimbursed, if at all, yet you provided the money."

Mr. Nissin smiled. "I know you are an honest man, Jamie. I'm sure in time I will be paid." He patted Jamie on the shoulder.

"Now, I suggest we should go; if you should be caught, it will mean your death. I can take you as far as my consulate, but not to Kemal's home."

"Sir, I hate to impose, but I cannot return to Kemal's villa the way I left it. If I could hide in your house until the call to Fajr, the sunrise prayer, I can make it through the streets without detection."

Mr. Nissin nodded and directed Jamie to his waiting coach. "Sunrise is at six," Mr. Nissin said, consulting his watch. "It is now ten past midnight. It will be safe for you to leave after five-thirty."

At Mr. Nissin's house, Jamie was offered food and beverages, for which he was appreciative since he hadn't eaten since morning. When he finished, Mr. Nissin showed him to a room with a bed.

"Rest. I will wake you in time."

❁ ❁ ❁

Just past five in the morning, Nissan woke Jamie and offered him a cup of coffee, which he gratefully drank.

"Jamie, take the purse Captain Sabatier returned. You may need this money."

"Sir, I can't take it. This is a small fortune."

"When I paid for the ladies' voyage, I didn't know the captain would return it. I trusted that you would pay me back. So take it and pay me when you are free."

Jamie was stunned. His life had been cruel for many months, but along the way he had found compassion: Malik, the de Aragon family, now Mr. Nissin.

"Sir, I will repay your money, but I can never repay your kindness."

Just as dawn was peeking out of the east, Jamie thanked the consul once again and entered the twisted streets of Tripoli.

From the mosques, muezzin were calling the faithful to prayer. People were emerging from houses, some rubbing sleep from their eyes as they walked to the nearest mosque.

Jamie mixed with the crowd and headed toward the mosque near Kemal's villa. He still had no plan how he would enter the compound. He hoped the stable door would be open, but like the others, the door was guarded day and night. How could he get the guards away?

Jamie stood by a pillar, trying to figure a way back in when he noticed a blind man outside the mosque, begging for alms.

"Alms for the afflicted. Alms for the love of God."

The man's eyes were wrapped with a dirty cloth and Jamie recalled Doctor de Aragon telling him about the scourge of trachoma. A few people tossed coins in his bowl as they passed by. He continued his begging for alms until the street was clear of people. Jamie was about to approach the beggar when the "blind" man lifted his bandage and began to count the money in his bowl.

The man's a charlatan, Jamie thought. Then an idea struck him. He walked from the pillar and, as he approached the beggar, the man quickly pulled down his bandage and cried out once again for alms.

Jamie towered over the man and in a commanding voice called out, "You are a deceiver. You are not blind."

Jamie tore the bandage from the man's eyes and knocked his stick aside.

The beggar tried to continue pretend to being blind. "No, no! Master, I have the affliction."

"You lie!" Jamie yelled.

He grabbed the man by the front of his jellabiya and pulled his knife.

The man suddenly cried out, "For the love of Allah, I'm a poor man. Don't kill me."

Jamie pressed the knife to the man's throat. "I will kill you if you don't do what I ask."

"Anything, master, anything."

"Pick up your bowl and your stick and come with me."

He shoved the beggar toward Kemal's villa. At the mouth of the alley near the stables, he stopped. A guard stood at the stable door.

"Go down to the guard and beg for alms. He will give you none. Curse him and run the other way."

"He will kill me."

"No. He will chase you away."

"If he catches me, he will beat me."

"Then it would be in your best interest he doesn't catch you," Jamie said. "Here is a silver coin, worth more than your lying hide. It is incentive enough for you to outrun him."

The beggar licked his lips at the sign of the silver and shrugged. "It is the will of Allah."

To make sure it was, Jamie gave him a push. The man walked down and begged. Just as Jamie predicted, the guard ran him off. The beggar cursed the guard, who chased after him, and as Jamie had suggested, fear propelled the man to run faster and escape.

Now it was Jamie's turn to run. He hoped he could alert George to unlock the stable doors. He took a deep breath and sprinted down the alley to the doors, reaching them just as the guard turned around and saw Jamie standing there.

"Stop!" he yelled in Arabic. "What are you doing there?"

Jamie froze as the guard came running back and drew his scimitar. Jamie put his hand in his jellabiya and gripped his knife. He would go down fighting. *At least*, he thought, *Claire and her mother are free.*

As the guard drew near, Jamie recognized him — it was Tariq, the Berber who Jamie had given the palm liquor to.

"Jamie, what are you doing out here?" Tariq asked in Arabic. He had not sheathed his scimitar.

Jamie backed away, afraid he would be struck down.

This time, Tariq raised his sword as to strike and demanded once again as to why Jamie was out of the villa.

Jamie tried to gather his wits. "I- I..."

"Speak." Tariq waved his weapon in Jamie's face.

"I heard a noise and some cursing, I opened the door to investigate, and I saw you chase that man down the alley." Jamie spoke in a loud voice, hoping to alert George.

"Why are you shouting?" Tariq asked in a voice almost as loud.

"Because you are waving that scimitar in my face and I'm frightened you will cut me."

Tariq lowered his scimitar but did not put it in his scabbard.

Then the door opened and George stuck his head out. "There you are, Jamie. I need help with the forge."

"What?" Tariq asked.

"I said I need help with the forge," George repeated, this time in Arabic.

"Ah," Tariq said, dismissing both of them with a wave of his sword.

Once inside, Jamie fell back against the door and wiped the sweat from his brow. "That was close. I hoped you would hear me."

"Well, you bellowed like a braying donkey. I couldn't miss hearing you," George said. "In all seriousness, I worried about you the whole night. How did you fare? Did you get the ladies on their way?"

Jamie related the night's events.

"Upon my word, you could have been killed more than once!"

"Well, my mission was accomplished," Jamie said. "Now, I could do with a bath, some clean clothes, breakfast, and coffee."

"I could use coffee myself. I didn't get a wink of sleep, worrying about you."

They cleaned up at the well. Jamie changed into his other djellaba and wrapped a clean turban around his head.

The two went off to the kitchen, where they found Tomaso in a highly agitated state.

"Where have you been, Sharpe? The master is returning today. He wants all in the household to attend him."

Jamie explained he had been helping George and now was looking for breakfast.

"Well, eat. Then come to the courtyard. Walling, you go to the stable and wait for Kemal Rais to return. Help with the horses, then go to the courtyard."

Tomaso turned to Dimas. "The master will be hungry. Prepare a meal."

The majordomo scurried out on his short fat legs, shouting to other servants and slaves as he left.

"I wonder what that's about," George commented between sips of Turkish coffee.

"We'll know soon enough," Jamie answered.

After they ate, George went to the stables and Jamie to the courtyard with the rest of the household.

George, and then Dimas, joined Jamie about a half-hour later.

"Well, he's here," George said, "but he went straight to his gulphor."

Jamie's prediction of soon enough stretched into two hours of waiting. Finally, Kemal walked into the courtyard. Everyone bowed.

"In a week, I leave for Derne in Barqa, the eastern province," Kemal announced. "I am to be the new admiral. Some of ye will be coming with me, the rest will be under the command of Tomaso. Lest ye think with me gone, ye may do as ye please, he will be assisted by Berber, Turkish, and Arab guards."

Kemal paused while Tomaso translated in English, Italian, and Maltese.

"I have very little room aboard me galliot, so I'll take only the essentials."

He pointed to the groom. "Usem will bring me horses and a few servants overland. Tomaso has a list of those who come with me. Now, return to yer work. Sharpe, Cutts, join me in my gulphor."

Jamie and Simon followed Kemal upstairs to his private quarters.

"Cutts," Kemal said. "Tomaso tells me ye're as good with the books as he is."

Simon nodded and smiled.

"Which means ye're taking money off the top."

Simon's smile disappeared and fear crossed his face.

Now, Kemal smiled. "A little *sariqat tafihat saghira*, petty theft, is to be expected, but too much and I'll have yer head."

Simon began to sweat. "Master, I swear I..."

"Stop now while ye're ahead." Kemal waved him off. "Ye will become majordomo at me house in Derne."

"Yes, Master. Thank you." Simon bowed low.

"There is no question that ye'll come as me secretary, Sharpe. I will bring yer friend, Walling, for with his strength, he can pull an oar better than most. As for the others from yer crew, they proved their worth. So they too will come."

"Thank you, Master." Jamie also bowed, relieved his friends wouldn't be left behind.

"Now leave, I've much to do in the next week."

Chapter 43

JAMIE RELATED THE NEWS to George and the others.

"Perhaps the harbor at Derne won't be as fortified as Tripoli," Fenton Webb said. "We may have a better chance to escape there."

"Let us hope so," Jamie said. "George, be sure to bring the grenades. When the time comes, we may need them."

The men went back to their daily chores. They didn't have to worry about packing, since they had little of their own possessions.

Jamie still owed money to Tomaso's cousin, Marco. He could pay him with the Danish silver, but that would bring suspicion. Fortunately, Kemal sent Jamie to buy flints.

On his way to the gunsmith's, he stopped at a moneylender who changed some of his coins into Venetian sequins, a common currency in Tripoli.

On his return, he asked Tomaso where he could find his cousin.

"Why do you want to know?"

"I have the last payment for him."

"Give it to me. I will see it gets it."

"No, I'll deliver it myself. I want to make sure he gets it. It is a debt I owe and I shall pay it."

"You think I'd cheat my own cousin?" Tomaso was indignant.

"I think you'd cheat your own mother. Everyone, including Kemal Rais, knows you alter the books."

"If you don't give me the money, I will strike your friends' names from the list going to Derne."

"Listen, you damn weasel, you'll get what's coming to you, but if you do anything to prevent my friends from going to Derne, I'll see you'll have a deadly accident."

"No, no." Tomaso raised his hands and backed away. "Your friends will go to Derne."

"Make sure that they do. Wet tiles are dangerous, a person rushing across the courtyard could slip and break his neck."

Tomaso nodded. His bluff was called and he backed down.

"Where can I find Marco?"

"He works in one of the castle kitchens. However, he can be found during the afternoon at the market at the Arch of Marcus Aurelius. He buys produce for the kitchen."

"I'll go now," Jamie said. "Give me some money so I may buy fruit. If you're good, I'll share it with you."

"Si." Tomaso nodded, cowed by Jamie's demeanor.

The best way to handle a bully is to stand up to him, Jamie thought as he walked to the market.

Jamie found Marco near a vegetable-seller, haggling over watermelons. Thanks to the American embargo, the market was low on foodstuff. Still, there were some crops grown in the country that were available, but prices were high.

Finally, Marco and the merchant were able to come to terms and Marco hefted a string bag full of melons. As he turned to leave, he spotted Jamie.

"Mr. Sharpe, *buon pomeriggio*. Good afternoon."

"Hello, Marco. I've come to pay the remainder of the money I owe you for getting my friends and me into Kemal Rais' house. You can buy your freedom now."

"No, not yet. You see, I must pay my cousin Tomaso a percentage."

"You mean he gets part of the money for allowing us to be slaves of Kemal Rais?"

Marco shrugged. "It is the way it is."

"Your cousin is a thief. He demanded I pay him the money I owe you."

Marco spread his hands. "*Si*, he's a thief, and I wouldn't have seen any of the money."

"Now that you have this money, why don't you just buy your freedom and leave?"

"I can't leave, not as long as your fellow Americans blockade the port. How will I live? At least I have food to eat and a place to sleep. After fifteen years, I wait a bit longer."

"Well, I wish you the best of luck." Jamie handed over the money. "I doubt we will meet again for I'm being taken to Derne."

"*Si.* My cousin tells me."

"I wonder why your cousin doesn't buy his own freedom. He must have plenty of money, taking from you, taking from Kemal, and for all I know, he gets money back from others."

"Ha! Tomaso could have been free years ago. But in Sicily, he was nothing. Here, he is the majordomo of an important house. He will stay until he dies."

Jamie just shook his head and bid Marco a farewell and good fortune.

Chapter 44

IT WAS TIME to leave for Derne. What little possessions Jamie and his friends owned were wrapped in small bundles. George had fashioned a tool chest with a false bottom. In it, he hid the grenades and Jamie's money.

Dimas smoked meat and fish for the journey and packed fresh fruit and vegetables.

Kemal sent his horses and his harem, along with other possessions, under strong guard on a caravan bound for Derne.

Jamie managed to say farewell to the de Aragon family when he was sent to purchase medicine for the voyage.

"Jamie, my elder brother, Amos, is a physician in Derne. I wrote to him when you first heard you were going there. Call on him if you need assistance."

"Thank you, Doctor de Aragon. You and your wife have shown me nothing but kindness. I wish I could repay you."

"Jamie, God will repay us. I would like to bless you before you go." He placed his hands on Jamie's head and said a prayer in Hebrew. "May God bless you and protect you. May God deal kindly and graciously with you. May God bestow His favor upon you and grant you peace!"

Jamie was awestruck. "Sir, my father blessed me and my sister before he sailed for China. It was the same blessing, although it was the King James Bible translation." Jamie repeated it. "The Lord bless thee, and keep thee; the Lord make his face shine upon thee, and be gracious unto thee; the Lord lift up his countenance upon thee, and give thee peace."

Jamie said goodbye to rest of the family. Abdullah presented Jamie with an ivory-handled dagger.

"Hide it from the devil Kemal Rais," he said.

Jamie left, knowing he might never see the de Aragons again.

Jamie returned to the villa and found Malik tending his beloved garden.

Trying not to choke up, Jamie said, "My friend and brother, I can never repay the kindness you have shown me. You've been my guide and teacher. I shall never forget you."

Malik smiled. "Young friend, you are a brave and honorable man. I shall miss our friendship. There are perils ahead. Face them as you have faced those in the past."

Malik raised his hand. "Jamie, before you go, if you permit it, I would like to give you my blessing."

Jamie nodded. He was honored to be blessed once again.

Malik spread his hands, palms up, and recited, "The Prophet Muhammad, peace be upon him, has said, 'I seek protection for you in the perfect words of Allah from every devil, and every beast, and from every evil eye.'"

Jamie, with tears in his eyes, took Malik's hand, held it for a moment, picked up his small pack, and bid farewell to his friend.

Kemal Rais' galliot was a small two-masted galley, with ten rowers to a side. It was armed with two six-pounder cannons mounted side by side in the bow, a number of swivel guns, six to a side, and four more swivels on the long quarterdeck. The cannon were fixed and could only be used if the bow was pointed straight at the target. The swivels were loaded with grapeshot, small metal balls packed tightly in canvas bags, which were devastating when fired at a mass of men. However, the real weapon of the galliot was its maneuverability. It didn't need wind, just the rowers seated on wooden benches. A long gangway ran down the middle of the boat from the quarterdeck to the cannon, dividing the benches. Two smaller gangways ran along the starboard and larboard rails. The long sweeps, or oars, fit under these side gangways and slid through holes on the gunwales.

Jamie, George, Mateus, and Fenton Webb were seated on the starboard benches, facing the stern. Dimas was sent to a small galley kitchen beneath the quarterdeck. Simon grinned a superior smile as Jamie and his friends were chained to the oars. He stopped smirking when Billy Scars, or Al-Nadba as he now fancied himself, grabbed him and slammed him down on a larboard bench. As he hammered the rivet of the cuffs around Simon's wrist, Billy Scars said with a sinister bent, "If you don't pull that oar hard, I'll whip the skin off your soft hide."

Simon started to protest, but Billy Scars backhanded him and said, "Shut your snifflin' potato trap! I don't answer to you no more, you bottled-headed fop."

Simon cringed. He couldn't understand what was happening. Wasn't he the majordomo? *Somehow*, he thought, *I'll get that bastard.* His thoughts of revenge were cut off by Kemal Rais shouting from the quarterdeck.

"It's more'n five hundred miles to Derne and you'll be rowin' more'n half of it. So I want you to put your backs into it. Thems that be free men, the rewards will be great once we get there and get to raidin' enemy ships. For those that ain't free, make it easy on yourselves by rowin' hard or the whips come out."

This message was repeated in Arabic by a thin, round-shouldered, gap-toothed man with a sparse beard. He was well-dressed in blue pantaloons, a white turban, an embroidered linen shirt, and red calf-skin boots. Two ornate pistols were stuck in his sash, and he carried a scimitar in a jeweled scabbard. He led the Muslims in prayers for a safe journey and against drowning.

Jamie wondered who he was, but as Billy Scars walked the gangway, swinging his whip, Jamie gripped his oars and commenced rowing.

It was dark as the galliot slipped out of the harbor. The oars were muffled by wrapping canvas around oar-locks to hide the sound from the American ships. Simon let out a low whimper, as his soft hands were already beginning to blister.

"Shut it!" Billy Scars said in a harsh whisper, shaking his whip in Simon's face.

The small galley clung to the shore, its shallow draft allowing it to move through the rocks and small islands. By morning, they were well away from Tripoli. Kemal Rais ordered the lateen sails raised, giving the men at the oars some respite. By late afternoon, they neared Misrata, a city near the Gulf of Sidra. Kemal planned to take on water and more provisions before crossing the gulf to Barqa or, as the Greeks and Romans called it, Cyrenaica. Kemal's plans were dashed when an American schooner was spotted closing fast on his vessel.

"Row, you scum! Row for your lives!" Kemal shouted.

Billy Scars cracked his whip and slashed down on freemen and slaves alike. The schooner had the wind and was closing. Kemal steered the boat closer to shore, hoping the American would follow and run aground. The galliot ran down the coast, dangerously close to shore. The schooner followed and soon was in firing range. A shot from a cannon landed close to the galliot, sending up a spray of water, drenching the rowers on the larboard side. Another shot flew over the boat and hit a bank of oars, sending splinters flying everywhere. The man in front of Jamie was pierced by a piece of a wooden sweep. He screamed and fell over his oar, his blood spraying Jamie.

"Pull, ye sons o' hell," Kemal cried. "Al-Nadba, take that man's oar!"

Billy Scars jumped to the bench, picked the dead man up, and heaved him onto the starboard gangway. He grabbed the oar and pulled hard.

Another shot from the schooner hit the forward mast, sending pieces of it crashing to the deck. Jamie looked up and his eyes widened in horror when he saw a heavy block had broken loose and was falling toward him.

Jamie tried to slide to his right as the heavy block came down, but chained as he was, he could only move a few inches. It was just enough. The block flew by so close he could feel the impact as it crashed to the deck, next to his leg.

Kemal, standing on the high poop deck, screamed at the men, "There's a small island ahead, between the mainland and the American schooner. The Yankees can't follow us! It's too shallow. Row, row for your lives!"

Row they did, with aching muscles nearly spent. Shots from the schooner's six-pounders rained down all around the galliot. Finally, the boat rounded the tip of island, out of range of the schooner's guns.

Even with its shallow draft, the keel of the galliot scraped a sandbar, making a low-pitch grinding sound before it floated off.

Kemal breathed a sigh of relief and gave the order to drop the anchor. The exhausted men fell over their oars.

Jamie looked around to see if his friends were all right. He took a deep breath when he saw all had survived. Even Simon Cutts was alive, but was whimpering and looking at his bloody hands. Others were not so lucky. Three of the crew were dead, speared by flying splinters, including the man who had sat forward of Jamie. Two others were injured from splinters and were bleeding. Kemal ordered Dimas to bandage the wounded. The dead were unceremoniously heaved overboard.

Kemal took inventory of his boat. The forward mast was split in half and the pieces were thrown overboard. Four oars were broken.

Checking the keel was another problem. They couldn't haul the boat to shore and careen it. So, one of his men swam under the boat to see what the damage was. He surfaced and told Kemal that the hull was intact, with only minor damage. Kemal checked the depth. It was two fathoms or twelve feet deep.

"The schooner's draft is probably close to that depth," Kemal told Billy Scars, "but the captain won't risk following us."

Kemal had Billy Scars row him to the island. They climbed a small rise to survey the situation. The American schooner was still nearby so Kemal's galliot couldn't come out from behind the island, at least in daylight. On his return to the boat, he conferred with the thin well-dressed man with the red boots and Billy Scars, then addressed the crew.

"We leave tonight. There will be a rising tide, so we hug the coast for a while. We make sure the Americans ain't following, then we will turn and cross the gulf. We have only one mast, so you will be rowing even more — and row you will. Any man who shirks will be given to the sharks. Now rest, for you will need your strength if we are to get out alive." He ordered rations and water to be passed. The men ate and drank, then closed their eyes, trying to get to sleep.

George, whose bench was just behind Jamie's, said, "Hell of a way to die at the hands of our own countrymen. But it would be worth it if a shot sent Kemal to Davy Jones' locker."

"I agree, but Kemal's a wily bastard. As the tide rises, he'll sneak out."

"And they say the Mediterranean is a tideless sea."

"Tides are small in most parts, but the Gulf of Sidra has tides."

"Aye, and sandbars and fast currents, if I recall what we read in school from the Roman, Cato, and the Greek, Strabo. And doesn't Virgil mention it in the Aeneid?"

"Yes, you're right," Jamie said and remembered the quote.

> *...inhospita Syrtis;*
> *hinc deserta siti regio, lateque furentes...*

George translated.

> ...the unfriendly Syrtis;
> on the one side a wilderness, a dry land, and wide,
> and the raging...

Fenton Webb, who was chained across from Jamie, asked, "What are you two talking about?"

"According to the ancient Romans," Jamie explained, "this gulf, the one they called Syrtis, is a dangerous place. The sea, the land."

"Things ain't changed much," Fenton said.

As night descended, the anchor was raised and Kemal ordered the oars out and muffled, with no lights showing.

The tide and current carried the boat out from behind the island. The lights from the American schooner could be seen, but it stayed away from the shore. The schooner's captain must have known of the gulf's currents and sandbars.

Kemal steered his boat south, away from the shore, and pushed the men to row harder. By daybreak, they were well away from the schooner. The sail was raised and the crew were allowed to rest. Jamie heard Simon crying and looked over to see his hands were bloody and raw.

Fortunately for Simon, Kemal also saw his hands and ordered Dimas to put some medicine on them and bind them up. When he was done, Dimas passed out food and a half-cup of water per man. Bruiser McPhee, now known as Al-Thawr, complained.

"This ain't enough water to drown a flea."

"Shut it," Billy Scars said, shaking his whip in McPhee's face. "We're short 'cause we couldn't take on water at Misrata, so if you want to drink, then row for Derne."

Luckily for the crew, the wind was in their favor and the galliot sailed out into the Gulf of Sidra. But by late afternoon, the wind died and the men were ordered back to the oars. It was difficult going. The crew had to struggle against currents and counter-currents as they crossed the treacherous gulf. They rowed on through the night, with even the toughest men beginning to falter. As they flagged, they were urged on by the whip. As day dawned, the galliot came to stop wallowing in the water. Billy Scars used his whip, urging the men to pick up their oars. Despite the beatings, none obeyed.

"Kemal Rais," Billy Scars said, "I can't drive them anymore."

Kemal nodded. "All right. Let them eat, drink, and rest. The town of Benghazi isn't far off. If the damn Americans ain't blockading it, we'll rest and provision there."

After an hour's rest, the men picked up the sweeps and rowed toward the small town of Benghazi. Two hours later, they saw the top of the white minaret on the Great Mosque. It was still an hour of hard rowing to reach the port. As they got closer, they saw a small xebec sail around a headland.

"Is she one of ours?" the thin English-speaking man asked.

"I hope so," Kemal answered. "She flies no flag." He ordered his flags raised.

As the two vessels neared, the men on the xebec opened the gun ports.

"Do they mean to fire on us?" the thin man asked. "Could they be Americans? Perhaps they added a captured xebec to their fleet.

After all, they burned the frigate *Philadelphia* using a captured boat flying Maltese colors."

"Al-Nadba," Kemal called to Billy Scars. "We turn to meet the xebec. We face them head-on so our cannon are aimed at their starboard side. When I call for it, we increase our speed. Any man that shirks is to be flogged."

In his broken Arabic, Kemal commanded his gunners to the load and prepare to fire on his command.

The exhausted men rowed as fast as they could, the galliot heading straight for the xebec.

"My God!" Fenton Webb yelled, looking over his shoulder. "I think Kemal means to shoot and then ram that ship."

Chapter 45

JAMIE AND THE MEN at the oars couldn't see what was happening.

"Faster!" Billy Scars yelled as he slashed his whip over the backs of the crew.

"Gunners," Kemal commanded, "light your matches!"

"*Tawqf!* Stop!" the man in the white turban yelled. "The xebec is Tripolitan. They raised the flag."

Kemal ordered the gun crew to stand down. "Backwater," he called.

The crew followed the order and the galliot pulled back from the xebec.

Kemal took a deep breath before he bellowed out in his bad Arabic, "Who the devil you is? Why didn't you show flag until we were near on you? You not recognize my flag?"

A young man in his mid-twenties came to the rail of the quarterdeck. He puffed up his chest, put his speaking trumpet to his mouth, and called down to Kemal. "I am Nabih ibn Ali Rais. And this is my ship, *Sarie*. Who are you, interloper, to question me? Answer quickly or my gunners will blow you out of the water."

The man in the red boots quickly translated.

Kemal turned red with anger. "*Abn hamar!* Son of an ass!" He could swear in Arabic quite well. He continued in his bastardized Arabic, "I Kemal Rais, Grand Admiral of Barqa. You dog, to me report."

"I- I...," Nabih started to answer.

"Quiet!" Kemal commanded. "Had you fired, you kill your admiral. Also Ottoman representative going to Derne." He pointed to the thin man in the calfskin boots. "This Demir Bey. Kill him, wrath of the sultan would you feel. Now, you young *majnun*, fool, send down water. My men die of thirst. Then take us in tow to bring to Benghazi."

❁ ❁ ❁

An hour later, the galliot was towed into Benghazi. The men were fed and had enough to drink. A number of the crew went to the *alhamaam*, the bathhouse, and then to the mosque. The slaves were held in a dungeon overnight.

The next day, Kemal Rais informed Nabih that he was taking command of the *Sarie* and sailing her to Derne. Nabih protested and the town governor pleaded with Kemal to leave the ship in Benghazi, but Kemal couldn't be persuaded. In his bad Arabic, he said, "She a swift ship as her name say. Draft is shallow. Also her cabin serves Demir Bey better."

Despite their protestations, the papers Kemal Rais carried gave him to right to take the ship.

The xebec was provisioned, the majority of the galliot's crew transferred, and with the galliot in tow, the *Sarie* set sail for Derne. The galliot was manned by a small crew of slaves, overseen by Billy Scars and a handful of trusted guards, including Bruiser McPhee.

Once away from the oars, Bruiser returned to his vicious ways, striking at the slaves, not for any reason, but for his own pleasure. He gave special attention to George, who had beaten him in a fight, and to Jamie, whom he hated on general principles. There wasn't much the men had to do, just keep the tow line taut. But Bruiser still laid it on.

Finally, Billy Scars, who was at the tiller, called down. "Bruiser, I mean Al-Thawr, lay off. Those men will have plenty of hard work to do once we reach Derne. No use flayin' the skin off'n so they be useless."

McPhee grumbled and cursed under his breath, but stopped beating the men.

Rations for the men were dried fish and water.

"At least it's edible," George said. "With Dimas transferred to the xebec, we're lucky we get any food at all."

"Take solace in the fact," Jamie said, "Bruiser and Billy Scars are eating the same rations."

"But they get to drink that palm liquor," Fenton Webb said, "though it be against their religion."

"They turned Muslim to save themselves from slavery and to become pirates," Jamie said. "They honor no religion."

"You down there on the benches," Billy Scars said. "Shut your gobs and get to backwaterin'. If the line goes slack, I'll let Bruiser loose."

It was nearly 150 nautical miles to Derne from Benghazi. The xebec was a fast sailer, but the galliot slowed it down a bit. Fortunately for Kemal Rais, there were no American warships this far east and the winds were with him.

A day later, they neared the harbor at Derne. From what Jamie could see, the harbor was small but well-guarded by a fort with cannon pointing out to sea.

There were a few fishing vessels in the harbor. Jamie had to chuckle to himself. This is Grand Admiral of Barqa Kemal Rais' fleet.

The *Sarie* and the galliot entered the harbor when a shot from a cannon crossed the xebec's bows. A call from the fort warned they were to tie up at a small wharf and wait. Kemal swore in three languages and the Turkish representative looked none too happy.

A few minutes later, a small contingent of soldiers emerged from the fort, led by an officer so young his beard was but a wisp. Just like the former captain of the *Sarie*, he approached the wharf in an inflated manner, waving his sword. He ordered his men to cover the intruders. Before he could say anything, Kemal let out a string of Arabic curses that would singe the beard of an iman, the least being, "*Kanat walidatuk qird!*" *Your mother was an ape.*

"Are there only fools here to shoot at xebec with flag of Tripoli flying?" Kemal shook his fist. "This our greeting? Where is governor and delegation from palace? Just lowly officer and squad of unkempt soldiers. Me Grand Admiral of Barqa and this, Demir Bey, the representative of the sultan."

The young man was stunned. One of his men covered his mouth to hide his laughter, enjoying his superior's discomfort.

Gaining as much composure as he could, the officer ordered one of his men to get a horse and ride to the palace. He begged Kemal

Rais and Demir Bey for forgiveness and asked them if he could escort them to the fort for refreshments while they waited for a delegation from the palace.

Kemal was still angry and told the young man not only would he and Demir Bey go to the fort, but he demanded food and water for his crews and ordered the young man to have a guard placed over his slaves. The slaves were unshackled and led off the boat.

The officer could do nothing but comply and orders were given. The slaves were ordered to sit on the wharf while the crew of the *Sarie* returned to the xebec to await the food.

"What of us?" Simon asked. "Don't we get food and drink as well?"

Billy Scars raised his whip and Simon cringed.

"Feed them too," Kemal ordered. "No more beatings for Cutts, unless I order it. He's me majordomo. That goes for Sharpe as well. I need a secretary who can write."

Simon breathed a sigh of relief. Jamie did as well, but worried about George and his other friends.

It wasn't long before food was delivered in huge pots. Several soldiers lugged them out to the dock. A big brute of a soldier carrying one of the pots cursed the crews, telling them the food was their rations and now they wouldn't eat until the next day. He hawked and was about to spit in the food.

"None of that," George said, shoving him away from the pot.

The big soldier drew his dagger and raised it. George used his forearm to block the strike and, with his other hand, twisted the knife away. The man was astounded — no one had ever done that to him.

"*Kalb kafir,*" he yelled, calling George an infidel dog.

George shrugged and tossed the knife in the water.

The soldier turned to his comrades and told them to beat George. None moved. Jamie, who now stood next to George, figured the big soldier was a bully and the others were glad to see his comeuppance.

The big soldier grabbed a musket from one of the other soldiers and aimed it at George.

"Stop!" Billy Scars yelled at the man. "These are men of Kemal Rais."

The soldier still pointed his weapon at George, not understanding Billy Scars. He cocked the musket.

Jamie shouted in Arabic, "These are Kemal Rais' men. He is the grand admiral. Hurt them and you will die!"

The soldier looked around, unsure of what to do. Billy Scars wrenched the musket from him and handed it back to the other soldier, then hit the big man so hard, he knocked him in the water.

Billy Scars gave Jamie a curt nod.

The crew from the xebec and the slaves were handed wooden plates and flatbreads. It was the usual fare of couscous and vegetables, but to the surprise of the crews, there was mutton mixed in.

The men greedily scarfed down the food while the garrison soldiers stood and watched sullenly but there was nothing they could do about it. None wanted to tangle with Billy Scars, not after they hauled their comrade out of the water and saw that his jaw was broken.

"That's something I never expected to see," George said, "Billy Scars coming to our defense."

"He's just protecting Kemal's property," Jamie replied. "He would like nothing better than to beat us bloody.

"Let's get the lay of the land," Jamie said. "As we rowed past the fort, I counted eight cannon all pointing out to sea."

"The town seems well fortified, the walls have loopholes for muskets," George said. "I see a deep ravine just west of us, what the Arabs call a *wadi*. Probably runs heavy with water during the rainy season."

"One thing I noticed is that the harbor is shallow," Jamie said. "No frigate will be able to come in close."

"Which means Kemal can sneak out in his xebec and stay out of range of a frigate's guns."

"It's all moot at this point," Jamie said. "Our navy's too busy blockading Tripoli to sail this far east. If they ever do come, a brig or schooner will be needed."

"What our navy needs are gunboats," George said, "Like the bashaw has."

"They may never come," Jamie said. "We're going to have to think of a way to escape."

Their thoughts were interrupted by the sound of clashing cymbals, drums, and reed instruments, including some type of bagpipe.

Approaching the fort was a man in a high turban riding a white horse. He was a bit stout but, on his horse, he looked commanding. He was preceded by a group of musicians and a troop of janissaries. When the procession reached the fort, the man in the high turban dismounted and a slave ran forward and held an umbrella over his head.

Hearing the music, Kemal and Demir Bey came to the entrance of the fort.

"I am Mustapha Bey, governor of Derne. I welcome you in the name of Allah."

Kemal was seething. "I thought I was expected. I flew flag of Tripoli and me own personal flag, but this boy" — he pointed to the young officer — "had the arrogance to fire a warning shot across my bows!"

Mustapha Bey turned to the chief janissary and said something. The janissary nodded and issued an order in Turkish to two of his men who seized the young officer and threw him to the ground. Two more began the bastinado. Instead of heavy palm branches, they used the flats of their scimitars to beat the soles of his feet. The man's screams echoed across the harbor.

Both Jamie and George flinched, finally turning away after twenty hits, but they could still hear the strokes. The beating went on and, at one hundred, Jamie stopped counting. The man no longer screamed, for he had passed out. The garrison soldiers were forced to stand at attention and watch, but two fainted.

Finally, after what seemed to go forever, the flogging stopped.

Kemal thanked the governor. Jamie noticed Demir Bey was visibly shaken, but the Turkish envoy said nothing.

"I assure you, Kemal Rais," Mustapha Bey said, Demir Bey translating to English. "The belongings you sent some time ago have been stored. A house not far from here has been set aside for your use. Had we known you would arrive this day, we would have had it prepared. It may need a bit of cleaning, since it has been empty for some months, but I'm sure your servants will see to it."

Kemal wanted to tell the governor to go to hell, but he knew Mustapha Bey was the bashaw's brother-in-law and the third most important man in the principality, so he held his anger inside.

The governor continued, "I will leave one of my janissaries with your people. He will assist and be a guide to the city. Now, if your excellencies will accompany me to my palace, I will have a banquet prepared in your honor."

Horses were provided for Kemal Rais and Demir Bey. Slaves kneeled and were used as mounting blocks so the two men could mount their horses.

Kemal leaned out of his saddle and said to Simon, "As my majordomo, I expect you to make sure everything be in order when I return." He tossed a purse to Simon. "This is for supplies, food, and spirits. I want it accounted for."

Simon nodded. "Of course, master."

"Tariq," Kemal called to the Berber, giving him an order in his poor French, "you in charge until I return. Watch these *spaleen*."

Tariq wasn't sure but imagined a spaleen must be a miscreant of some sort. While the governor's party rode off toward the palace, Kemal's household retrieved their belongings and were marched to their new home.

Chapter 46

IN A VERY SMALL GARDEN with a fountain below the gulphor, Jamie looked about the house and grounds.

The house was nothing like the villa in Tripoli. It was smaller, the ceiling lower, the walls pierced with loopholes for muskets. The slave quarters were cramped. The barracks for the sailors and guards were outside the wall, as was the stable. Even the courtyard was tiny. The harem's quarters still overlooked the garden. Jamie found the main garden lush, although overgrown with weeds.

"I'll spend hours getting the gardens in shape," he said to George, who had joined him.

"The stable hasn't been mucked out for some time and is full of biting flies," George said, "and God knows what other vermin are hiding in there."

The kitchen, located between the courtyard and the main garden, was dirty; grease and other grime permeated every corner. The rest of the house wasn't in any better condition.

In typical fashion, Simon looked around in despair. As majordomo, it was his job to get the place ready for Kemal Rais. "He'll whip me. I'll receive the bastinado. What am I to do?"

Jamie laughed at Simon's discomfort, yet he knew if action wasn't taken soon, they would all feel Kemal's wrath.

"Simon, you're used to ordering people around, but the servants you had at home knew what to do without being told. Here, you'll have to direct them."

Simon scratched his head and then bellowed out in English, "Clean this place up." Of course, no one understood him except for Jamie's people and Kemal's renegades. He yelled once more in English. "I'm the majordomo. Do what I say!" No one moved.

He continued ranting until Jamie finally took over. Pointing to various servants and slaves, he gave orders. Some to clean and prepare Kemal's gulphor, others to clean the various rooms. He told several to help Dimas clean the kitchen. Billy Scars and his men refused to help.

"That's fine with me," Jamie said. "When Kemal returns and sees you doing nothing while others are working, he'll punish you."

Billy Scars, stood for a minute, unsure, and finally ordered the crew to pitch in. George pointed to two Arab sailors and Bruiser McPhee, telling them to help clean the stables.

"I ain't taking orders from you," Bruiser said. "I ain't gettin' dirty cleanin' 'orseshit."

"Just do it, Bruiser," Billy Scars said. "If it don't get clean, Kemal'll find out you didn't help, he'll cut your gizzard out." He turned to Jamie and demanded, "What the hell are you going to be doing?"

"I'm going to the market to buy food and other provisions."

"I ain't giving you permission to leave."

"You don't have to. Tariq is in charge. He gave me permission and is sending the governor's janissary to direct me to the market."

Billy Scars grumbled and kicked one of the sailors to make him work faster.

Jamie turned to Simon. "Give me the purse."

"Damn me," Simon said defiantly, "but I ain't giving you the purse."

"We need food. Kemal Rais will be angry if we don't buy it."

"I shall buy it, then," Simon sniffed.

"You can't bargain in Arabic. You can barely give orders. Remember, Kemal wants an accounting. You're bound to be cheated."

Simon reluctantly handed the purse to Jamie. "See that you get a good price and don't forget to buy spirits."

Jamie counted out the money. There was enough silver and copper to provision the larder for some time to come, if he could carefully bargain.

Billy Scars insisted Tariq send two of his guards with Jamie to the market. When they arrived, the place was a wonder to behold.

Unlike the one in Tripoli, which had been affected by the blockade, the market overflowed with produce. Because Derne sat in a lush valley, tomatoes, peppers, peaches, figs, and squashes were among the many fruits and vegetables that flourished here. Lamb, mutton, and goat meat were also in abundance. Even if there should be a blockade, Derne would survive as long as there was abundant rain.

One of the guards, Kasim, shoved Jamie. "Move, dog, and make the purchases."

The other guard, Nadim, said, "I have not seen such plenty, not since the infidels blockaded Tripoli. No wonder this one gawked."

Kasim grumbled, but let Jamie shop.

Jamie bargained hard, buying fresh fruits and vegetables. At a butcher's stall, he bought lamb, mutton, and goat. The butcher's apprentice was tasked with delivering it to Kemal's house. The butcher assured Jamie he knew the house well. Jamie gave the apprentice a few coppers and he added the produce to his cart.

Kasim gruffly reminded Jamie, "Dog, don't forget the spirits."

The other guard, Nadim, just laughed. He was easygoing, but a follower.

The janissary, who identified himself as Kuzey, was corpulent and looked a little dissipated. Jamie remembered his friend Malik once telling him the janissaries had been known as the fiercest warriors in the Turkish Empire, but many had become rebellious and were not as stalwart as they had been in centuries past. Kuzey seemed to fit the new mold.

Jamie nodded and they found a Christian merchant selling spirits at the edge of the market. He had a small tavern and was doing a booming business in a country where liquor was supposedly prohibited. But the people of Derne didn't seem to mind. Many homes had grape arbors and made wine.

The merchant sold mostly wine, but also had a small supply of French brandy. Jamie bargained for it and was able to buy the entire stock. He also bought palm wine and some local concoction made with grapes and other fruits.

Kasim demanded that Jamie buy him some wine. Jamie refused.

"The money belongs to Kemal Rais. I must account for all of it."

"Christian dog." Kasim drew his pistol.

Nadim put a restraining hand on his colleague. "No," he said in Arabic. "Kemal Rais does not allow it. This one is worth money in ransom."

Kasim nodded, then backhanded Jamie across his face. Jamie fell hard to the ground.

Jamie shook himself and climbed to his feet. The guards were already drinking the brandy. Without a weapon, he was helpless to stop them. He gathered up the few jars he could carry and left the market. His face bore a red mark where Kasim had struck him.

While the guards imbibed, Jamie wandered away, taking in the fortifications of the town. The houses and walls were built from stone and dried mud-bricks, then plastered over with more mud and whitewashed. Some of the houses had loopholes in the walls for muskets. Besides the cannon at the water battery where they had come ashore, there was a large mortar on the grounds of the palace. With the shallow harbor, it would be difficult for the navy to come in close.

He wondered if there was better anchorage up the coast — perhaps overland might be a better way to attack. But the navy didn't have enough men to come overland. He remembered William Eaton telling him a troop could march from Egypt. That seemed impossible. Derne may be a fertile place, but from what he gleaned from talks with Malik, the land to the east was a desert.

There would be no rescue soon, as the mail had been delayed at Malta. It could take months or even years to be redeemed. Kemal could keep the money and not free Jamie and his friends. He had kept Claire and her mother, despite knowing that the Swedish captives were to be free.

Escape was a viable option. If he and George, along with Fenton, Dimas, and Mateus could steal a small boat, a fishing vessel perhaps, they could make their way to Malta. Planning and executing an escape would take time and luck.

Chapter 47

BACK AT THE HOUSE — Jamie couldn't call it a villa — progress had been made. The cleaning was going well. Simon, remembering the little Arabic he had acquired, was happily giving orders.

Jamie was pleased to see the butcher's apprentice had delivered the food to the now-scrubbed kitchen. Dimas already had the ovens lit and was beginning to prepare a meal.

Jamie went to the courtyard in search of Tariq. The Berber wasn't there, but Jamie saw the courtyard had been cleaned of debris, the marble scrubbed, and the fountain flowed with cooling clean water.

Relishing his status as majordomo, Simon approached Jamie and demanded the receipts for his purchases.

"Here they are." Jamie handed the papers to Simon. "Of course, they're in Arabic and you can't read them."

"The food was delivered. Where's the liquor?"

"There are three stone jars of wine in the kitchen."

"That's all you bought? With the money in that purse, you should have purchased much more. How much money did you keep?"

Jamie was tempted to strike Simon. Instead, he stepped in close to him and said, "I'm no thief like you. Never accuse me again. I'll explain to Kemal when he returns."

Simon took a step back. Fear showed in his eyes, but the look quickly turned to hate. Jamie shrugged his contempt.

Tariq called to Jamie. "Where are Kasim and Nadim?"

"I saw them last in the market with the janissary. Kasim struck me down, then he, Nadim, and the janissary took the French brandy and got drunk."

Tariq swore in Arabic, Berber, and French and grasped the hilt of his scimitar. "I'll deal with them." He waved Jamie off.

❁ ❁ ❁

Soon, Dimas and two slaves served a sumptuous dinner in the courtyard to slave and freeman alike. Many had never eaten as well in their whole lives. Billy Scars and the sailors ate with everyone else, although they grumbled there was no liquor.

"Next time you go to the market, you make sure you bring back liquor, Sharpe," Billy Scars said. "There must be taverns run by Christians or Jews that sell the stuff."

"Are you going to use your own money," Jamie asked, "or Kemal Rais' to pay for it?"

"None of your mouth, Sharpe, or I'll cut your tongue from your head."

"You could try."

Jamie stood. George scrambled to his feet.

"*Tawqf!*"

Tariq drew his pistols, and the other guards their scimitars. Tariq yelled at Billy Scars in Arabic, who understood little of it. But he was wise enough not to challenge the armed Berber. He raised his palms and backed up, a false smile on his face.

Strangely, it was Bruiser McPhee who translated Tariq's words. "He said, 'to back off.' Sharpe's the Rais' secretary."

"When the hell did you learn the heathen tongue?" Billy Scars demanded, forgetting he was now a Muslim.

"One of the Maltese slaves taught me. I sit enough at the oars and sleep in the same hovel as these buggers. I ain't treated as well as you. So I had to learn."

Billy Scars scratched his head. "Well, I'll be damned."

"You will, indeed," George said.

Billy Scars turned red and started for George but, with one look from Tariq, he turned away and stalked out of the courtyard.

"I'm not afraid of him," George said in French, "I've been waiting for a chance to fight him."

Tariq answered, also in French, "Don't be so quick to clash with him. He is free, you are a slave. He is Muslim, you are Christian. If you won a fight with him, you would be punished, even possibly killed. Don't provoke him. I will not always be around to intercede."

George nodded. "*Merci, Tariq.*"

❁ ❁ ❁

Jamie met with George, Fenton, Mateus, and Dimas. He told them what had happened at the market.

"We must find a way out of here," Fenton said.

"We will. I scouted the harbor. If we can steal or buy a fishing boat, we can sail to Malta."

"If me and Mateus get our old job of fishing back," Fenton said, "we might be able to steal a boat."

"We must wait until we are sure," Jamie said. "We've only been in Derne a day. We need time and a plan."

"You're right, Jamie," George said, patting his friend on the back. "I only wish we had allies in this town."

"We might have one. Doctor de Aragon's brother, Amos, is here. He too is a doctor. Ephraim sent a letter to him, asking him to help us should we ask. I will contact him as soon as I'm able. Until we have a plan in place, we bide our time and follow the rules."

Chapter 48

KEMAL RETURNED THE NEXT DAY, having spent the night at the palace. He was red with anger.

"I'm grand admiral of nothing!" His bitterness was acute. "My fleet is a galliot and a small xebec. I can commandeer a few fishing boats, that's all! The bashaw sent me here to appease his son-in-law."

Jamie hid his smile. He wondered how long it would be before Kemal realized what he had already seen when they entered port.

Kemal yelled, "Sharpe! Get yer lazy arse in the garden and clean it up." He raised his riding crop for emphasis.

Turning to Simon, he said, "You, Cutts, bring me liquor."

Simon shook with fright. "Master, there are only a few jars of local wine. Sharpe had plenty of money to buy more, but he must have pocketed it."

"What?" Kemal roared.

"I t-told him to buy spirits, but he didn't."

"That's right," Billy Scars said maliciously. "I also told him to buy wine and spirits.

"Drag that *amadán* bastard back here!" Kemal resorted to Irish, calling Jamie a fool.

Billy Scars happily complied. He ran to the garden, where Jamie was trimming a grapevine.

"Sharpe," he yelled. "Get over here."

"I'm busy and I don't answer to you."

"You'll answer to me, you will."

Billy Scars prodded him with a knife. The blade went into Jamie's side, drawing blood. Jamie stumbled and fell.

Billy Scars dragged Jamie to his feet, pulled him out of the garden, and heaved Jamie at Kemal's feet. Jamie was bleeding from a cut to his side. Billy Scars used a scrap of cloth to wipe the blood off his knife.

"He give me lip, so I had to cut him."

Kemal cursed and struck Jamie hard on the head with the weighted end of his riding crop, then slashed the wound on his side with the whip end.

"Why didn't ye buy spirits, ye damn idjit?"

Jamie was bleeding heavily from his wounds, trying not to cry in pain. He pressed his hand to his side, blood oozing between his fingers.

Kemal raised his whip again and Jamie managed to answer.

"The guards stole the French brandy I bought. There is some wine."

"What guards?" Kemal demanded. "Where in the hell is Tariq?"

Tariq was summoned and Kemal ordered him to name the two guards that had accompanied Jamie to the market, along with the janissary from the governor's palace.

"Kasim and Nadim. The janissary is called Kuzey."

"Bastinado the scum," Kemal ordered.

"They haven't returned. When they do, I'll see to their punishment," Tariq said in better French than Kemal could muster. "The janissary, I have no power over."

Kemal grunted. "I'll speak to Governor Mustapha. You take care of the other two."

The Grand Admiral of Barqa looked about his new quarters. "Damn small. But at least clean."

"I made sure of it," Simon bragged. "I had everyone working until the place was spotless."

Kemal nodded. "Ye done well. I was wise to make ye me majordomo."

Simon beamed. "I strive to do my best for you, Kemal Rais."

Kemal reached into to his purse and handed Simon a few Venetian coins. "Buy yourself some better clothes. It won't do for me majordomo to go about in them rags."

George was kneeling by his friend, who had collapsed to the floor. He cursed Simon for the scoundrel he was. "Did you hear that weasel? He took credit for your orders."

Jamie didn't answer.

George wiped the blood away from his friend's head and saw a large knot. But it was the cut to Jamie's side that concerned George more. It was bleeding severely. George ripped the sleeve off his own shirt and pressed it into the wound.

"Dimas, help me." George knew he had some small skills at medical arts.

Dimas ran to Jamie and knelt down.

Kemal looked over. "Get up, Sharpe," he commanded. "Ye're gettin' blood on the tiles."

George looked up with hatred in his eyes. "He's unconscious."

Dimas had sent for his bag of medicines. When it arrived, he applied ointment to the wound in Jamie's side and packed it with lint, but he couldn't wake him.

"He is hurt, master. I've stopped the bleeding, but this is beyond my poor skills to aid him. He has lost blood. He needs a doctor."

"A doctor?" Kemal bellowed. "He's malingerin'."

"No, master," Dimas insisted. "The cut was deep. I packed it, but it will still bleed."

"Damn. I need him alive. I've got to find a doctor."

"Sir, if I may," George spoke up, "Doctor Ephraim de Aragon's brother practices in Derne."

"Ah, the Jewish doctor." Kemal suddenly remembered de Aragon speaking of his brother. "Tariq, find someone who knows the doctor and bring him here."

As the Berber raced off, Kemal told Dimas to make sure Jamie didn't die. Dimas nodded and asked George to move Jamie into the room off the kitchen.

George picked up his friend and carried him to Dimas' pallet.

Kemal shouted to Simon to clean the blood off the tiles. He turned to Billy Scars. "You fool. What did ye have to knife him for? I need him for the ransom."

"Like I said, he gave me lip. I hit him, he hit me back," Billy Scars answered, "so I gave him a bit of blade."

"Ye gave him more'n a bit. He dies, the ransom comes out o' yer hide."

Billy Scars nodded. If push came to shove, it would be Kemal that would taste more than a bit of the blade. He hoped it wouldn't come to that. He needed to show loyalty until he was made a reis and commanded his own ship.

Jamie had gone into shock. George and Dimas worried for his life.

"He's come through so much," George said. "Floggings, beatings, blows to the head, but he always survived. Now this. If he dies, I'll kill Kemal and Billy Scars."

Dimas put his hand on George's shoulder. "He's not dead yet."

Chapter 49

JAMIE LAY UNCONSCIOUS and burning with fever when Doctor Amos de Aragon arrived. The doctor was older than his brother, his beard was gray, his shoulders a bit stooped, but his eyes were alert and his hands steady. He checked Jamie over, examining the wound on his side first, then the bump on his head.

He spoke English with an accent but was clear enough for George and Dimas to understand. "He has lost a great deal of blood, but packing the wound with lint helped staunch it from further blood loss. Now the lint must be removed and the wound cleaned. Boil water and put this needle and these probes in it."

"The tools must be clean, yes?" Dimas asked.

"Yes. We physicians have known since Abraham that cleanliness helps prevent sepsis." He reached into his medicine chest and removed two vials and a pot of honey. "I mix rose water, spirits of pine, and honey. It will cleanse the wound and prevent infection."

After the wound was cleaned, he took a needle and threaded it with catgut.

"You do not use cotton thread?" Dimas asked.

"If I don't have catgut made from the intestines of sheep. But this dissolves on its own. I must clean it first with a solution of potassium hydroxide."

"P-potassium...?" Dimas asked.

"Potassium hydroxide. Never mind. If you have to suture, use cotton thread, but boil it first." The doctor took up the needle and sutured the wound. "Now, he must rest. I will give him Peruvian bark for his fever. Feed him broths made from the marrow of sheep and beef bones. No muscle has been cut, nor a vital organ. I will return tomorrow. Make sure he lies still so he doesn't tear the sutures." He added, to Dimas, "You saved him by packing the wound."

"I know only a little of medicine, but for Capitão Jamie, I must try."

"What of his bump?" George asked.

"Ice would bring down the swelling, but alas, none can be had here. It is not a serious blow — the scalp was cut, but not deep, and the swelling will go down — he may have a headache for a few days, but it will pass."

Doctor de Aragon packed up his chest and was ready to take his leave when he was accosted by Kemal Rais.

"Will he live?"

"He has lost much blood. But I believe God will look kindly on him. Keep him quiet and make sure he gets nourishments. If the fever breaks, he can be taken outside to get sun. In a month, if all goes well, he can do light duty."

"I need him to work," Kemal said. "Who will tend my garden?"

The doctor shook his head. "You have other slaves."

"None who have been trained by a master gardener."

"In a week, if he's strong enough, he can direct someone to do the work." Doctor de Aragon tried not to show his frustration.

"All right," Kemal said. "Make sure he'll live."

"If my instructions are followed, he should live. Let your cook attend to him. I will return tomorrow. Now I must report to the governor and attend to his needs."

Jamie struggled through the night. He was in and out of consciousness. He was delirious, sometimes calling out his for his mother. Other times, he fought to get up, only to be held down by Dimas or George. But early the next morning, his fever broke and he fell into a deep sleep.

The doctor returned as promised, accompanied by a tall, wiry young man in his late twenties. His beard was full but didn't hide his handsome features.

"This my son, Alon. He is my assistant," Doctor de Aragon explained to Kemal. "I wish him to examine the patient."

The doctor and his son found Jamie sitting up. Dimas was feeding him marrow broth, as he was still too weak to feed himself.

Alon de Aragon pushed back his sleeves to reveal well-muscled arms. Dimas brought him a basin of water and the young man washed his hands with soap. He sat next to Jamie and took his pulse.

"Steady," he commented. "How do you feel?"

"Pain, headache," Jamie managed to whisper.

"I'm sure," the younger de Aragon said. He removed the bandage and examined the wound. "I see no putrefaction around the sutures. Keep it clean," he said to Dimas. "I'll mix a tincture of Peruvian balsam, which you can apply to the wound. It will help in the healing."

The elder de Aragon nodded his approval. To Jamie, he said, "My son has learned his lessons well. You will heal."

"Doctor," Jamie said in a weak voice, "they tell me you saved my life. I owe you many thanks."

"You can thank your friend, Dimas. Had he not packed the wound, you would surely have died from blood loss. I told Kemal Rais that you need rest and won't be able to work for a month. You should regain your health before that, but I wanted to give you extra time to heal. In a week, you may sit in the sun and take short walks about the garden. Increase the walks every day and, by month's end, you should be healthy enough to resume your duties."

"I am once more in debt to the de Aragon family," Jamie said.

"I know of your plight. My brother has written to me. He thinks highly of you and asked me to aid you in any way I'm able. I shall do so."

"Doctor, my friends and I plan to escape. I don't know when, but we must leave this place lest we die here. We need a boat."

Doctor de Aragon pulled at his beard. "I can do nothing now, but I'll be alert for opportunities. You can't leave until you are well. So until then, rest and follow my instructions."

In a week's time, Amos allowed Jamie to take short walks in the garden. Still weak and in pain, it was a struggle just to get out of a chair. Amos sent Alon to walk with Jamie and watch his recovery.

"Your strength will return soon," Alon assured Jamie. "You have a strong constitution, which helps. Next week, I will give you a series of exercises to build you up."

Jamie laughed and winced. "I've always had plenty of exercise, usually chopping wood, manning my sloop, fencing, rowing."

"The exercises I prescribe will build your body in specific ways. My father was a doctor to the janissaries in Constantinople and learned how they trained for strength and agility. I know it works because he made me follow their exercises. He even hired a former janissary to teach me to fight and use a sword, although Jews are forbidden to use arms."

"You should go to America," Jamie said. "My grandfather served with a Major Franks, a Jew, during the American Revolution. Good doctors are always in demand."

"Perhaps someday," Alon said. "First, I must go to Constantinople and meet my bride."

"Your bride? You haven't met her?"

"No. It was arranged by her father and mine. She comes from a prominent Polish Jewish family. Her father is a doctor to the sultan."

"I've known of arranged marriages in America. However, I wouldn't marry anyone I didn't love first."

"From the way you say that," Alon teased, "I believe you have met someone."

Jamie nodded, thinking of Claire. He hoped she was safe and wondered if he would ever see her again.

"I'm sure my fiancée is the woman I'm destined to marry." A smile crossed Alon's face. "From her correspondence, I can tell she is a wonderful and intelligent woman. She is a poetess and writes with such emotion." The smile left his face, replaced by a sudden sadness. "Yet, it may be years before I can meet her. The governor won't let me leave. He says because of the war with the Americans, no doctor can leave Derne. Her beautiful letters will have to sustain me until then."

"We are both cut off from women we love," Jamie said, his face, too, a mask of sadness.

Chapter 50

WHEN THE TWO who had stolen his brandy were found days later in a brothel, Kemal had them seized.

They begged forgiveness, but Kemal was too incensed. First, they were bastinadoed, then had their right hands cut off. The only way they could live was to beg. The governor banished the janissary that had aided the guards.

Jamie was healing faster than expected, but the doctors and his friends kept the information from Kemal Rais. Still, Kemal ordered a desk to be set up in the garden where Jamie was expected to work on Kemal's correspondence, mainly letters to the bashaw asking to return to Tripoli or, if not, to at least send him more vessels.

Kemal finally relaxed a bit when his harem arrived from Tripoli, along with his favorite horses.

By month's end, Jamie had to return to the garden to work. While it had been cleaned of debris during his convalescence, he had to take care of the plants. He became concerned when it ceased to rain. So far, the well had enough water, but he used it sparingly.

Jamie was able to produce lāgbi, the palm liquor, which Kemal consumed in large quantities. But Kemal wanted stronger spirits and the best the market could produce was wine. No more spirits from Europe had arrived, due to the American blockade.

In one of his drunken rages, he forced his way into Amos de Aragon's house and demanded he turn over his medicinal spirits. Amos gave him some and promised more.

Once governor Mustapha Bey found out, he admonished Kemal for being a bad Muslim. "de Aragon is my personal physician. From the spirits, he makes medicine. Never bother him again."

Just as the bashaw had done, the governor insisted Kemal purge himself, go to the hills, and seek out a holy man.

While he was away, Jamie and Alon came up with a plan. Alon gave Jamie a small copper alembic. In essence, a still.

As he handed it to Jamie, Alon told him that Miriam, a Jewish woman — an alchemist living some centuries earlier — invented the alembic.

Jamie distilled wine into a harsh brandy. When Kemal returned, he stayed sober for a week, then demanded drink. He was greatly surprised when Jamie gave him a jar of the brandy.

It was vile stuff, but Kemal drank it with pleasure.

Two months had passed since Jamie was stabbed. He had completely healed except for a scar. Thanks to Alon's exercise regime, his strength and agility was back. During his convalescence, Jamie asked Alon to help him read and write Arabic. Malik had given him some lessons, using the Qur'an as a primer, but Jamie hadn't had much opportunity to work on it. He was a diligent student and, in a few weeks, he could read and write slowly.

One day, Alon told Jamie, "My father is trying to procure a boat. You must escape before January. After that, the harbor isn't safe due to harsh north and east winds. Boats are usually brought ashore as they could be destroyed by the winds."

Plans were made. They would gather supplies and Amos would find a boat.

Late in September, word came from Tripoli via a Tunisian ship that, in August, the Americans had attacked and managed to destroy a number of the bashaw's gunboats. When the word finally reached Jamie and his friends, they were elated. The navy was striking back.

As well, a new squadron arrived and added to the fleet already there. A new commodore took over command from Commodore Preble.

"I hope he's a fighting commodore like Preble," Jamie said.

Demir Bey was to be sent back to Constantinople to apprise the court of the events in Tripoli. Kemal Rais was ordered to take the Bey to Crete to transfer to a Turkish ship.

After he left Crete, Kemal was to patrol the waters off of Derne. Kemal sobered up as best he could and took his xebec and the galliot out to sea. He knew he was no match for an American warship, but at least he could warn the governor if the Americans were approaching.

Unfortunately, George, Mateus, and Fenton were made part of the crew of the galliot. The plans to leave were abandoned for now.

"It's good news our navy is on the offensive," Jamie told the others before they were sent to the oars, "but for us, it means we will be captives still. We may have to wait until spring to try and escape if the weather turns as bad as Alon said."

A cloud of disappointment descended on Jamie and his friends.

With Kemal gone, Jamie experienced more freedom. Simon tried to rule him as he did the rest of the household, but Jamie was having none of it. Simon complained to Tariq, who asked if Jamie was tending the garden and helping in the kitchen.

"Yes," Simon had to admit.

"Then why do you bother me? You may be majordomo, but Jamie is the secretary and head gardener."

The drought continued. It hadn't rained since July. It was up to Dimas and Jamie to do the marketing, as Simon couldn't or wouldn't learn enough Arabic to bargain. What once was a thriving market was now short of food. Jamie was surprised how fast produce and meat became scarce.

Alon said, "From time to time, the weather changes and famine occurs. Many people store and preserve for that time. When there is drought, people buy out the market. Obtain what you can and have Dimas preserve produce and smoke meat. Use water only on the produce, not the flowers. There are some herbs and flowers that can be used for medicine. Those, I will show you. Try to save them if you can."

Whenever he could, Jamie would go to the harbor and study it carefully. He knew if there was to be an escape, he would have to get by the water battery unseen. The winds were also a problem. They began to shift as predicted and sailing out might be difficult or even not possible. They would have to row.

Jamie continued to worry and pray for his friends. If Kemal should encounter an American warship, he might leave the slower galliot to the mercy of the American's guns.

❁ ❁ ❁

Toward the end of October, Jamie breathed a sigh of relief when Kemal's xebec sailed into Derne, followed shortly by the galliot.

Once the crew was ashore and back at Kemal's house, Jamie was overjoyed when George came into the garden. They greeted each other like brothers.

"George, how was it?"

"It was actually boring for most of the time. Fortunately, there was enough wind to sail the galliot, so we only had to row occasionally. When we did, Billy Scars or Bruiser used the whip more than was necessary. We saw no American or Neapolitan warships." George smiled.

"Our supplies were running low, so we returned to get more. We should be here at least two weeks."

"It doesn't give us much time," Jamie said. "We must find a boat, stock supplies, and be ready to leave at a moment's notice."

❁ ❁ ❁

Two days later, Kemal sent for the doctors.

"There is something wrong with my first officer, Omar," he explained. "His eyes, they burn, and he moans in pain. You must do something."

They examined Omar and Alon turned to Kemal. "I believe it is trachoma."

His father concurred.

"Can you cure him?"

"We can treat it with lemon juice," Amos said.

Billy Scars and Bruiser were called in to hold Omar down. Amos applied the juice with a small cotton swab to the eye lids. Omar cried out in pain and cursed in Arabic. Amos ignored the curses and said, “Blink often and do not touch the eye. I’ll make a poultice of fig leaves that may help.”

“But will it cure him?” Kemal asked again.

“At this stage, perhaps. But there is no way to know for certain. The disease is rampant, a scourge. He must rest for now. You have Atropa belladonna growing in your garden. It is highly poisonous, but I will dilute it enough so it can help him sleep. Either my son or myself will return tomorrow.”

“Poison, you say. Will it kill him?”

“Not in the dose I’ll give him. It will ease his pain. I do recommend that it be handled with care. I’ll inform your gardener, Sharpe.”

“When can Omar sail again?” Kemal demanded.

“I suggest you find a new officer. He may never recover.”

“Damn it,” Kemal said. “This place is cursed. First I’m greeted like a pirate, then I have no fleet. An overzealous retainer stabs my secretary. Now a drought has struck and my first officer is going blind.

“Cutts!” he bellowed. “Bring me some of that brandy.”

Kemal retired to his gulphor to get drunk, cursing all the way.

Alon went to the garden to gather fig leaves. Jamie joined him.

“We have a boat,” Alon said. “A small fishing vessel, but large enough for you and your companions. It is in a cove just west of the wadi. Here is a map I’ve drawn so you may find it. I don’t know how all of you will manage to get to it.”

“I have some ideas. The next time I go to the market, I’ll slip down to the shore and look the boat over.”

Chapter 51

TWO DAYS LATER, Jamie left the nearly barren market and crossed the large wadi, now dry with nary a trickle of water. He followed a path down a bluff to a tiny cove. A wooden boat known as a felucca lay hidden between two dunes. If he didn't know where it was, he would not have found it. He removed the tan canvas covering and inspected it carefully.

The boat was eighteen feet long with a broad beam. She was rounded at stem and stern and decked. She'd be a slow sailer, built for fishing, not for speed. Her lateen sail wasn't new and had several patches, but was serviceable, as were her mast and spars. Four sets of oars were laying in her bottom. From what he could tell, her hull was sound, but he didn't know how long she'd been out the water and her planks would probably leak. He wished he could take her out and let her hull swell, but it would be too dangerous. He covered the felucca with the canvas.

Later, he called his friends together.

"Today is Sunday, October twenty-eighth. We must leave the night of the thirty-first. That is Samhain, known to some as Hallowe'en. Kemal still celebrates it. Last year, he killed Badr, the chef, because he baked the bairín breac with cloth inside, which meant bad luck. This year, Dimas will make it with coins inside, which means good luck. He'll love it and get drunk or go to his harem or both. That is when we make our escape."

Fenton said, "Me and Mateus are locked up at night in the slave quarters. Same for George in the stable. You're locked in the garden shed."

George spoke up. "The stable is outside the walls. The door to the paddock isn't locked. I'll go out that way. If Usem should wake, I'll overpower him and tie him up."

"All good," Fenton said, "but what about the guards? You have to go by their barracks to get in."

"Most will be asleep and we've timed the guards on patrol," Jamie said. "George will sneak by."

"How will you get into the house?" Fenton asked. "The door is barred."

"Dimas isn't locked up," George said. "He will unbar the door."

"Yes," Dimas said. "I have freedom of house, kitchen, and garden, so I can prepare food for household."

"Once I'm in," George said, "I'll break the locks on Jamie's shed and the slave quarters door and let you and Mateus out, along with the rest of the slaves."

"The guards'll be bound to wake once they hear the other slaves," Fenton said.

"That's to our advantage," Jamie explained. "Slaves will be milling about, not sure what to do. The guards will try and round them up and, in the confusion, you'll head for the door where Dimas will be waiting with food and water. George will lead you to the wadi, where we will meet up."

"I believe it will work," Fenton said. "What about you, Jamie?"

"I'll be in the gulphor, collecting weapons, a compass, my sextant, and hopefully my watch. With Kemal gone to his harem, it will be easy.

"I'll go with you, Capitão," Mateus said. "You need help with weapons."

The next three days were filled with anxiety. But all tried to keep busy. Dimas gathered the stores and the water they needed for the voyage. Jamie began to hide garden tools that Fenton and Mateus could use as weapons near the slave quarters.

When the de Aragons came to check on Omar, Jamie told them of their plans.

"It will be fraught with danger," Amos offered. "I could give you opiates to put into the guards' food or drink."

"No," Jamie said. "They would eventually figure out where they came from. You have done enough. We want no suspicion to fall on you."

"I could give you money. You'll need it once you reach Malta."

"We have money. I have Danish silver. We should be all right."

"I can call upon God to bless and keep you from harm."

Jamie was touched. "I will always hold you and your family in my prayers. I will never be able to repay my debt to the de Aragon family."

"Go with God."

Alon also offered his blessings. He added, "Jamie, do not sail to Malta, at least not directly. Sail east toward Egypt. Kemal will assume you will be going to Malta and he can overtake your boat. Sail east and he won't think to search in that direction."

"Thank you, Alon. I would never have thought of that. I just wanted to get to Malta."

"I have one more thing I can give you. I stole Omar's charts of the Mediterranean. He will never need them again. He will be blind — I tried but he can't be cured. I will hide them in the felucca."

Once again, Jamie was overwhelmed. He fought to hold back tears. Kindness by the de Aragons, Malik, Marco Cardullo, and even Tariq had seen him survive.

As the sun set on the night of the thirty-first, the faithful were called to prayer. Kemal stayed in his quarters, waiting for his bairín breac. For some superstitious reason, he expected the contents of the bread to be guided by the hands of fate, although he gave Dimas the symbols.

Dimas prepared the bread, adding the dried fruit. Next, he reached for the coins, but they were gone. So was the ring. He searched around the kitchen but could find neither. All that was left was the pea, stick, and cloth. Dimas broke into a cold sweat. If he didn't find the coin or at least the ring, not only would the plan fail, but Kemal might kill him.

Only one person had reason to see him fail — Simon. Simon always resented that the kitchen was Dimas' domain. He had tried to use his position as majordomo to take over, but Kemal told him to let it be as long as Dimas cooked as well as he did.

Now, Dimas was furious. He picked up a heavy cleaver and walked to Simon's office. Simon was drinking tea and was startled to see the cook.

"What do you want? It ain't a market day, so I have no money to give you."

Dimas brandished the cleaver. "You know what I want. You steal coins and ring for Kemal's bread. I heard what you do to Badr, you don't do that to me. Now, give back the coins."

"You're mad. Now, get out before I call the guards and have you bastinadoed."

"You call guard and I tell them you steal coins. What you think will happen to you? Kemal will cut off your hand, maybe kill you. Now give me coins or I call the guards myself."

Simon tried to look defiant, but Dimas stepped closer and slammed the cleaver down on Simon's desk, only inches from his hand. Simon drew it back quickly.

"My God, Dimas, I was only having some fun. I wasn't going to keep the coins." Now it was Simon's turn to sweat.

"Give," Dimas demanded.

Simon reached into his desk, took out the ring and gold pieces, and handed them to Dimas. Dimas pocketed them and as he left, said, "Thieves lose hands in this part of the world."

Simon sat there shaking, cursing under his breath. But suddenly, he became suspicious. What made Dimas so bold? Was it more than his usual fear of Kemal?

Chapter 52

DIMAS DELIVERED THE bairín breac to Kemal and turned to leave.

"Stay here," Kemal ordered. "I want ye to see me fortune. This past year was a disaster. Lost the Irish singin' women, became the admiral of nothin', no prizes to take in this end of the sea. For yer own sake and me own, there better be good fortune this year."

As Kemal picked up his knife to cut the bread, Simon burst into the room.

"Master, don't eat that! It may be poisoned."

"What?" Kemal turned the knife toward Dimas. "Poison me, will ya?"

"No!" Dimas backed away at the sight of the knife. "I did not. I prove it, I eat the bread."

Kemal paused and looked at Simon. "Are ye sure?"

"He's started acting bold. Threatened me with a cleaver, he did. Claimed I hid the coins for the bread. I didn't," Simon lied. "I wonder if he didn't put belladonna berries in the bread. It grows in the garden."

"He lies," Dimas said. "The coins..."

"Shut yer gob. You said you'd eat it, go ahead." Kemal cut a slice of the bread and then held the knife to Dimas' throat.

Dimas couldn't be sure if Simon had slipped some of the berries into the fruit at the same time he stole the coins. Swallowing hard, sweat on his brow, Dimas took the slice and ate it.

Minutes ticked by and he seemed no worse for it. After a while, Kemal became impatient.

"He ain't dead, not even sick."

"He's up to something," Simon said. "I feel it."

Kemal looked hard at both men. "Keep an eye on him. I'll sort it out tomorrow. Now, let me see me fortune." He opened the bread and the gold coins spilled out. "At last, fortune follows. Now get ye from me sight."

After they left, Simon turned to Dimas. "I'll be watching you."

"I will tell Kemal you stole coins."

"How could I steal the coins when they were in the bread? You're a fool. He'll never believe you."

Dimas found Jamie and told him what had happened.

"While Simon's watching you, I'll be watching him. Now we wait, while Kemal gets drunk."

One of the kitchen slaves sought out Jamie. "The master wants more brandy."

Jamie nodded. He had already distilled a large batch. He handed a jug to the man, hoping it would soon render Kemal dead drunk. Now he wished he had taken the opiate, not for the guards but for Kemal. Jamie knew Kemal's capacity for drink was huge and it might take hours before he succumbed.

As the slaves were rounded up and locked in their quarters, Jamie could hear Kemal singing at the top of his lungs, still awake. If he didn't fall into sleep by Isha, the night prayer, it would be very dangerous to try and take weapons and navigational instruments from him awake, even drunk.

Finally, the escapees heard the muezzins call the prayer. It was the dark of night. Jamie reckoned it was past 2 a.m. Dimas had gathered the food and water and placed the supplies by the kitchen entrance to the courtyard. At last, Kemal was silent.

Fenton and Mateus left their pallets and stood by the door of the slave quarters.

Jamie paced in his small shed. He checked the edges of the dagger Abdullah had given him, then tucked it in his sash. The waiting made feel like he was on a precipice, ready to fall. Barely realizing he had just done it a minute ago, he checked the knife again.

What if Kemal wasn't passed out drunk? Would he have to try and kill him? Would Kemal awake the guards? Where was George?

Had he been caught? Maybe Simon had seen Dimas and alerted the guards.

George had gathered his tool chest and selected a pry bar to break locks. He had no second thoughts — either the plan would work or they would fail, but to do nothing was worse.

Usem had gone to the mosque — he wouldn't have to overpower the groom who had been kind to him. Usem hadn't locked the door. George didn't have to cut through the paddock and possibly startle the horses, which could alert the guards. He peeked out, watching the courtyard door across the yard. A guard walked by, yawning, and rounded the corner. It was now or never. Only a tiny sliver of the moon was visible. He dashed across the dark yard to the courtyard door. He tried it and it was still barred. Then he heard the scimitar chain on the guard's scabbard jingling — the man was returning. George hefted the iron pry bar. If Dimas didn't open the door in the next ten seconds, either the guard or George would be dead.

Chapter 53

"WHAT THE HELL are you up to?"

Dimas had his hands on the bar of the door. At the sound of the menacing voice, he turned to see Simon brandishing a heavy piece of firewood.

"Get away from that door or I'll brain you."

Simon was bigger and probably stronger then Dimas. But the Portuguese cook hadn't survived sailing on ships with rough men without learning a few tricks. He pulled a paper packet full of ground pepper from his sash and tossed the pepper into Simon's eyes. Simon dropped the firewood and, before he could scream, Dimas clobbered him with the piece of wood. Simon fell and Dimas unbarred the door. George slipped in, just as the guard rounded the corner. Dimas closed the door and dropped the bar back in place.

George took one look at the situation and sized it up. Simon was stirring and George struck him hard on the jaw. This time, Simon was out cold.

"Find something to tie and gag him," George said.

Dimas ripped up Simon's pantaloons and used the strips to gag and tie him. George picked up Simon as if he were a rag doll and threw him over his shoulder.

"Go back to the kitchen and wait," he said to Dimas, before running to the garden.

At the shed, he set Simon down, broke the lock, and let Jamie out. Jamie looked at the trussed-up Simon.

"Throw him in the shed," Jamie said. "I'd take him with us, get him back home to face justice, but he'd be too much trouble. We'll be lucky to get away without him as a burden."

Before they left the shed, they wedged it shut with a heavy rake.

The slave quarters were between the house and the garden.

At the door, George said, "Stand back."

He used the iron pry bar to break the lock. He lifted the heavy bar and swung the door open. Fenton and Mateus dashed out, followed by several slaves who wandered out, bewildered.

George handed Jamie a bundle from his tool chest. Mateus rummaged through the shrubs and found three hoes that Jamie had stashed there. Fenton and Jamie each took one. More slaves came out of their quarters as George and Fenton went off to get Dimas. Once found, the three of them would leave by the courtyard door.

Jamie and Mateus headed through the dark house for the gulphor. A lantern lit the landing above them. A shadow flickered in the light.

"There's a guard by the door," Jamie cautioned quietly.

He led the way up the stairs. One creaked underfoot and Jamie and Mateus froze. They waited a minute and when nothing happened, they climbed more stairs to the top. The guard was leaning against the wall, his musket next to him. He seemed to be dozing but, just as Jamie and Mateus reached the landing, he opened his eyes. It took him a second to reach for his musket. Jamie leaped and swung the hoe. It connected with the guard's head and he fell to the floor in a thump. Mateus rushed in and grabbed the musket. Jamie took the man's scimitar.

"Try not to use the musket," Jamie warned. "A shot will bring the guards."

He checked to see if the man he had struck was still breathing. He was, but out cold. They unwound his turban and used the cloth to tie and gag him.

Jamie put his ear to the door. "I can't hear anything. Kemal is either asleep or in his harem."

He cautiously turned the handle on the door and slowly opened it. He peered inside. The room was dimly lit by a small lantern. Jamie could make out several empty brandy jars scattered on the floor. The air was hazy and smelled of hashish.

Jamie squinted though the haze but he couldn't see Kemal. He mouthed "Harem" to Mateus and led the way into the room. He pointed to a cabinet where Kemal kept his pistols, muskets, and swords. Mateus nodded and began to gather them, along with powder and ammunition. Jamie's own weapons, the Highland pistols and the claymore sword, were hanging on the wall. He quickly took them down. His dirk was there as well and he shoved it in his sash. Jamie strapped on his sword and loaded his pistols.

He needed his sextant, a box compass, a telescope, and his chronometer. Kemal's sea chest sat in a corner. It was locked, but Jamie pried it open with his dirk. He found his navigation instruments in a leather satchel and removed the chronometer. It was neither wound nor set. It would be difficult to navigate without accurate time. Kemal had a large ship's clock on the wall. Jamie hoped it was accurate and set his watch by it. He put the timepiece back in the satchel and hung the bag over his shoulder.

Mateus opened the cabinet and found ammunition, a ten-pound powder barrel, six pistols, three muskets, four scimitars, and a cutlass. "Capitão, how will we carry all of this? It is much heavy."

He pointed to Kemal's sea bag. "Put the weapons in that."

Mateus stuffed everything in the bag. Jamie signaled it was time to go. Without warning, the door from the harem opened and Kemal swayed in the doorway, obviously drunk and stinking of hashish. Trying to focus, Kemal squinted and saw Jamie and Mateus.

"What!" Kemal slurred. "What the hell are ye doin' here?"

Before Kemal could call for help, Jamie cocked his fist and smashed him in the nose. The pleasure of hearing it crack was short-lived, as a eunuch armed with a scimitar ran into the room, quickly followed by another, who stopped to help Kemal to his feet. Unlike their master, they were sober. The first one slashed at Jamie, who parried the cut with his claymore and, before the ringing from the clash of blades subsided, Jamie riposted and stabbed the man in the chest.

The other eunuch, seeing his comrade go down, screamed for help and pulled his pistol. However, before he could fire, Mateus jumped in front of him. They wrestled for the pistol. In the struggle, the weapon discharged and the ball struck Mateus in the stomach. Jamie fired one of his pistols at the eunuch, killing him instantly. He hoped the guards were too busy at the slave quarters to hear the shots. But what was done was done.

Kemal, his nose broken, his eyes glassy, barely able to stand, drunk, and now feeling the pain, tried to figure out what had happened. His eyes focused for a moment.

"Sharpe," he slurred.

Kill him now! Jamie thought. He raised the sword, but he couldn't do it, not while Kemal was so drunk, and full of hashish. Instead, he hit him with the flat of the blade, knocking him out. Kemal fell next to his dead eunuchs.

Mateus stood, but fell back almost instantly.

"Mateus!" Jamie cried and knelt by his friend.

The wound was deep and bleeding heavily. Jamie ripped the turban off one of the dead eunuchs and used it to staunch the bleeding.

"Mateus, can you walk?"

"No, Capitão," he said. "*Minha vida acabou.* My life is finished."

"Don't say that," Jamie pleaded.

"It is true. Now you must go. The shots could have aroused the guards. It is all right, Capitão. I die free, not a slave. I ask God to forgive me for my sins, which are many."

"He will, he will." Jamie quoted John 15:13. "'Greater love hath no man than this, that a man lay down his life for his friends.'"

Mateus smiled briefly and passed.

Jamie closed Mateus' eyes, then wiped his own as he straightened up. He reloaded his pistol, put his satchel in the sea bag, and slung it over his shoulder.

Jamie took one more look at Mateus and left the room. He stepped over the door guard and made his way down the stairs.

Billy Scars led the guards and armed sailors in trying to round up the slaves in the courtyard, but the frightened men ran in every direction. In the dark chaos, guards sometimes struck each other, but even so, at least four of them stood guarding the doorway, blocking escape.

Jamie backed out of the courtyard. Billy Scars hadn't seen him and he wanted to keep it that way. His only way out was through the front door of the house. He hoped that George and the others had reached the wadi by now.

A guard stood in front of the front door and Jamie jumped back behind a corner. He set down his bundle, cocked his pistol, but as he did, an explosion went off close by. Startled, the guard opened the door to see. Jamie ran up behind him and hit him over the head with his pistol. He looked out onto the street, for the moment, it was empty, as the sound of the explosion kept people inside their houses.

Jamie knew the hue and cry was out. Soon, the town would be crawling with janissaries, soldiers, and watchmen searching for the escaped slaves.

Jamie heard another explosion. George was making good use of the grenades.

George had given him two grenades. He lit one with his tinderbox and tossed it back down the hall, hoping it would slow pursuit. He snatched the guard's cloak, threw it on, and put up the hood. He picked up the sea bag and ran from the house. He had to make it to the wadi to meet up with the others.

He had a good half-mile to go to reach the rendezvous. He knew running would draw attention, so he slowed to a walk. Ahead, a man holding a lantern in one hand and a pistol in the other was moving straight toward him. There was no place to hide. If challenged, he'd have to kill the man before the man killed him.

As the person neared, he recognized him, it was Tariq, the head guard. At the same moment, Tariq recognized Jamie. They aimed their pistols at one another.

Chapter 54

TARIQ AND JAMIE locked eyes, pistols pointing at each other.

Jamie called out to Tariq. "*Alssalam ealaykim, ya sadiqi.*" *Peace to you, my friend.* He lowered his pistol.

"*Alssalam ealayk,*" Tariq answered automatically. Then he shook his head and lowered his weapon in turn. "Jamie," he continued in Arabic, "you should not be out here. My duty is to bring you in."

"My friend, I can't go back. I will not face Kemal's punishment, nor be a slave a moment longer. I intend to escape and I do not want to shoot you. You are a good man, Kemal is not. He isn't a good Muslim. He's a hypocrite."

"Jamie, my duty..." He hesitated. "I haven't always been righteous – I'm fond of drink – but I believe in Allah. It is true, Kemal doesn't believe in anything but drink, women, and plunder." Tariq rubbed his forehead in anguish. Finally, he said, "Ai! Go with my blessing to you and yours. However, should I see you again this night, I must kill you, so for the love of God, please don't let me see you."

"Thank you," Jamie said, his voice cracking in gratitude.

Tariq walked past Jamie and headed back to the house. Over his shoulder, he said, "And if I were you, I would pull that cloak tighter to hide your pistols and sword."

Jamie nodded, picking up his bundle. Keeping to the shadows and doorways, he continued toward the wadi and the appointed place.

As he slipped down into the ravine, arms like iron gripped him around the throat. He struggled, but the grip was too strong.

"Stop!" Fenton Webb called out. "It's Jamie!"

"Oh my God," George said. "Jamie, I didn't recognize you with the cloak over your head. I thought you were the watch trying to stop us."

Jamie rubbed his throat. “Remind me never to make you angry, George,” he croaked. “I should have called out, but all I thought about was escape.”

“Where is Mateus?” Dimas asked.

“He died,” Jamie said, with tears in his eyes. “He died saving me from a bullet. I- I wanted to get us all free, I failed.”

“No, Capitão Jamie,” Dimas said. “We all understood the risk. Mateus was a brave man, but he would not want you to grieve. As I’m sure you recall, his surname was Balduino. It means ‘bold friend’.”

Jamie wiped his eyes and took a deep breath. “We aren’t free yet,” he said. “We must get to the boat and be on the water before sunup.”

Jamie led the way to the boat. They quickly uncovered it, piled their supplies inside, dragged it down to the water, and launched it. They scrambled aboard. Jamie took the tiller while the others manned the oars. Water seeped in between the dried-out seams, but the wood would soon swell.

“We row north before we turn east. I want to be out of the range of the cannon at the water battery and the mortar at the palace before we can bail the boat.”

The men put their backs into it. Jamie steered the course until they were a half-mile out.

“Dimas, take the tiller, I’ll row.”

Jamie knew Dimas wasn’t used to the oars as the others were and felt he had to do something to ease his conscience over the death of Mateus.

By daybreak, they were several miles north of Derne and Jamie called a halt to the rowing. There was about a foot of water in the bottom of the boat.

“We’ll have to bail, then can raise sail as we have wind. We will sail northeast until it’s safe to turn toward Malta. Hopefully, Kemal will expect us to sail northwest.”

It took little time to bail the boat.

“Before we step the mast,” Jamie said, “there are things that must be done. First, we must pray for a safe voyage.”

The men bowed their heads as Jamie led from what he remembered from the Book of Common Prayer. "O eternal Lord God, who alone spreadest out the heavens, and rulest the raging of the sea; who hast compassed the waters with bounds, until day and night come to an end; Be pleased to receive into thy almighty and most gracious protection, the persons of us thy servants, and the boat in which we serve..."

Dimas uttered a prayer in Latin and, when finished, crossed himself. The men sat silent for a moment. Then Jamie asked George to take one of the silver coins so he could place it under the mast, as was the tradition.

Once the mast was raised, Jamie said, "We must remember our brother, Mateus Balduino. So, if Dimas would hand me a small portion of wine, I will christen our little boat *Balduino*." He poured the wine over the bow. "We pray our 'Bold Friend' will take us to safety."

Jamie returned to the stern and took the tiller.

"Now, men, we raise sail and leave this terrible shore. And may God grant us a safe voyage."

Chapter 55

THE LITTLE BOAT sailed with the wind astern. At the moment, the seas were running light and making headway was no problem. They sailed all night, taking turns on watch. Jamie insisted there be no lights, except for a shielded lantern set below the stern seat so the man at the tiller could watch the compass.

The next day, with George at the tiller, Jamie fixed their position at noon and examined the charts that Alon had stowed under the deck.

"We're averaging six knots. We've come nearly forty-two nautical miles. We'll sail northeast for at least three days in hopes of fooling Kemal. If he believes we're sailing to Malta, he won't find us. But looking at these charts, once we turn west, we should sail to Syracuse in Sicily, instead of Malta."

"Why?" Fenton asked.

"Because the American squadron is stationed there. It's not without risk. There are hostiles in the waters — Turks, Greek and Albanian pirates, as well as renegades from Napoleon's army."

"Sailing to Malta has the same risks," George said. "I say we try for Syracuse. It'll further put Kemal off our track."

Dimas and Fenton nodded their assent. Dimas passed out the rations and they ate their first meal since leaving Derne.

Every half-hour, Fenton scanned the horizon with a telescope Jamie had taken from Kemal. "So far, no pursuit," he said.

Jamie nodded and took over the lookout position. He saw a sail, hull down, heading southeast, but it was miles away.

As night fell, the first full day out was without incident. Jamie broke the watch into four-hour shifts: four on, four off, Jamie and Dimas on one team, George and Fenton on the other.

The next day passed as the first had, as they sailed farther east. On the third day at noon, Jamie took a reading with the sextant.

"We've gone far enough east. It's safe to turn northwest and cross the Ionian Sea for Syracuse."

While the wind should have been in their favor, it suddenly died.

"Looks like we row," George said.

They took to the oars and, all that day, they rowed west. By nightfall, they were exhausted. Dimas prepared a meal of cold couscous, dried mutton, and weak coffee he brewed over the lantern.

"I wish we had brought bricks to make a small stove," Dimas said. "I could serve a better meal."

"This is fine," Fenton said. "I've had me worse food on some of the ships I sailed. But when we get to Syracuse, I'll have me meat and apples or whatever fruits they got there. Aye, and rum or gin or a good wine."

"We'll all celebrate," Jamie said. "I'll buy us the finest food Sicily has to offer. But first, we have to get there. Back to the oars."

But they didn't have to stay at the oars long. Just as the wind had died earlier, it came up strong. When night fell, they went back to two hours on, two hours off.

❆ ❆ ❆

A little past midnight, George woke Jamie.

"Lightning." He pointed to the east. "I smell rain and the wind is rising. I think we're in for a blow. I took a reading on the North Star before it clouded over. We're near Crete. I think we'll be in the teeth of the storm in an hour. We could run toward Crete and seek shelter."

"Aye," Jamie said, "and if we shelter in Crete, we'll be in Ottoman territory."

"Look," George said, pointing to the chart. "There are two small islands off the coast of Crete. We could try and shelter there. I saw them when I was chained to the galliot's oars. One of the slaves, a Greek Christian, said the islands were no longer inhabited."

Jamie looked at the chart where George had marked their position. "We could make the island by morning, but it will be rough seas ahead. The larger island is marked Gondzo or, in Greek,

Gavdos. Gondzo must be the Turkish name. We'll sail for there and hope what the Greek said was true."

The storm overtook them as predicted. Jamie had to shout over the roar of the storm to order reefing the sail. George and Fenton struggled to shorten the canvas. The wild wind nearly drove Fenton overboard, and only by grabbing his belt was George able to drag him back before he was lost to the raging water.

The boat was tossed into high waves and deep troughs, and like so many storms, the wind would often change direction, throwing the boat up, down, and sideways.

It was up to Fenton and Dimas to constantly bail as Jamie and George sailed the pitching boat toward what they hoped was safety. Lightning flashes illuminated the faces of the terrified men determined to sail their frail craft.

Finally, through a slate gray sunrise, Jamie thought he could see a smudge on the horizon. George aimed the telescope where Jamie pointed.

"It looks like land."

They sailed for another hour, rain pelting their faces. They were soaked to the skin. It was a miracle their sail had held together as long as it had, but it began to shred.

As they drew closer, lightning flashes revealed a barren coast.

"Let's hope its Gavdos and not Crete," Jamie said. "We have to stand off until the storms lessens more or we'll be driven into who-knows-what."

Trying to hold their position without an anchor and the sail shredded was near-impossible.

The men were shaking with cold as large waves drove them toward the rocky shore. Without warning, a terrible shudder ran through the boat as it smashed into a submerged rock and water rushed in.

George, standing lookout on the small deck, was thrown overboard and a wave washed over him.

"George!" Jamie yelled.

Suddenly, George emerged from the sea like Poseidon, shaking water as he stood.

"It's shallow," he yelled over the sound of the rain and surf. "Small beach to the left." He pointed. "Pull the boat up."

They jumped into the surf and dragged their damaged craft to the beach. They fell to the sand, exhausted, wet, and cold. They lay there a few minutes until Jamie struggled to his feet.

"Get up. Get up! We shall die here if we don't find shelter and build a fire."

The others fought to get to their feet.

"Save the food and the instruments," Jamie said.

They gathered the food and Jamie filled the satchel with his navigation aids. Tripping and falling often, they staggered inland, always uphill, in hope of finding safety as the storm increased again. The wind screamed in fury, lightning zigzagged in a slash across the sky. They stumbled on as thunder boomed and then, in a lightning flash, Jamie thought he saw a small structure.

"This way," he shouted.

The next lightning streak illuminated a stone hut only a few yards ahead. Jamie led the way. He pushed aside a low weather-beaten wooden door and crawled through the opening in the small shelter, followed by the others. They all collapsed on the floor. With what little light shone through the door, Jamie noticed the structure was round and shaped like a beehive.

"Shepherd's hut," Dimas said. "Many like it in Portugal. Maybe goatherd, by stink in here."

"We need a fire," Jamie said.

Opposite the door was a small hearth with a stack of unburned wood. Shivering from the cold and close to shock, Jamie's hands shook as he struck his tinderbox until he was able to get a spark. In a few minutes, he got a fire going.

"Strip off your clothes. We have to get dry."

All the men were shivering as they undressed and gathered close to the small hearth. George dragged the wooden door shut. The smoke was vented out through a small stone chimney. The smell of pine rose from the hearth, and the wood popped and set out small sparks. Soon, the little hut was warm and getting hotter. The men gradually warmed up.

Dried rushes covered the dirt floor. They were relatively clean, which led Jamie to believe the hut had been inhabited recently. Perhaps that's why there was a supply of firewood. He was too exhausted to give it any more thought.

They all laid down and began to drift off to sleep.

Jamie wasn't sure how long he slept. What woke him was a baby's cry.

Chapter 56

JAMIE WAS SURE he was delirious. A baby outside? Then he heard it again, the cry defiantly coming from the other side of the door.

He woke the others. "Get up. There's a baby crying outside!"

"What?" George said, stretching and rubbing the sleep from his eyes. Then he heard the crying as well. "My God, a baby here."

Dimas broke into laughter.

"What's so damn funny?" Fenton asked.

Dimas crawled to the door and pulled it open, still shaking with laughter as a black nanny goat walked into the hut. "You never heard a goat bleat?"

The others fell into laughter.

"A goat, a damn nanny goat," Fenton roared.

"Jamie, all the time you spent on your grandfather's farm and didn't recognize a goat bleating?" George thundered with laughter.

Jamie turned a bright shade of red.

"Don't be sheepish," George said. "Perhaps I should say don't be kiddish!"

The others laughed harder at Jamie's expense.

After he gained control of his laughter, Dimas said, "Her udders are full. No kid. Means she needs to be milked. Find pot."

They rummaged through their gear and found a pot. Dimas milked the goat.

The warm milk was passed around and the men all drank, still trying to control their laughter. Jamie laughed at his own expense. It had been a long time since these men had anything to truly laugh about.

Suddenly, Jamie stopped laughing and said, "If there's no kid, this goat's been milked regularly. There must be people on the island. I was too damn tired last night to think clearly."

"I guess the Greek slave got it wrong," George said.

The men grew silent, realizing they were still in danger.

Jamie spoke up. "We'd better get down to the boat and see the damage and collect our weapons."

"I wish we had brought them with us last night," Fenton said.

"I think all we wanted to do was get out of the storm." George said. "At least we have our knives."

They threw on their now-dry clothes and crawled out of the hut. The sky had cleared during the night and the sun was shining brightly.

Jamie consulted his watch. "It's nearly noon, I can't recall a time I slept so long. We were truly exhausted."

They made their way down to the beach where they had dragged the boat ashore. Off to their right was a narrow peninsula pointing southeast.

"According to the charts, that's the most southerly point in Europe," Jamie said. "If we landed on the other side of that rocky jut of land, I'm not sure we would have survived. It is all cliff and rocks. We were lucky to walk away."

"I ain't so sure we was lucky," Fenton said, pointing to the boat. "She's stove in."

A jagged hole in the bow was obvious to all.

George looked the boat over. "She's beyond repair. I could patch the hole, but one large wave would break it open. The planks are split and the rest of the hull is damaged as well. If our friend Brad were here, he might be able to fix it, seeing as his father was a boat-builder. The best we can do is try to salvage what we can, cut down some of the trees, and build a raft. But it's a long way to Syracuse."

Jamie nodded. "If it comes to that, then that is what we'll do. But if there are goatherds on the island, they may have a vessel. Let's see if we can find them."

Their weapons were still there and the gunpowder was sealed in jars. They armed themselves and headed for higher ground, climbing a steep goat path that wound its way through pine trees and juniper shrubs. They saw more goats and a few sheep, but no herders.

"No guard dogs," Fenton said. "I wonder why?"

"No wolves on the island," Dimas said.

They reached the clifftop, where they were buffeted by winds from the sea.

"We must have climbed a thousand feet or more," George observed, his breath coming in small gasps as he threw himself down on the sparse grass.

Jamie caught his own breath, took out the telescope, and began a visual sweep of the island.

"Quite a few sandy beaches. Too bad it's winter. I wouldn't mind a dip, get the smell of mildewed clothes off me."

"After the drenching we got, I'll stay with the stink," Fenton said.

Jamie continued to look through the telescope. "There!" He pointed inland. "Two goatherds and a flock. Just down in the valley to the north. We'll approach with caution. There's a trail leading down that way, a mile as the crow flies, but as my grandda used to say, 'Yer nae a crow, Jamie lad.' So we follow the path."

The path, little more than a goat track, was full of it twists and turns as they made their way down.

They were sweating by the time they were halfway down. The temperature was probably close to seventy-five and the sun was high. They found a small stream and refreshed themselves before continuing on.

Finally, when they were close to the herders, they lay low, hidden by a bend in the path. The herders rested in the shade of a pine while their goats nibbled on the grass and brush.

"I'll approach alone," Jamie said quietly. "The rest of you hide yourselves and cover me should anything go wrong."

Jamie showed himself and, in Greek, called out, "Good day to you. I come in peace."

The surprised herders leaped to their feet. One was a man about forty, the other a boy of twelve or thirteen. The older man shoved the boy behind him and drew a knife from his belt.

From his point of view, he saw before him a ragged bearded ruffian armed with pistols and sword, who spoke a strange and accented dialect of Greek.

"*Fýge!*" Go away!

"I mean you no harm," Jamie said. "My comrades and I were shipwrecked last night in the storm. We seek a way off the island. A boat, is there a boat?"

The man looked worried, "You are pirates?"

"No, we are Americans. We escaped from Derne."

"From the Arabs?"

"Yes," Jamie said. "We just want to go home, but we need a boat."

"No boat. Not for many days."

"We need food and shelter. I can pay." He produced a silver Danish coin.

"How many are you?" the herder asked.

"Four."

"I think he tells the truth, father." The boy spoke up. "He is armed and could have killed us."

"Hush, Iskandar, let me think." He stood awhile, ran his hand through his mustache, then finally said, "Yes, my son is right."

Jamie breathed a sigh of relief and called the others from their hiding place. He introduced them and the herder shook their hands.

"*Eímai o Theódoros kai aftós eínai o gios mou, o Iskantár.*"

Jamie translated for Dimas and Fenton. "He is Theódoros and his son is Iskandar."

After the formalities, Theódoros invited the castaways to share bread and cheese and some strong red wine.

When they finished, Jamie questioned Theódoros about a boat. And translated his answers for the others.

"Boats come to take the cheese we make from the milk. No boats come for many weeks. Maybe they come in two weeks or three. But I must warn you, Turkish soldiers come with them to protect shipments from Greek pirates. If they find you, they will send you back to the Arabs."

"The United States is not at war with the Ottoman Empire. We are only at war with the Regency of Tripoli."

"I'm a simple man," Theódoros replied, "but I do know the Turks will send you back. They share the same religion. And the Pasha of Tripoli sends tribute to the sultan, and the sultan will send you back in chains."

After Jamie translated for his friends, George asked Theódoros, "How many soldiers come with the boats?"

"Eight, ten, no more."

"How many boats?"

"Two. One for the soldiers, one to carry cheese. Sometimes they bring goats."

"We thank you for your hospitality," Jamie said, "and we will leave you to your goats."

"Where will you go?"

Jamie described the hut they were using. "It saved us. We were able to build a fire. If we hadn't, we would have died from the cold."

"Father!" Iskandar looked stricken. "They can't stay there. Dryas uses that hut."

"Who?" Jamie asked.

"Dryas. The Turks call him Meşe, which means 'oak.' He is the headman for them here, He calls himself *Evgenis* Dryas, noble Dryas. He is a Greek lackey of the Turks. His brother is the captain of the soldier's boat. Dryas keeps a flock, but mostly he makes sure we supply our quota of cheese. He is a strong man and has a gun and sword. He has two followers, Niilo and Castor. Both are strong men."

"We are armed and don't fear them," Jamie said.

"But if they are killed or attacked, when the soldiers come, they will punish us, probably kill us."

"We won't let that happen," Jamie assured Theódoros.

"I know, father," Iskandar said. "There is the cave where we sheltered with our herd during a storm. It is high up and maybe was once used by those that came before. Perhaps where St. Paul sheltered on his voyage to Rome."

"Ah, my son is a bright boy. He can read and write and is taught by the priest, Ambrose, who lives in the hills not far from the cave. Yes, the cave is ideal. From there, you can see the beach where the boats land. Dryas and his minions will never go there. They believe that part of the island is full of ghosts from ancient times. The witch Calypso enchanted Odysseus for seven years on this island and it is believed it was her cave."

"This is Ogygia? The island from the Odyssey?" Jamie asked.

"So says the learned priest, Ambrose."

"We will go there," Jamie said. "First, we must return to the hut and retrieve our belongings. Then, hide the remnants of our boat."

"Iskandar will go with you to make sure it is safe. Then he will lead you to Calypso's cave. Later, he will bring food. There is a spring there, so you will have water."

Jamie translated for Dimas and Fenton. Then they bid farewell to Theódoros and followed Iskandar. As they neared the stone hut, two men were approaching from the other direction.

"Dryas!" Iskandar cautioned. "Niilo is with him."

Chapter 57

"*PÍGAINE NA KRYFTEÍS!*" Iskandar said, telling them to go hide. "If they see you, they will try to take you prisoner or even kill you. Then, they kill my father and me."

Jamie and his friends ducked behind a hillock. They checked their muskets and pistols.

"I'll go to them and try to prevent them from going into the hut," Iskandar said. The boy strode down to the hut and called out greetings. "*Geia, Evgenís Dryas.*"

Dryas, a broad-shouldered man in his mid-thirties with a bristle of beard and mustache, scowled at Iskandar. "What are you doing here, boy?" He placed one hand on the pistol in his sash and the other on the hilt of a rusty scimitar that he carried without a scabbard.

Niilo, a tub of a man, shook a heavy club in Iskandar's face.

"Searching for a nanny and kid that became lost in the storm. A brown goat with a white spot between her eyes. The kid was brown as well, with white legs. Have you seen them, noble Dryas?"

"No. We search for my own goat. A nanny as well. Black."

"I saw such a goat only this morning." He pointed to a very high ridge, away from where the fugitives hid. "I was on the other side, so I couldn't reach it."

Dryas cursed. "*Kólasi!*" *Hell!*

"Come, Niilo. We'll find her. She's my best producer." Without another word, Dryas walked off, followed by Niilo.

Once they were out of sight, Iskandar signaled it was safe for the men to come out from hiding.

"You're a clever lad," George said. "Dimas milked a black nanny goat this morning."

"The goat has probably wandered back to the herd or mingled with another one. There are ten other herders on the island."

"For an uninhabited island," Fenton said, "this place is getting mighty crowded."

"Now, we must hurry," Iskandar said. "Clear your belongings out of the hut and then hide your boat. I will gather firewood to replace the wood you used last night."

George and Jamie stripped off their clothes, dragged the broken boat to deep water, and sank it. They swam back to shore.

Jamie and George used Iskandar's wool cape to dry off.

"Damn, that water's cold," Jamie said. "I take back my thought of wanting to swim."

They dressed hurriedly and gathered their belongings.

Then, they quickly followed Iskandar, first up a narrow path, then down through a deep ravine and once again up along a steep ridge. They continued up, avoiding other herdsmen, until they reached a high wooded area. It was almost dark, but Iskandar knew the way.

"Not far now," the boy said.

Then they heard clicking of beads and a voice chanting in Greek.

"Holy God, Holy Mighty, Holy Immortal, have mercy on us. Holy God, Holy Mighty, Holy Immortal, have mercy on us. Holy God, Holy Mighty, Holy Immortal, have mercy on us. Glory to the Father and the Son and the Holy Spirit, now and forever and to the ages of ages. Amen."

"Father Ambrose," whispered the boy in Greek, "it is Iskandar."

The priest rounded the path. He was dressed in a worn black cassock and a tall black brimless hat. He carried a stout walking staff. His long beard, white with age, swept his chest.

"Have I not watched you as you climbed to these heights?" he asked, also in Greek. "You bring visitors and, by the look of their torn and tattered clothes, I suspect they are shipwrecked men and not hermits such as myself seeking God's grace."

"We're Americans," Jamie said in Greek. "We've escaped from the Bashaw of Tripoli."

"Americans," Father Ambrose answered, in English now. "You speak a rather accented and classical Greek."

"You speak English, Father," Jamie said, surprised.

"I have had the opportunity to learn a number of languages." The priest smiled, showing teeth as white as his beard.

Jamie looked him over. Despite the many wrinkles on his sun-darkened face, he moved with robust energy. His eyes as blue and deep as the ocean, peered at the castaways through round glasses held together with string.

He addressed Iskandar in Greek. "Where do you take these men?"

"To Calypso's cave. I must hide them from Dryas and his men."

The priest nodded. "A good place for hiding. But for how long?"

"Until we can get a boat and sail to Sicily," Jamie said.

"The only way you will get a boat is to steal one," the priest said.

"We can pay for a boat. We are free men." Jamie said, then introduced himself and his companions.

"I have never met Americans, but I've read of you. You fought the British and won your independence. We Greeks have not yet freed ourselves from the Ottoman yoke, but there are those of us who will continue to struggle until we are free," Father Ambrose said with a mixture of sadness and pride. "Fear not that I will reveal you. You are safe in these hills and in the cave of Calypso. The ignorant Dryas and his men fear these forests and hills."

He turned to the young herder. "Iskandar, it grows late. Return to your father, for he must be worried. I will lead them to the cave."

"I will bring food tomorrow," Iskandar said. "You are safe with Father Ambrose."

The men thanked the boy and Iskandar hurried down to find his father.

"A smart and good lad, that," Father Ambrose said, watching the boy bound down the trail, surefooted even in the twilight.

The priest set a fast pace and led the way up a bit further until they reached a small clearing and, behind it, a dark opening.

"Behold, the cave of the enchantress, Calypso."

The cave was well-hidden from the sea. Twisted cedar and junipers grew before the entrance. The cavern was large, going back at least twenty feet. Father Ambrose lit an oil lamp and led the way in. He held the lamp high and the men could see faded paintings on the walls.

"Minoan," the priest said. "Painted by a lost civilization."

"The cave of Calypso is a bit different than Homer described it," Jamie said. Then he quoted some of the Odyssey, in Greek.

> Then, swift ascending from the azure wave,
> He took the path that winded to the cave.
> Large was the grot, in which the Nymph he found
> (The fair-hair'd Nymph with ev'ry beauty crown'd);
> She sate and sung; the rocks resound her lays;
> The cave was brighten'd with a rising blaze;
> Cedar and frankincense, an od'rous pile,
> Flamed on the hearth and wide perfumed the isle;
> While she with work and song the time divides,
> And thro' the loom the golden shuttle guides.
> Without the grot a various sylvan scene
> Appear'd around, and groves of living green;
> Poplars and alders ever quiv'ring play'd,
> And nodding cypress form'd a fragrant shade;
> On whose high branches, waving with the storm,
> The birds of broadest wing their mansions form,
> The chough, the sea-mew, the loquacious crow,
> And scream aloft, and skim the deeps below.
> Depending vines the shelving cavern screen,
> With purple clusters blushing thro' the green.
> Four limpid fountains from the clefts distil;
> And ev'ry fountain pours a sev'ral rill,
> In mazy windings wand'ring down the hill;
> Where bloomy meads with vivid greens were crown'd,
> And glowing violets threw odors round.

Fenton and Dimas stood bewildered, but George and Father Ambrose smiled with delight.

"You are a man of learning, Mr. Sharpe," the priest said. "For that alone, I must protect you and your friends." He made the sign of the cross. "My abode is but a short walk from here. I will bring some goatskins for you to rest upon. Build a fire if you will, but alas, no cypress wood. You must do with cedar and juniper. And no vines with clusters of purple grapes either. I will also bring cheese and bread and some greens. I shall return presently."

The men set down their belongings and built a fire back from the entrance. True to his word, Father Ambrose returned, carrying a bundle of goatskins and some food and wine.

"Eat," the priest said. "You must be hungry. Then rest. I will return tomorrow. Iskandar will bring food and I wine. I would talk with you. It has been a very long time since I spoke with learned men."

They thanked the priest and he walked away, clicking his beads.

"It has been quite a day," George said. "In fact, it has been quite a week. I'm for sleep."

"Do you think we need to keep a watch?" Fenton asked.

"I'll keep watch for a while," Jamie said. "It's dark and I doubt anyone would dare the trail. A slip or false turn and they would plummet to their death."

The others wrapped themselves in the goatskins and curled up near the fire. Jamie sat at the cave entrance and absentmindedly chewed on a blade of grass. His thoughts were of home and of Claire.

I pray she's safe. I pray she and her mother are in Boston or very much near it. I know my mother, sister, and father will take them in.

I worry about getting home. These men are my responsibility. We must steal or buy a boat, sail across dangerous waters. If we do make it to Syracuse, I wonder if Brad will be there. Brave Brad, I miss him. I know he was aboard the Constitution. *I recall Horace Long telling me Brad fought a duel with Geoffrey Horne and wounded him in the hip. I miss him, but thank God George is here. I wouldn't have survived without him.*

Chapter 58

THE MEN WERE ABLE to rest and relax for the first time in months.

The food that Iskandar and the priest brought was plain but nourishing. The men became stronger after days of hardship. Jamie led them through the exercises that Alon had taught him.

Jamie and George looked forward to Father Ambrose's visits. They discussed philosophy, religion, and politics. He brought books written in French, Latin, and Greek, which both men devoured with passion. He helped them with their Greek, he taught them some Turkish, and they in return told him about America.

The priest's glasses came apart one day when the string holding the frame together broke. George asked to see them.

"The frames are made of coin silver. The hinge is broken. I can repair it."

George took some tools from his chest, including a small crucible that he had used to fix gun locks. He shaved off a piece of the Danish silver and melted it in the crucible.

"Now, here's the difficult part. I don't have a mold, so I'll try and shape it by hand."

After several tries, George was satisfied and fixed the new hinge on the frame, using silver as solder. "Try them now, father."

"Thank you, my friend," the priest said, hooking the glasses over his ears. "I was always afraid of losing the lenses. Without my spectacles, I could no longer read. No new ones would come from Crete. I must survive by my own hand and by the kindness of the herdsmen."

"Why don't you go back to Crete when the boats come and get new glasses?" George asked.

"I can never leave the island until the archbishop in Crete allows me. And I doubt he ever will. I'm an exile." Ambrose explained,

"You see, I believe Greece must be free of Turkish rule and have said and written as much. However, the church is afraid they will be punished if there is an uprising. Under the Ottomans, we may practice our religion but must defer to the Muslims. Many of our churches have been turned into mosques. But the church continues to bow to the Turks. The Patriarch at Constantinople is under the thumb of the sultan. There have been patriarchs who have rebelled and, let me say, they have not died of natural causes. So I stay on the island, hoping for the day I can return to my studies on faraway Mount Athos, the holy mountain. There is an academy there, the Athonite, which will lead a free Greece into the enlightened age. It is a place of great learning where ancient philosophies and modern sciences are taught. I left there to take the message to Crete, but alas, I stepped on the toes of the hierarchy and so I stay on this island. I serve the people here as it the will of God, until he softens the hearts of those that sent me into exile."

Jamie and George listened to the old man and showed him great reverence for his intellect, being attentive to his teachings.

They admired his courage. He stood to the oppressors in the church and to the Turks. If the Turks found out he'd helped hide them, he would surely be executed.

Storms came often and the men hunkered down in their cave, knowing no boat would venture out from Crete. After a particularly violent storm late in the month, the skies cleared. Fenton was scanning the sea off of Crete with the telescope when he saw boats approaching.

"They're coming," he shouted to the others. "Boats, two of them, about ten miles offshore."

He passed the glass to Jamie.

"They're headed for the cove below," Jamie said. "Gather our supplies and weapons. We must get down to the beach and prepare a welcome."

It was a tattered lot that started down the trail toward the beach. Many of their clothes had rotted away and they didn't dare bring the goat skins with them for fear of implicating the herders. They carried only the belongings they had brought with them.

Halfway down, Father Ambrose waited on the trail.

"Try not to kill anyone. It will go hard on the islanders. The boat, the one the soldiers ride in, is the most seaworthy. Wait until night before you take the boat." Then he blessed them. "Go with God, my children."

"Father, if I ever get to America, I will try to send you books. And George has melted some silver coins and left them in the cave, so they won't be recognized by the Turks as Danish silver. They are for you and for Theódoros and Iskandar."

"I will use the silver to send Iskandar to school. Send books of science to the academy on the holy mountain. Now, I must also go to the beach, but by a different path. They will have a few books, some soap, and a perhaps some clothes for me. I'm sure there will be no reprieve."

"When you see me, please do not acknowledge that you know me."

He turned and disappeared into the forest.

They made their way down, stopping every so often to see how far out the boats were. Jamie was able to make out the crew of both vessels. The one with soldiers was a two-masted felucca, about thirty feet long and partially decked. The other boat was larger and open. That boat was wide in the beam and trailed the other boat by a mile. It waddled more than sailed.

"The priest was right. The soldiers' boat is the one for us."

"How many soldiers?" George asked.

"I count eight and a crew of four."

"Bad odds," George said.

"George, what could go wrong? We've been blessed by two Jewish doctors, a Muslim soldier, and an Orthodox priest," Jamie said with a smile. "Still, we will proceed with caution."

They neared the beach and entered a grove of junipers. The twisted trunks and low hanging needles gave them enough cover so they were well-hidden.

As the boats closed, the sound of a brass horn could be heard across the water. In a while, answering calls from trumpets and conch-type shells were blown from around the island.

The boat with the soldiers sailed up to a small wooden pier. The soldiers, led by a fat sergeant, got out and immediately strung hammocks, then went to sleep. After the crew secured the craft, they too, strung their hammocks.

"Siesta," Dimas whispered.

"They must be very tired after sailing, what, twenty, twenty-five miles?" Fenton said sarcastically. "This should be a good time to seize the boat."

"Not while the other boat is still out there," Jamie said. "If they see us, they'll turn around and notify the authorities on Crete. We'll wait until dark and then surprise them."

They hunkered down in their grove, unseen, quietly planning their attack.

Heading the call of the trumpet, the herders carried large wicker baskets full of cheese down to the beach.

Father Ambrose ambled down after a while and the Greek boatmen asked for blessings. The captain of the larger boat handed the priest a small crate, probably containing a few books and some supplies.

The herders were given crates and barrels as well. Some were given letters but needed Father Ambrose to read them.

As evening approached, fires were lit along the beach. Some herders had departed, but most stayed, including Iskandar, Theódoros, and the headman, Dryas, along with his henchmen, the rotund Niilo and a brute of a man Jamie guessed was Castor.

Dryas was in deep conversation with the captain of the boat that brought the soldiers. Jamie remembered they were brothers.

As dark descended, some men drifted off to sleep. Dryas, his henchmen, his brother, and the sergeant sat around a blaze and drank heavily from stone jugs. Young Iskandar skirted around them, carrying driftwood for his fire, but Dryas reached out with a shepherd's crook and tripped the boy. The lad fell and cut his arm on a rock, causing Dryas and his cronies to roar with laughter.

"Take the wood," Dryas demanded and Niilo jumped to obey.

When Iskandar protested, Castor kicked him.

Up the beach, Theódoros saw what was happening and drew his knife. Father Ambrose rushed to him to stop him. If Dryas saw Theódoros with a knife, he'd shoot him before he could get within ten feet.

"Now!" Jamie said. "George and Fenton, cover us." He motioned to Dimas to follow.

"All of you," Jamie called in Greek. "You are under our guns. Make a move and you will be shot."

Those on the beach were stunned. They couldn't see into the dark, as they had been staring into the fires. One of the soldiers reached for the stacked muskets and George fired, the ball landing in the sand between the man's feet. The soldier let out a yelp and jumped back, raising his hands.

"You, "Jamie commanded, "the big man with the saber, toss it into the sea."

Dryas hesitated and Jamie drew one of his pistols. The steel weapon reflected brightly in the firelight. Dryas tossed the sword away and it landed in the surf.

"Now, all of you, stand facing the sea. The first man who turns around will be shot."

"I think he is a desperate man," Father Ambrose said. "We should obey."

That's all it took. The Greeks lined up and faced the sea. The Turkish sergeant didn't hesitate either and told his men to line up and turn to the sea as well.

Dimas collected the muskets and put them in the smaller boat. Then he relieved the men of their knives and tossed them in the larger boat. He retrieved several lengths of rope.

Fenton and George joined Jamie and Dimas and began to load the boat with their belongings. Dimas took the baskets of cheese that belonged to Dryas and set them in the boat as well.

"*Ochi!*" Dryas yelled. *No!* "*Aftó eínai dikó mou!*" *This is mine!*

George walked over to him. "I'm so sorry," he said in Greek. "I'll fight you for the cheese."

"What? No. If I win, you will kill me."

"No, I'll let you live."

"I won't fight."

"Coward," George said. "But I will take your pantaloons. They will probably fit me

"My pantaloons?"

"As you can see, I am in tatters. We were shipwrecked and I need some clothes. In fact, we all need clothes. Your shirt is too small for me, but the pantaloons look right, as do the stockings."

George pulled Dryas' pantaloons off, to the laughter of several people, including the fat sergeant.

As he tied Dryas' red sash around his waist, George turned to the sergeant. "Don't laugh, oaf. While your belly is so large I could never wear your pants, your shirt and jacket should fit me well enough."

The shirt was relatively clean, the red jacket soiled with food stains but wearable.

Fenton, Dimas, and Jamie were able to find clothes that fit them among the soldiers. Fenton took particular enjoyment in stripping Castor and Niilo and he was none too gentle. In fact, he gave Castor a particularly hard kick.

Jamie ordered the sergeant to tie up his men, the herders, and the priest. Once it was done, Dimas tied up the sergeant and checked the other bindings. He tightened several of them and actually loosened Father Ambrose's, as well as Theódoros' and Iskandar's.

"Well," Jamie said, as he wrapped a turban around his head, "It's time for us to leave. We will leave the larger boat at the south point."

"Wait, you take my boat?" Dryas' brother protested. "You can't."

"I'd say it's worth something." Jamie tossed two silver coins at the man's feet.

"That should buy you a new boat."

With that, Jamie and Dimas climbed into the smaller boat, George and Fenton into the larger. Sails were raised and the men set out, supplied, dressed, and ready to attempt the crossing of the Ionian Sea to Sicily once they dropped off the larger boat as promised.

Chapter 59

DURING THE DARK of night, they set sail and headed west.

"Here we are again," George said. "Let's hope this boat brings us to safety."

"Aye," Fenton said. "I just hope there are no more storms like there were the last few days. That gale would have sunk a larger vessel than this one."

"The wind is with us and we will reach Syracuse, God willing," Jamie said, moving the tiller to adjust his course.

They sailed through the night. By daylight, the seas roughened, but no storms were in sight.

Dimas passed out the food, dried goat and cheese. They even had some arrack, the harsh anise-flavored Turkish liquor that they found in the little cuddy under the deck. Jamie allowed each man a small dram as a way of celebration.

At noon, Jamie took a reading. "We've come 43.5 nautical miles and, so far, no pursuit. It's still a long way to Sicily, more than four hundred miles. We've plenty of food and water, the boat is sturdy — we will make it. Still, we must maintain lookouts. We don't know who sails these waters. The British or French will press us into their navies. Pirates will try to take us. Turks will probably kill us or make us slaves."

"I'd rather be dead then be a slave again," Fenton said.

"We are well-armed, if it comes to that, and we won't go without a fight. Now, back to the old watch, four on, four off."

They sailed through the day with no incident. As night fell, they sailed on, always watchful.

At two in the morning, Jamie roused George.

"What?" George asked, rubbing the sleep from his eyes.

"I see lights to the north."

George looked in that direction. "Aye, and moving toward us. The wind is with them and they'll be on us by daybreak."

"There is no place to hide," Jamie said. "At sunrise, we'll take down the sails and mast, and hope that our profile is so low we won't be seen."

Dimas and Fenton awoke and were informed of the situation.

"If it's a British or even a French vessel, we will run up the Ottoman flag. Neither country is at war with the Turks," Jamie said. "If it is a Turkish vessel, we may be left alone, but if it does approach, I will not surrender. Load all the muskets."

They watched through the night. The day arrived cloudy and gray as they took down the mast. The vessel was at least ten miles away and heading right for them.

Jamie trained his telescope on the oncoming vessel. "A brig, and a trim one. English, I'd guess. We'll change course and hope she'll pass us."

They rowed southeast and hoped the brig would sail west. Their hopes were dashed when the vessel also altered its course to southeast.

"She's headed right for us. Raise the Turkish flag and step the masts. We'll raise sail as well. Now that we're spotted, no need to row."

Jamie kept the craft on course, hoping those on the brig would think they were fishermen or merchants and would pass by them.

"Wrap turbans around your heads," Jamie said, "so when they take our measure, they may think we're Ottomans and leave us alone."

"What if they hail us?" George asked.

"If they hail us, I'll answer in Arabic. We can't fight a brig. The best we can do is bluff."

Chapter 60

Aboard the Brig, November 21, 1804
Off the Coast of Crete

THE CAPTAIN SHOWED great confidence in this tall midshipman with the reddish-brown hair. The young man had proved himself in so many ways to be an excellent officer. It wasn't often a midshipman would be officer of the deck. With the second lieutenant injured in the storm, the captain had chosen the midshipman he had the most trust in. The young man, in turn, was diligent in his duties.

A younger man, also a midshipman, stood by the starboard rail. He was midshipman of the deck, among whose duties it was to make sure the lookouts were vigilant. He also kept his eyes on the horizon. He raised his telescope and trained it on something that caught his eye.

"Sir," he said, addressing the older midshipman, "I see what I believe is a small vessel off to starboard."

The officer nodded. He took his own telescope and climbed halfway up the mainmast rigging. He trained the glass to where the younger man was pointing.

"You are correct, Mr. Danielson, there is a vessel out there," he said. "I can't make it out, but we should be upon her within the hour. Please notify the officers of the tops, fo'c'sle, and lieutenant of marines to keep a sharp lookout and report when they can identify the vessel."

He climbed down from the mast.

The younger man jumped to the orders. When he returned to the quarterdeck and asked, "Should the captain be notified?"

"Not yet. I'll let you know. Now, if you please, note the time in the log when you first spotted the vessel and that the appropriate officers were notified. You have sharp eyes, Mr. Danielson. Excellent job."

Midshipman Danielson smiled at the compliment. After all, it came from one of the heroes who was engaged in the burning of the *Philadelphia.* Admiral Lord Horatio Nelson himself was reputed to have called it "the most bold and daring act of the age."

The brig, the fastest in the squadron, was closing on the small vessel. The senior midshipman used his telescope to try and identify the boat.

"Mr. Danielson, do you recognize the flag?" he asked, testing the younger man.

"Aye, sir. Ottoman. Could it be a fishing boat from Crete, blown off course?"

"We will soon find out. Notify the captain."

The young man quickly obeyed.

It wasn't long before the rotund captain mounted the quarterdeck —the captain who had been aroused from sleep and hadn't had time to comb his curly dark hair.

"Well, it seems we have a bit of excitement this morning," the captain said, raising his own telescope to look at the boat.

"A felucca, by the look of her. Turkish or perhaps from Tripoli. Though she's far from Africa and close to Crete. She could have been blown off course during the gale. Though it's difficult to believe she could have survived that blow. Even we had to reef sails and wait out the storm. She's probably a fishing boat from Crete. Still, she may need assistance. Or she could be a smuggler or even a pirate. To be safe, we'll check her out. I believe she's spotted us, for her mast and sails are raised. Have the bosun summon Lieutenant O'Bannon."

Shortly, the handsome lieutenant of marines joined the captain on the quarterdeck.

"Lieutenant O'Bannon, muster your marines. We will investigate yonder boat."

"Aye aye, sir. It will give my boys some action after being kept below during the storm."

The drummer summoned the marines, some of whom were ordered to the starboard rail, others to the tops.

A square-faced man of about forty came on deck, a saber strapped to his waist and a brace of pistols shoved in his belt. He was quite muscular and carried himself with military bearing.

"I heard the drum. Is there to be a fight?" he asked, perhaps a bit eager for a brawl.

"I doubt it, but to make sure, I've ordered the marines out." The captain explained about the vessel, which was running with the wind, trying to get away. "She can't elude us. We'll be on her in the next few minutes. Seems there are at least four aboard, although more may be hidden under the deck or beneath the rail. They're wearing Turkish garb and a mix of uniforms of some sort." He handed his telescope to the man. "I've been informed it was your stepson who first caught sight of the boat. Sharp-eyed lad. You should be proud, sir."

The man smiled and looked over at young Eli Danielson, who turned a bright red. By this time, the other officers and two other civilians were on deck, watching as the brig closed on the boat.

"Hail them," the captain ordered.

The midshipman picked up the speaking trumpet. "Unknown felucca, heave to and identify yourself."

A bearded man, his face burned dark by the sun and wearing a turban, stood and yelled back, but his voice was lost in the wind.

"They are a motley-looking crew," the marine officer said.

"Aye," the captain replied. "The boat is riding high. I doubt it's carrying much cargo. I'd venture they're fishermen from Crete. Still, I'd like to have a closer look."

The captain turned to the senior midshipman and told him to pick a crew and lower a boat. Mr. O'Bannon sent two marines to join the midshipman's crew.

A boat was lowered and six armed bluejackets, a marine corporal, and a tall marine private pushed off from the brig with the midshipman in the stern sheets. As they approached the felucca, it was hailed once more.

"Identify yourself."

"*Hal 'ant Anklyzy?*" the man with the dark beard called back.

"What language are they speakin', sir?" the corporal asked.

"Arabic, I think."

"Can you understand what they be askin'?

"I think they're asking if we're English. Damned if I'll answer them."

He called back to the felucca. "Prepare to be boarded."

"I demand to know who I'm speaking with," the man from the felucca called back.

"You speak English, do you?" the corporal said, standing and raising his musket. "You look like renegades or deserters to me, dressed as you are like Turks or Ay-rabs. You don't get to demand."

"Belay that, corporal," Midshipman Bradford Welles said. "I'll seek your advice when I ask for it."

"Sorry, Mr. Welles, I forgot my place." The corporal sat down.

"Even if they are renegades," Brad said, checking his own pistol, "they don't present much of a threat to the *Argus*, nor us. Just make sure your muskets are primed."

Brad Welles addressed the men in the felucca. "We are from the American brig *Argus*, whose guns you are under and my men are armed as well. Now enough of the pleasantries, prepare to be boarded." Brad stood and drew his cutlass.

"My God," the bearded man called when he saw Brad stand. "Brad Welles!"

"What? Who? Jamie, Jamie!" Brad could hardly believe his eyes. Another man stood next to Jamie. "George!"

The crew of the longboat didn't know what was going on. The tall marine private, breaking discipline, suddenly gave out with a cry, "By Saint Jude, the saint of lost causes, Jamie Sharpe and George Walling, I thought you were dead for sure. And there's Webb and Dimas too."

The corporal tried to pull him back down, but was shrugged off.

The boats closed and old friends reached across and embraced. There was much questioning and all talking at once, and the tall marine joined the reunion.

"Ben Murphy!" George exclaimed. "The last I saw of you, you were in the bottom of a Royal Navy longboat, being pressed into service. Now you're here."

"I was pressed in the Royal Navy, but when we made Gibraltar, I saw the American squadron," Ben said. "I remembered the German fellow, Anton Gunther, used a barrel as a float and swam ashore at Horta in the Azores. So I done the same. I threw a barrel in and used it to reach the *Constitution.* Mr. Welles recognized me and convinced the commodore to let me join the Marines. I knew I'd never be a sailor, but I know how to use a musket, seein' I was a sergeant in the army. And Jamie, thanks to you, I ain't afraid to go to the tops no more."

"There is much catching up to do," Brad said, "Let us repair to the *Argus* and then we can share our stories."

Chapter 61

JAMIE, GEORGE, FENTON, AND DIMAS were clean-shaven, dressed in clothes from the slop chest, and waiting to tell their stories to the captain, Master Commandant Isaac Hull, and Mr. William Eaton, Eli Danielson's stepfather.

But first, they asked Brad about news from home.

"George, your family is well, but worried beyond belief. They for sure thought you were a captive somewhere on the Slave Coast. They never gave up hope."

"They never received our letters?" George asked.

"When Commodore Preble found out the consul at Malta hadn't send on any messages from Tripoli, he was furious. The letters have been sent now, but who knows how long it will take for them to reach home?"

"So it's true what Captain Sabatier told me," Jamie said. "What news of my family?"

"Just like George's, they haven't given up hope. Your father returned from China with a rich cargo. Before I left, I heard that John Adams was acting as your family's lawyer and demanding that South Carolina extradite Nehemiah Cutts back to Boston. Your grandfather was ready to go to Charleston and drag Captain Cutts back."

Jamie gave a low chuckle. "And what of my sister, Maisie?"

Brad turned red and hemmed and hawed. "Uh... that is to say, I mean... Dash it all, Maisie and I are engaged."

Jamie laughed hard at Brad's discomfort. "By jove, Brad, that's wonderful news! But be aware, Maisie has a mind of her own."

"Aye." Brad laughed. "Indeed I know it."

Eli Danielson, who had been sitting quietly by, now said, "All Brad talks about is Maisie Sharpe."

"Belay that, you young rascal," Brad said, as the others laughed.

Their laughter was interrupted by a marine. "Excuse me, Mr. Welles, captain's compliments, you and these rescued gentlemen are to join him in his cabin."

The cabin was crowded with the ships' officers. Mr. Eaton introduced himself, a Scotsman named Richard Farquhar, and an Italian gentleman named Mr. Busatile as representatives of Hamet Karamanli, the deposed Bashaw of Tripoli.

Captain Hull addressed Jamie and his friends. "I see you gentlemen have eaten and had a bit of a rest. We would be interested in your story and how you came to be off the coast of Crete."

"It is a very long story, sir," Jamie replied.

"Pray, tell it," Captain Hull said with a smile.

Jamie and George told the full story from their kidnapping through the events aboard the *Beneficence* through their rescue by Captain Sabatier through the capture of the *Barbara Allan* through the harrowing days of captivity to their escape from Derne.

"Remarkable," William Eaton said. "You men have endured and survived great challenges. Mr. Walling and Mr. Sharpe, I have need of you for a special mission, but of course, Captain Hull may want you as well."

"Indeed," Captain Hull said. "I could use brave men such as you aboard the *Argus*."

"I'm an experienced topman, Captain," Fenton Webb said. "I'll be glad to join your crew. Seein' as you're part of the squadron fightin' Tripoli. I want a crack at them bastards, pardon me, sir."

"You are pardoned, Webb," Captain Hull said with a smile. "Dimas?"

"I too would stay aboard if you can use a cook."

"Navy fare is rough, but a man who can cook is man after my own heart," Hull said, patting his round belly.

"And you, Mr. Walling, you are still a midshipman," Hull continued. "As I indicated, I'm sure I could use you. However, you heard Mr. Eaton requesting that you join him for a special assignment. A dangerous one, I might add, and after you hear what it is, you may refuse."

Hull turned to Jamie.

"As for you, Mr. Sharpe, I can't order you, but Mr. Eaton has requested you join him as well. But I will let him explain." Hull turned to Eaton.

"Mr. Eaton, would you enlighten these gentlemen as to your plan?"

"Mr. Walling, Mr. Sharpe, now that I've heard your remarkable story about your time in and escape from Derne, I could use your aid in my mission. For you see, I plan to travel to Egypt, find Hamet, the rightful Bashaw of Tripoli, gather an army, sail to and capture Derne, then go on to Tripoli to depose the usurper, Yusuf, and place Hamet on the throne. So what say you gentlemen? Will you join me?"

"I've a score to settle with Kemal Rais and Yusuf," Jamie said. "I shall go with you, Mr. Eaton."

"And I," George said.

"Then it is settled," William Eaton declared. "We shall go to the hostile shores of Tripoli and end this war.

Historical Notes

Jamie Sharpe and the Pirates of Barbary is a work of fiction. However, certain events described in the novel actually happened.

It is true that the regency of Tripoli (modern-day Libya) declared war on the United States in 1802. As one of the Barbary States, the others being Tunis and Algiers, Tripoli demanded payment from a number of countries or they would capture their ships and put their crews into slavery. When Tripoli thought the United States was not paying enough, it declared war.

Commodore Preble's was the third squadron sent to the Mediterranean, but was the only one ready to do something other just than observe.

Preble's action aboard the *Constitution* when challenged by the British frigate *Maidstone* happened as described. He did not know he faced a frigate but thought he was up against an eighty-four-gun ship of the line. Still, he was prepared to fight when he ordered his gunners to "Blow your matches, boys."

The grounding and capture of the USS *Philadelphia* was a combination of bad luck and perhaps too much bravado. Captain Bainbridge was a man of extraordinary bad fortune. He lost a ship during the Quasi-War with France. After delivering tribute to the Dey of Algiers, the Dey forced him to fly an Algerian flag on an American frigate and carry tribute from Algiers to the Ottoman Sultan. Bainbridge redeemed himself in the War of 1812 when, in command of the *Constitution*, he fought and sunk the HMS *Java*. Still, he was known as a martinet and many men refused to sail with him.

The burning of the *Philadelphia*, led by Stephen Decatur, Jr., was a daring and dangerous venture as described. It has been purported that British Admiral Lord Horatio Nelson called it "the most bold and daring act of the age."

Was Gavdos Calypso's island as mentioned in the *Odyssey*? Perhaps. Other suggestions are Malta, the Nile, Atlantis, and somewhere in the Atlantic Ocean. For the purposes of this book, Gavdos will do.

The United States Consul at Malta was Joseph Pulis, who was Maltese, not an American. This was not unusual at the time. President George Washington appointed the first 17 U.S. consular officers: 12 consuls and 5 vice consuls. The nominees were Americans engaged in trade in the city to which they were assigned; where none could be found, foreigners were appointed.

Much of the historical details in the book were drawn from the scholarship of Richard Zacks (*The Pirate Coast: Thomas Jefferson, the First Marines, and the Secret Mission of 1805*); A.B.C. Whipple (*To the Shores of Tripoli: The Birth of the U.S. Navy and Marines*); Ian W. Toll (*Six Frigates: The Epic History of the Founding of the U.S. Navy*); Frank Lambert (*The Barbary Wars: American Independence in the Atlantic World*); Joseph Wheelan (*Jefferson's War: America's First War on Terror, 1801–1805*); Louis B. Wright and Julia H. Macleod (*The First Americans in North Africa: William Eaton's Struggle for a Vigorous Policy Against the Barbary Pirates, 1799–1805*); Stephen Clissold (*The Barbary Slaves*); and websites too numerous to list.

About the Author

A historian by training, GARY R. BUSH writes fiction for adults, young adults, and children.

He is co-editor of the anthology *Once Upon a Crime*, a collection of short stories from some of the world's best mystery authors. His stories have appeared in numerous anthologies. He is also the author of the children's graphic novel *Lost in Space: The Flight of Apollo 13*. His historical novel, *Jamie Sharpe and the Seas of Treachery*, won the Midwest Book Award for the best YA novel.

Away from writing, Bush enjoys sailing and has sailed on the Atlantic, Pacific, and Lake Superior. He has always loved stories of adventure and the sea.

Bush lives in Minneapolis with his journalist wife, Stacey.

www.ingramcontent.com/pod-product-compliance
Lightning Source LLC
Chambersburg PA
CBHW071415200726
48294CB00002B/402